Theatre in the Solovki Prison Camp

Theatre in the Solovki Prison Camp

Natalia Kuziakina

formerly of the St Petersburg Institute of Theatre, Music and Cinematography

Translated from the Russian by **Boris M. Meerovich**

Routledge
Taylor & Francis Group

LONDON AND NEW YORK

First Published 1995
by Harwood Academic Publishers.
Reprinted 2004
by Routledge,
11 New Fetter Lane, London EC4P 4EE

Transferred to Digital Printing 2004

Copyright © 1995 by Harwood Academic Publishers GmbH.

British Library Cataloguing in Publication Data

Kuziakina, Natalia
  Solovki Prison Camp Theatre. — (Russian
Theatre Archive, ISSN 1068-8161; Vol. 3)
  I. Title   II. Meerovich, Boris M.
  III. Series
  792.0220947

ISBN 3-7186-5439-3 (hardback)
ISBN 3-7186-5440-7 (paperback)

Contents

Introduction to the Series

The Russian Theatre Archive makes available in English the best avant-garde plays, from the pre-Revolutionary period to the present day. It features monographs on major playwrights and theatre directors, introductions to previously unknown works, and studies of the main artistic groups and periods.

Plays are presented in performing edition translations, including (where appropriate) musical scores, and instructions for music and dance. Whenever possible the translated texts will be accompanied by videotapes of performances of plays in the original language.

List of Plates

(Between pp. 86 and 87)

Nos. 1 to 4. Caricatures by Ver. *SLON*, 1924, Nos. 5, 7–8.
  1. Pilgrimage to Solovki.
  2. From Our Aphorisms
  3. Felling Logs – Our Shock Workers.
      (Dedicated to the 10th platoon)
  4. Caricature of I.S. Levkassi.

Nos. 5 to 10. Organizers of the theatre.
  5. I.A. Armanov as Krechinsky in the play *Krechinsky's Wedding*.
  6. M.S. Borin as Raspliuyev in *Krechinsky's Wedding*.
  7. I.S. Panin.
  8. N.K. Litvin.
  9. B.N. Shiriayev.
  10. B. Glubokovsky with actors on the Solovki (at Kem?).

  11. Front page of *The New Solovki* newspaper, 7 June 1925, with portraits of A. Nogtev, Solovetsky Camp Chief, G. Bokii, OGPU Collegium Member, and F. Eichmans, Camp Chief Deputy.
  12. Character reference of N. Litvin, from the minutes of the USLON Central Attestation Commission, 12 September 1925.
  13. Permit of G.M. Osorgin's wife to visit her husband, issued 24 August 1928.

Nos. 14 to 17. Plays of the 1st Department Theatre:
  14. *The Decembrists* by N. Lerner, director Borin (?), 1926.
  15. *The Warrant* by N. Erdman, director Glubokovsky, 1926.
  16. *Masquerade* by M. Lermontov, director I. Kalugin, 1929.
  17. *A Lyre for Hire*, 1932 (?).

  18. I. Terentiev. Self-Caricature, *Teatr (Theatre)*, 1987, No. 5.
  19. The Povenets Propaganda Brigade named after Firin. Singing verses on a good attitude to horses. In: *The Stalin Canal*, 1934, 313.
  20. Theatre at Tuloma. General view. Banner says 'Welcome'.
  21. Jazz-band in the Tuloma theatre.
  22. Final scene of Griboyedov's comedy *Woe from Wit*. Tuloma theatre, 1934.
  23. Scene from play by unknown playwright, Tuloma theatre, 1934–35 (?).
  24. Scene from comedy by unknown playwright. Tuloma theatre, 1934–36 (?).
  25. Theatre at Medvezhiegorsk. Destroyed by fire during World War II.
  26. Leading figures at the Central WSBC Theatre.
      Right to left: D.M. Person, I.I. Vovk, S.A. Taneyev, Misha (lighting engineer), A.G. Alexeyev, and (in armchair) B.S. Pshibyshevsky, 1936.
  27. Concert programme and bill for A. Arbuzov's play *Tania*, 1939.
  28. Barracks on Anzer Island. Photograph by Yu. Brodsky.
  29. Stage director A. Kurbas. Photograph from camp case file.
  30. Bill for N. Pogodin's play *Aristocrats*. Director A. Kurbas, Solovki theatre, season of 1936–37.

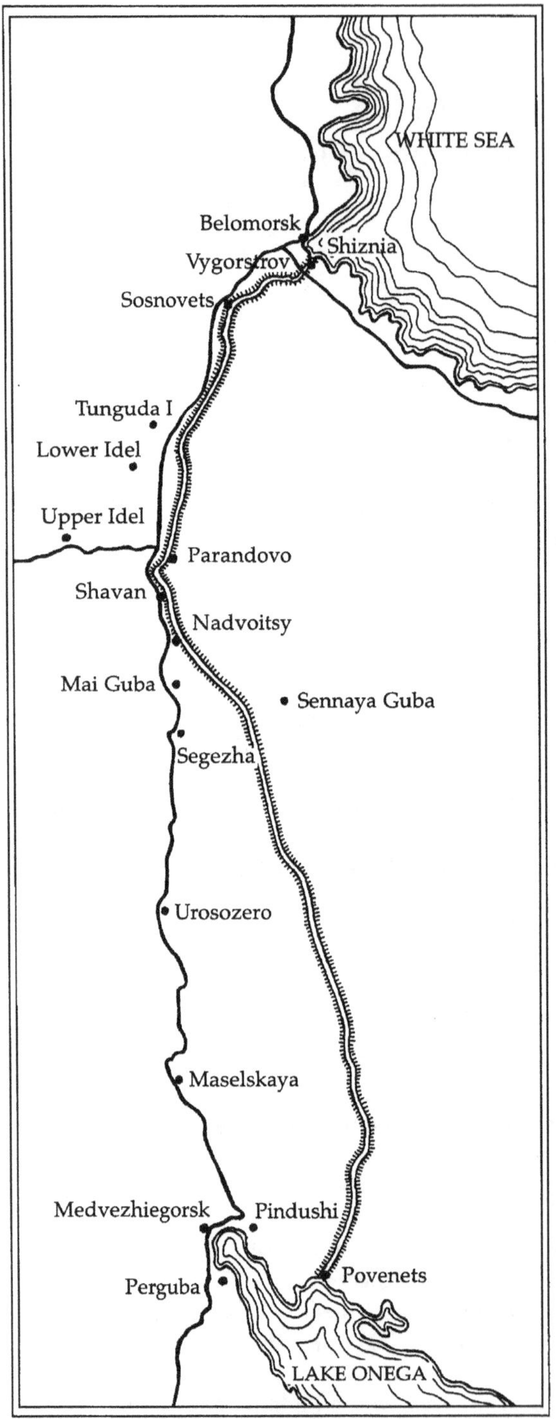

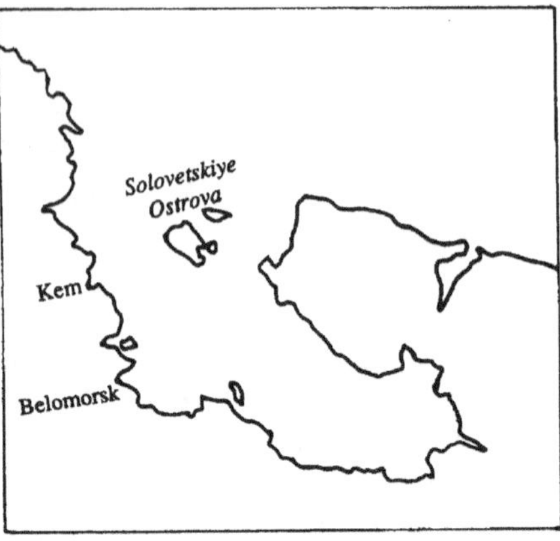

The Solovetsky islands

Main sites of prison camps involved in the construction of the WSBC, along the only reliable transport artery: the Murmansk–Leningrad railway. Canal route to right of railway line.

Preface

It is extremely difficult to write about the camps after the publication of *The Gulag Archipelago*. Indeed, Alexander Solzhenitsyn broadly and powerfully outlined the issues of that life, about which many preferred to know nothing. Though created in secrecy, behind closed doors, his book breathes freedom of thought and expression.

The *Archipelago*'s felicitously resilient, buoyant forms constitute a kind of archipelago all their own, self-contained and obeying its own inherent laws. The writer confidently draws into a single stream material that could seem too heterogeneous and aesthetically contradictory: his own recollections and the evidence of hundreds of prisoners, documents and civic passion. The sounds of camp life (so keenly heard by Solzhenitsyn) swell in a crescendo. Thoughts and feelings still aglow mingle in a single mighty tide, sweeping the reader along.

My particular task was that of the historian, not the artist. My book deals with the role of stagecraft in the system of prison camps and, naturally, with the fates of its creators and spectators.

Prison camp theatre is a theme justified by actual life, even though the marriage of such concepts as 'theatre' and 'prison camp' may appear, to the ordinary mind, preposterous.

Decency militates against art in shackles. If art is the result of creative effort by spiritually free individuals, how, then, can it realize itself under compulsion and oppression? Here fate pulls the strings in the jailer's hands, jerking the actors like puppets in a round-dance when they really feel like crying. One is profoundly sorry for the actors, but where does art come in?

Our subject, let us admit, evokes doubts also from the viewpoint of drama study: were the camp's stage productions of any genuine artistic merit at all? Could any real theatrical gems in their own right be discovered there? For did not the convicts use forms most probably already tried out on the professional stage?

Such misgivings seem justified. They were shared by the stage director, Boris Glubokovsky, who wrote a lengthy piece on the activities of the Solovetsky Theatre (1927) and by the author of a volume of Solovki memoirs, Boris Shiriayev (*The Inextinguishable Lantern*, 1954). Glubokovsky asserted:

> Considering the Solovetsky theatre, one cannot speak of its company as something definitely formed, or of a trend dictated by some special artistic purpose. Yet one may discern in it the threads of a strong social bond between the footlights and the audience. And wherever there is a social bond, wherever there is a spectator, there is theatre; wherever there is a special spectator, there is special theatre. And of this special theatre one should speak not in the language of the art critic, but in the language of the public man and of the sociologist.

Yet Glubokovsky also saw the camp theatre's aesthetic features: 'A will for the theatre, for theatricals, for pure theatre, are, indeed, manifest in the productions of the Solovetsky theatre'.[1]

Does this mean that the performers and spectators are of greater interest than the stage, that is, the play itself? Right, says Glubokovsky. The unusual mode of existence, the monstrous social crucible, unimaginable in a stable society, in which the Solovetsky spectator was grilled, all this gave birth to a special theatre, which played a tremendous role in the life of the inmates, incommensurate, as it were, with narrowly aesthetic standards.

Glubokovsky's thoughts found confirmation when, half a century after the closure of the Solovetsky prison camp, the few, but all the more important, memoirs of former convicts were published. To most of the prisoners the theatre was more than simply a place of recreation or aesthetic delight: it was a place where one could return to one's former normal life as a free citizen. In that inhuman world the theatre unfurled the banner of humaneness, and this earned it the gratitude of its spectators. D.S. Likhachev recalled:

> In spring, on a white night, I had the good fortune to watch *The Solovetsky Review*. The impression it made was tremendous. Why do I say 'white night'? I recall how we all came out of the darkened theatre (lights were not switched on for a long time after the last scene of twinkling distant fires) to be welcomed by a sky – at once light and somehow papery-blue. Together with the white buildings, the stirring of the air, the absence of the cries of the seagulls (on a white night the seagulls did go to sleep, after all), all this was quite exceptional and seemed unreal, as if in a dream.[2]

The emotional shake-up in this instance (and it was not unique) was the result of the play's aesthetic effect, of the theatre having delivered its full impact. For this reason the author was able to single out prison camp theatre as a special theme for study.

And the most suitable means for studying it at the present time is via the genre of historical essay. It would be fitting to have a series of articles on artistic phenomena in the life of the largest camps and political isolators, for it is only now that the doors leading to the cellars of various archives are at long last creaking open.

Solovki is just the right place to start. For it is there that the system of prison camp–art relationships is most fully represented, a system that was emulated, whether spontaneously or deliberately, in other places of confinement. The theatrical spectacle of the Solovki, and eventually of other settlements in the White Sea–Baltic Canal zone (Medvezhiegorsk, Tuloma, Mai-Guba, and others) presented in the 1920s and 1930s the various forms in which stage art was preserved under adverse conditions.

Three kinds of material, unequal in scope and merit, are available to the historian of camp theatre.

Official documents – orders of the day and reports of the cultural and educational departments and sections (CES) under which the theatres were placed – are, so far, extremely scanty. Camp documentation has not yet been declassified and many archives were destroyed for various reasons over the years.

A thin folder with material on the Central Theatre of the White Sea–Baltic Canal (the WS–BC combine) for 1935 to 1938 is today the only one of its kind.

Light could be shed on the fates of many actors and stage directors by the dossiers containing their letters, permits for visits by relatives, photographs, complaints, etc. True, working with dossiers and files is especially difficult. In addition to the investigators' outright provocations, and the prisoners' self-accusations, any single fact in a case may be buried under double and triple layers of fiction; at any moment pure truth may be followed by outrageous lies.

Most of the files remained in the place of indictment (Moscow, Leningrad, etc.) and the search for them is hindered. The case files which accompanied a prisoner to camp were more often than not destroyed. Camp files with the records of an inmate's transfers, workdays, sentence cuts or extensions and destiny (served full term, died, exiled, etc.) have also largely disappeared.

This is why the historian lives, as it were, in a world gone deaf; he cannot hear the people of those years. But suddenly, occasionally, human speech breaks through: the personal file of G.M. Osorgin, captain in the Lifeguards, preserves a letter from his wife, written in Moscow in anticipation of a visit to her husband in September 1928.

> Just a fortnight remains before our meeting. All the time I am in a
> kind of silly confusion, either due to agitation, or to excitement. . . .
> The four months that I haven't seen you, though I do not regret
> our Butyrka (prison) meetings, I have been constantly thanking
> God that you are alive there.[3]

Making up to some extent for the shortage of official information is a special kind of publication, peculiar to the Solovetsky Islands: the special camp's monthly journal *The Solovetsky Islands* and the daily paper *The New Solovki*.

The voice of the Solovki resounds loudly and at times is quite expressive. Of course, the reporters are from the very start in a false position, and their reports are rather one-sided, turning a blind eye to the other side of events. Or, compelled by the administration (or, possibly, owing to their own zeal), they even deny any untoward facts in the camp's life. Nevertheless, despite all the distortions and evasions, the Solovki press is absolutely indispensable material. The history of the theatre from 1924 to 1926 is reflected in the pages of both the journal and the paper with rare completeness. It is thanks to these publications, that the titles of plays, the names of stage directors and actors, and brief descriptions of the productions have come down to us.

Recollections by former Solovki prisoners, as well as by convicts working on the WS–BC, make up the third, ample but contradictory, source. Solovetsky reminiscences have peculiarities of their own: partly written in the 1920s and 1930s, hot on the heels of events, they naturally pay tribute to social journalism. At the same time, afraid of revealing the real names of still-living people and in order not to attract the KGB's attention to them, the authors avoided concrete characterizations and resorted to omissions and changed names. The result is schematicism and depersonalization.

In *Red Hard Labour*, Julia D. Danzas, as if anticipating her reader's disappointment, seemed to be exonerating herself:

> I am unable to give a full description of what went on at the
> Solovki, for this would fill up volumes and call for the composure
> of an historian working through documents, without constantly
> seeing before his eyes the actual picture of that horrible night-
> mare. . . . The day will come when this history is written, and
> those who read it will blush with shame for mankind.[4]

The cautious Danzas published her recollections in Paris in 1935, in French, without indicating the author's name, which, in view of the presence of vicious KGB residents abroad, is quite understandable. Neither did she mention any other names, nor succumb to the temptation to portray any of the convicts who had surrounded her. Today this evokes deep regret – without people, nothing but a schema remains.

Recollections set down by Solovki inmates in the 1940s and 1950s are different: names appear, as a rule, of people no longer living, with the stories of their lives.

But here the reader should beware of a lurking pitfall, about which the literary critic, Academician Dmitry Likhachev, duly cautions us:

> Recalling now what happened 60 years ago, I come to the conclusion that what is most difficult is to restore the date of this or that event. In my mind's eye I clearly see people, visualize their faces and the features of nature surrounding the Solovetsky Monastery, the platoons, I can hear the roll-calls, the crackling of rifle fire as people are shot, I recollect conversations, but to arrange them all in chronological order is most difficult. As if my memory keeps photographic and audio records of events and conversations, but all in disarray.[5]

Again, Likhachev cautions that 'most imprecise in memoir literature are conversations written down from memory. Unless the writer kept a diary, all that appears in inverted commas as direct speech is largely fantasy'.[6]

This is not only a matter of the imperfection of human memory. Camp life itself, where thousands found themselves in the most harsh contraposition to authority, to the environment and to one another, abounded in denunciations and provocations that in those years were perceived by many as being quite serious and tended to confuse them utterly. In the autumn of 1929 a large group of former officers, seamen and intellectuals, part of the camp élite, were shot at the Solovki, allegedly for plotting to kill the guards, seize ships, and escape, fighting, via Kem to Finland. The inmates believed the story. In *Red Hard Labour* M. Nikonov-Smorodin devotes a whole chapter entitled 'The Solovetsky Conspiracy' to this event: the plans of the underground group were related to him by one of the plotters, the energetic agronomist Petrashko. Within a few hours of the uprising there were sudden arrests, followed on 22 November by the shooting of 63 people, including Petrashko himself.[7]

Nikonov-Smorodin's figures are all wrong: in fact 51 people were convicted of conspiracy, of whom 36 were shot on the night of 28–29 October. More important is that the conspiracy was apparently concocted by the Cheka men themselves, and insinuated, through provocateurs, into the minds of a small group of prisoners. Some even then guessed at the truth.

Case No. 885 of the investigation into crime on the Solovetsky Islands contains the following statement:

> I had known several of those shot, lived with them for some time, and may assert that these people were simply incapable of such a crime. I heard that one or two provocateurs had been working in this case who were, by the way, also shot to cover up any traces, and that in fact there was no such plot. The whole business is fantastic and is worth checking.[8]

At the time nobody, of course, bothered, but today a publication by I. Chukhin corroborates the idea that the case was a frame-up.[9] Provocation spread like circles on water, distorting everything.

There are plenty of fantasies in Solovki memoirs and to check them would take considerable effort. In his book *The Solovetsky Monastery Prison Camp. 1922–1929. Facts – Conjectures – 'Latrine Buckets'*.[10] M. Rozanov demonstrated how imprecise are various recollections. The words 'latrine buckets' are used here in quite an unexpected, purely Solovetsky context: in everyday prison life a latrine bucket is a tub in a prison cell in place of a toilet. But Solovki took pride in the fact that the cells were not locked up for the night so that anyone could go outdoors whenever nature called. Because of this, 'latrine buckets' in the camp meant unverified rumours.

Rozanov did not escape errors, either, nor Likhachev fantasies. One of these is connected with the 1929 conspiracy, and the personality of the above-mentioned Osorgin and his wife Alexandra Mikhailovna. 'Georgy Mikhailovich Osorgin, Chief Clerk at the Medical Care Section, who had given relief from hard work permits to many intellectuals, was arrested…. Unexpectedly Osorgin's wife arrived for a meeting, and he was, on his word of honour (to think, that such a thing was then possible!), let out of the punishment cell.'[11] His wife was not told he was about to be shot and, upon taking leave of her, he returned to die.

The touching story of Osorgin's gallantry and love is recalled by others, too, perpetuating respect for an out-of-the-ordinary, brilliant personality, prepared for unexpected feats. He was, indeed, sent to a punishment cell for 30 days in May 1929 for 'his criminal activities, which found expression in exceeding his authority, as Chief Clerk at the Central Infirmary'.[12] This, possibly, was the time his wife arrived for a meeting. Osorgin was sentenced to death on 24 October 1929 and shot (died, says the case file) on 10 February 1930. And, according to circumstances, that last-hour meeting of camplore could not have taken place, for no meetings were permitted in winter, the link with Kem being maintained only occasionally, by aircraft.

The banal idea of the imperfection of human memory reconciles the historian with the inaccuracies he finds in texts written long after the event, and pointing them out is all that one can do. It also allows this author to count on the leniency of readers of the book before them, for it is likewise bound to contain some errors of 'ignorance'.

In a book about convicts I would like to pay due respect to the memory of those who perished in that special world. Alexander Solzhenitsyn's *The Gulag Archipelago*, which proved a shocking revelation to millions of readers, remains for me a book of tremendous moral fortitude.

Nevertheless, I would like to point out that Solzhenitsyn's remark about 'silent Solovki' was not quite true, and due entirely to the fact that at the time he wrote *The Gulag Archipelago* the relevant papers and journals were unavailable to him. No, the Solovki did not keep silent! The islands spoke to the whole country, and this constitutes one of the features of the Solovki press, not limited to the years 1924 to 1926 within the camp's walls. And what it had to say has lost neither its interest nor its edifying message.

Yet there is still another thing that seems to me important. This is our shared concern over the fate of art in the twentieth century. This century has twice seen the collapse of an enormous country, Russia. The downfall of so vast an empire is a prolonged and painful process. Attempts to save the country, which took 70 years amidst unprecedented sacrifices, ended in a shambles.

How does art stand up to such convulsions? What is the meaning of such historical ordeals to those involved in creativity?

The camp experience, according to the writer Varlam Shalamov, adds to 'mankind's negative experience'. What, then, under such conditions, is the quality of art – 'mankind's positive experience'?

What art opposes to the chaos of destruction and nonexistence, is, apparently, an inherent culture of developed forms, a concentration of reason and sensation. Form resists destruction and is even capable of subordinating to itself its spontaneity. And it is here that the force of art manifests itself, it is here that its everlasting battle against the entropy of the spirit is joined, and waged by exponents of the arts on behalf of man's salvation. Protecting the personality against destruction and self-extermination is the road for true humanists of our day to tread.

Today this road is harder than ever before. Yet any other leads to moral degradation, cynicism and occupational vacuity, however loud the phraseology camouflaging it. For this reason, the story of the camp theatre goes beyond its narrow historical aspect. It is aimed at drawing the mind of the reader, to a larger or smaller extent, to the problems of today. One may be aghast at the twentieth century's 'negative experience'. But what can be done to prevent it from crossing the threshold into the twenty-first?

In collecting material for this book I was helped by colleagues at the St Petersburg Branch of the *Memorial* Society – I.A. Reznikova, T.L. Dolgaya and T.F. Kosinova, who told me of their archival findings, and by V.V. Ioffe, who shared with me literary sources from his extensive library.

Special thanks are due to former Solovki inmates, whose reminiscences proved particularly useful: I.N. Rusinov, V.I. Tsekhansky, I.A. Vekentiev, I.P. Levitskaya; and to relatives of some of those who perished – I.P. Gordon, V.Yu. Gessen.

The unwavering goodwill of the staff of the State Historical Archives of Karelia, Petrozavodsk, very much facilitated the search for relevant materials.

I profited much from the valuable advice unstintingly given by A.V. Melnik and A.A. Soshina of the Solovetsky Museum, just as I did from the file they had drawn up.

Thanks are due to film director V.B. Meleiko for his kind permission to reproduce photographs he used in the making of the 1992 documentary *The Canal*, St Petersburg.

To all whom I have mentioned, as well as to those whom I have inadvertently left out, my profound gratitude.

Lastly: having landed in the winter of 1942 in prison (because of my own stupidity, incomprehensible to any adult), I pledged to write down all that I witnessed. I was 13 years old at the time. The decades that passed demonstrated the flimsiness of a child's experience matched against the sufferings of millions. But the pledge, once given, was not forgotten.

By publishing this book, I am paying an old debt and honouring, at least in part, my promise to tell the story of those who lived and perished in that world.

Natalia Kuziakina
St Petersburg
1992

PART ONE

1 From monastery to concentration camp

> *'Well, for such arguments that Kant ought to be
> seized and packed off, say, for three years to the
> Solovki!' Ivan Nikolayevich quite suddenly blurted
> out. 'Ivan', Berlioz whispered, embarrassed. But the
> suggestion to send Kant off to the Solovki, rather
> than shock the foreigner, sent him into raptures.
> 'Exactly', he shouted. 'That's the place for him!'*
>
> M. Bulgakov, *The Master and Margarita*

The transformation of a monastery into a prison camp – an unheard-of sacrilege to believers – befell many large and, before the revolution, rich cloisters at that time. The call for mass terrorism unleashed on 5 September 1918 throughout Russia and the revival of the medieval institution of taking hostages, Dzerzhinsky's assertion of the 'infallibility' of the secret police, whatever atrocities they perpetrated, and many other things brought about the prompt isolation of hundreds and thousands of people.

Prisons could not accommodate all the arrested. The only place where inmates could be herded on a mass scale and kept under guard were the monasteries (in Moscow, the Andronikov, today the Andrei Rubliov Museum of Old Russian Art, among others). From abodes of spiritual salvation they were converted into dens of disease, suffering and death for multitudes.

The new powers did not reach out to the Solovetsky Monastery at once. Even among such mighty northern pillars of Orthodoxy as the St. Cyril Monastery on the White Lake, and the Balaam on an island of that name in Lake Ladoga, it was by far the most distant and independent. Surrounded by huge votive wooden crosses along the coast, it proudly raised the green domes of its cathedrals, amazing all by its wealth and splendour.

The Solovetsky Archipelago, Solovki for short, comprises several rocky islands in the White Sea: the Great Solovetsky, the Great and Minor Muksalma, Anzer, the Big and Smaller Zayatsky, Kond, as well as a group of tiny islets – the Kuzova and Parusniye, nesting grounds of the rackety Solovetsky seagulls.

These bits of land, gifts of an ancient glacier, now hilly, now flat, are very small indeed. The main one, the Great Solovetsky, running north to south, is 25 km long and from 7 to 16 km wide; Anzer is 16 km long, 6 km wide, and separated from the Great Solovetsky by a strait. The Great Muksalma is 10 km long and 6 km wide; in 1865 it was linked to the Great Solovetsky by an arched bridge of large boulders, the 'dam'. The islands are 40 to 60 km from the nearest mainland. There stand the settlements of Kem and Sum, which belonged to the Novgorodian Burgomistress Martha, who donated them in the fifteenth century to the monastery with all its forests, ploughlands, villages, and other possessions.

What did the Monastery's legendary founders, the Balaam monks Sabas, Zosimus, and later, Gherman bring the Solovki? Piety and humility, as related in their *Lives*? A search for the ideal hermitage? Or a passion, unrestrained even by humility, for the exploration of new lands and a thirst for self-assertion? For only the staunch and courageous could have survived in that harsh realm.

True, the islands' nature and climate are peculiar, much better than on the mainland, if compared to the self-same Kem (today a city and station on the St. Petersburg–Murmansk railway), which is a dreary spot: the littoral is flat, lifeless, unrelieved by any natural vertical. All around are marshes, with ribbons of wooden sidewalks from grey house to brown. In winter an icy wind from the ocean sweeps right through the scattered houses. And perhaps the fantastic displays of the aurora borealis are the only thing to brighten up the silent shores and the frozen, humpy sea.

When one is acclimatized to the Solovki, the extremes of northern nature are quite tolerable: winter is relatively mild, without excessively severe frosts. And the terrain is astonishingly picturesque with forested hills and hundreds of lakes. The monks Sabas and Gherman, who had visited the Solovki previously, must have had souls responsive to beauty, for, having observed this island, of rare charm in summertime, they resolved to stay there. Sabas, having returned to the mainland, soon died, and a year later Zosimus and Gherman went out to the island again – an event dated 1429 by historians – and founded there a monastic community.

The monastery was granted an independent and full title to the Solovetsky Islands by the Novgorodian Burgomistress Martha

Boretskaya. It remained now for the monks to establish themselves on the remote desert islands.

Hard manual work became the prime source of life on the Solovki. The monks laboured hard and long throughout the summer, for the soil, strewn with rock and stone, bore no grain, yielding scanty hay; vegetables, like potatoes, cabbages and turnips, bitten by night frost, were not as tasty as on the mainland. While the monastery was taking root, food was gathered 'underfoot' – mushrooms and berries – and taken from the sea by fishing and by hunting white dolphin and seals. Eventually a kitchen garden was cultivated near the kremlin, and a good cattle farm was built on the Great Muksalma. Later still reindeer were released into the forest. They yielded skins for footwear, and wool for mattresses and pillows.

Winter, naturally, brought chores of its own: felling trees, which grew on the islands very slowly. Very soon timber had to be imported from the mainland. Generally, staple supplies had to be stored up, because for five months, from December to May, the mainland was cut off. In emergencies only did the dwellers of the seacoast risk crossing to the mainland by 'karbas' boats – wooden sloops that were dragged over the ice and then sailed amidst floating ice floes. The venture was always deadly hazardous and remained so even in the twentieth century, as described by journalists in the pages of *The New Solovki*.[1]

The history of the Solovetsky Monastery has been described fully in the literature.[2] A substantial monograph, *The Achitectural and Art Monuments of the Solovetsky Islands*, under the general editorship of D. Likhachev, who also contributed the introduction, has been published. As a student, Likhachev was exiled to the Solovki in 1928. For him, as a Petersburger, here was the first Russian monastery whose vaults he entered. As he was leaving the camp in 1931 to join the builders of the White Sea–Baltic Canal, where for shockwork preterm release was promised, he could not have imagined that he would ever be dealing with Solovki history as a scholar. Let us quote a remark of his:

> The Solovetsky Monastery contributed to the history of Russian culture its famous collection of manuscripts, its sixteenth to eighteenth-century stone edifices, a unique Old-Russian ensemble of civil engineering and architectural structures, its priceless collection of icons, now scattered about many museums of the Soviet Union. Its importance in the history of the Russian North from the middle of the fifteenth to the early eighteenth century is tremendous.[3]

The history of the embattled Russian North involved the monastery's hard-working monks in complicated missionary work to spread Christianity among the surrounding tribes (Karelians, Lapps, Finns, and others) and in the overall colonization of the territory. The black soutanes of the Solovetsky monks could be seen throughout the White Sea littoral, setting up salt works, felling timber for the Monastery, subjugating new villages. The Russian historian, Kliuchevsky, remarked in an early work, *The Economic Activities of the Solovetsky Monastery in the White Sea Area* (1866), that 'in the history of this cloister the economic and spiritual activities of its monks appear so closely intertwined, that one unfailingly accompanies the other everywhere'.[4]

Philip Kolychev, the monastery's superior for 20 years (from 1546 to 1566), left a special mark on its history. Wealthy and endowed with an indomitable spirit of creativity, he was one of those rare souls who seem capable of changing the world by their sheer creative energy. It is to him that the Solovetsky kremlin owes its gems: the Church of the Assumption, the Cathedral of the Transfiguration, the refectory chamber and the other stone edifices that formed the heart of the monastery. The main structures of the kremlin, built under the guidance of Novgorodian master masons, stand to this day in various states of preservation.

They should be seen, and best of all on a summer night, when, against the strangely pallid sky, 'one dawn hastens to oust the other, leaving the night but half-an-hour', to quote Pushkin. Or at the time of the brief incomparable sunsets, with their unearthly crimson, dark purple to violet tints in the deep velvety blue of the heavens.

These are moments when the huge boulders, of which the tall walls are built, coated with bright reddish lichens, are strikingly impressive. As if hands other than human had hoisted them up, one upon another, to soar there till the end of time. And rising still higher above the fortress walls, also as severe and forbidding as a castle, looms the huge, white Cathedral of the Transfiguration, unlike anything else, austere and lonely. As if the same inspired hands that had so easily thrown up the walls placed the bricks, caring less for straightness of line than for strength of masonry, destined to endure!

Such were the impressions of the geographer and historian S.V. Maksimov. When he visited the Solovki in 1856 he was stunned by those walls, their stones 'as if wedged in there by non-human hands and force'.[5] If even to people of the past two centuries the mighty, harsh Solovetsky cathedrals seemed creations of 'non-human hands', what can be said of the feelings of the monks and peasants of long ago, who visualized the stern beauty of those churches as a design executed and sanctified by God?

Meanwhile, at the time the monastery flourished, 'the community was preoccupied with many quite secular cares' (Likhachev). Enroachments by Swedes, Germans and Dutchmen and the military revolts and civilian riots of the sixteenth century spurred the continuation of Kolychev's building projects, even after he was murdered on the orders of the Tsar Ivan the Terrible in 1570. Walls, five to seven metres thick, in those times absolutely impregnable, sprang up around the monastery.

An elongated pentagon in plan, the fortress is protected on one side by the sea and by the Holy Lake on the other. These natural defences were augmented by eight battle towers: the monastery's triangular head with the White Tower stood on the bank of the Holy Lake, while its blunt rear, with its St. Nicholas and Watch Towers, climbed a low hill hugging the woods.

In the middle of the seventeenth century the monastery displayed valour of the highest order when, in 1657, it spurned the newly printed liturgical books decreed by Patriarch Nikon (himself a one-time Solovetsky monk) to replace the old ones. The Russian Schism assumed and gave voice to the general discontent throughout the land, especially in the north. Moreover, the Schism's religious aspect as such was fundamental; Nikon's reforms proved alien, hostile and incomprehensible. The north resolutely rejected them.

The Solovetsky monks, having reinforced their ranks with Don Cossacks, runaway serfs and other rebels, refused to bow to Nikon, and so a military expedition was dispatched to subdue the monastery. The monks, with up to 700 defenders, withstood an 8-year siege (1668–76), and only thanks to a traitor were the troops able to break into the kremlin. Of the 400 defenders only fourteen were spared, and the dead were left unburied, covered with stones.[6] I. Syrtsov held that 'the Solovetsky rebellion imparted strength and prestige to the Old Believers' cause.... The fruitful soil they had cultivated soon gave birth to the famous Vygovo Hermitage, which flourished and fertilized virtually the entire Russian Schism for nearly 200 years'.[7]

The Old Believers were numerous in the north; they suffered persecution and extermination for centuries. Villages on the banks of

Vyg Lake and the river Vyg, settled by Old Believers, disappeared under the waters as late as 1933.

The rout of the Solovetsky Monastery in the seventeenth century undermined its influence on the life of the north. When the crown expropriated monastic estates in 1764, it seemed the Solovki would dwindle altogether. Of course, the monastery fell into decline. However, it did not take the community too long to get back on its feet again.

The monastery's wealth was built up from all kinds of donations. Yet the Solovki's main asset was a happy balance between incumbents and temporary sojourners. For centuries the island's population never exceeded 900 to 1,000. The ratio of monks to those who worked with and for them, was rather erratic, but within limits: in 1649 there were 350 monks and up to 600 servants and labourers, in 1674 there were 200 monks and 300 novices. Novices were aspiring priests, not yet ordained (vacancies were scarce), who, while awaiting their turn, worked in various capacities. There were also the so-called yearmen, who came for a year or two or longer (having taken an oath, as penitents, or, if teenagers, as apprentices), and who worked without pay for bed, board and cloth.

Living in the monastery at the beginning of the twentieth century were 230 monks, up to 500 labourers and a number of yearmen, all in all, some 800 to 900 people. This unique, age-long population stability sustained monastic life in equilibrium. Work was looked upon as a spiritual mission, while, because of unpaid labour, the community's wealth kept mounting.

Any work on the Solovki rocks was arduous, and the construction of a dam and of canals took its toll of maimed lives. In 1926 some old papers, dated 1865, turned up on Anzer Island. One of the monks wrote: '...just consider the plight of the yearmen, those labourers for free: of weak constitution, too young and unseasoned for this truly Egyptian task, which strips them of health for ever.... Yet the Solovetsky superior cares nothing for the health of the unpaid year-labourers, who get their limbs broken and crushed by the rocks, and their innards ruined and their navels torn'.[8]

But this, apparently, was considered of no matter at the monastery: primordial barbarism went hand in hand with ecclesiastical enlightenment in the island's everyday life.

In the eighteenth century the Solovetsky Monastery assumed a new and far from easy function: in addition to being a place of confinement and incarceration for members of the clergy, which was the case throughout its existence, it turned into a political prison for lay persons, exiled at the command of the authorities, often for life.[9]

Until the middle of the seventeenth century people were incarcerated on the island in small casemates of stone. There were also pits in the ground, officially termed 'of prime severity'. A royal ukase of 1742 ordered all prison pits to be filled in with earth, and in 1758 a special inspector checked on compliance with this, but the monks, according to the historian G. Frumenkov, covered the pits for a time with boarding, after which they put them to use again.

How long could one endure in a pit? According to Frumenkov, Ivan Buyanovsky, a defrocked priest, sentenced in 1722 by Peter I to a ground jail 'for all time', was still languishing there in 1751, 29 years later. Two peasants held a record: Anton Dmitriev spent 62 years at the monastery, of which 48 years were in solitary, while Semion Shubin, 'for blasphemously abusing the Holy Sacraments and the Holy Church', was imprisoned for 63 years.

Piotr Kalnishevsky, the last Cossack Hetman of the Zaporozhie Host in Little Russia, as the Ukraine was styled before 1917, proved toughest of all. At the head of the Zaporozhie Host, Kalnishevsky fought the Crimean Tartars and the Turks in the Russo-Turkish war of 1768–74. In the middle of the campaign he was awarded a diamond-studded gold medal for valour, and the Host was given thanks.

Yet, no sooner did the war end in Russian victory than it was decided to get rid of the wilful Cossacks. On 3 August 1775, a ukase by Catherine II proclaimed to the populace that 'the Zaporozhie Host has been utterly destroyed, with the extermination for the future time of the very name of the Zaporozhie Cossacks...'.[8]

Kalnishevsky, who at that time was already 84, simply disappeared. And only a hundred years later the exiled historian P. Yefimenko heard by sheer chance from peasants in the village of Vorzogory on the White Sea, that back in the early nineteenth century there had lived in confinement in the Solovetsky Monastery some Cassack chieftain, whom they had seen in person. Thus, a trace was found of Kalnishevsky, exiled to be 'tamed'.

He had lived on the Solovki since 1776, where he was incarcerated in a casemate of the White Tower, isolated from the whole world. The peasants recalled that Kalnishevsky was taken out for a breath of fresh air three times a year: at Easter, on the Feast of the Transfiguration and for Christmas. He spent 16 years in a stone cubby-hole, and then another nine in a somewhat better cell, 25 years in all.

In 1801, upon the ascent to the throne of Alexander I, the Privy Expedition was abolished and the prisoners in its custody freed. Kalnishevsky was graciously 'pardoned'. The old man, who had gone completely blind and wild, decayed like the rags he wore, retained, nevertheless, a clear mind. He asked to be left in the monastery, where he soon died in 1803 at the age of 112 years.

A newly built three-storey prison stood in the first section of the kremlin and drew the eye, according to M. Kolchin, 'by its red roof, rising above the monastery walls, and the barred windows of the third storey'. Having become a fixture, it introduced into the monastic life certain moral aberrations. Although inmates were maintained at the cost of the treasury, they were treated so mercilessly that they frequently went mad.

The liberal journalist and future writer for the Nazi paper *Völkischer Beobachter*, Vasily Nemirovich-Danchenko, found only two inmates in the prison in 1872 and was truly aghast at the cells within a damp wall and the double bars: 'Oh, God forbid that anyone should experience such terrible years of solitary confinement and enslavement. Better death!'

Gradually, the spirit of liberalism reached the Solovetsky prison. In 1886 the military platoon which had guarded the prisoners was sent away. M. Kolchin's essays about the Solovetsky prisoners appeared in the pages of the press and were later published as a book. The medieval image of the Solovetsky prison was at variance with the humanitarian demands of the times, and the prison, where only one inmate remained, was at last closed in 1903. The building was converted into a hospital.

At the beginning of the twentieth century the Solovetsky Monastery, with its strong peasant element, could boast of a rich and diversified economy, which had developed, unit by unit, over the centuries. All kinds of produce were processed in its own workshops and facilities to meet the community's needs. A candle works was operating, from which hot water went to hothouses to grow melons, watermelons and other delicacies for the table of the Father Superior and the presiding elders. There were also tailors, cobblers, carpenters' workshops, plumbers and tin-smiths, gold- and silversmiths, a lapidary workshop and stone-cutters, harness- and cart-makers' shops. Strong hands were required for net-making, for the building and repair of seagoing vessels, in the granaries and the flour-mill, in the lime kilns, for hunting and fishing, at the tannery and brick works, on the cattle farm and in the stables. The icon-painting workshop opened a general education school to train peasant youngsters.

In the 1880s the monastery purchased two steamships to bring pilgrims over from Archangel and Sum; these flew their own tricolours bearing the letters 'SM'. In 1892 a lithography shop was established to print postcards of Solovki sights, and on a canal linking the lakes an electric plant was built in 1910, one of the first in Russia, which brought light to the monastic cells and the monastery's three guest houses. This was especially appreciated during the short autumn days and long, dark winter.

For the Russian North the Solovki became a centre of religious pilgrimage and tourism. 'Our Solovki is a Russian Mount Athos,' the monks used to state proudly.

The ritual of pilgrim ablutions in Holy Lake was carefully followed, and two bathing sites, for men and women, were maintained. The rules of behaviour were stringent: the day began at 3 a.m. and there were hours in church and visits to chapels. Peasants, who made up the majority, were settled in the guest house twenty to a room; intellectuals of other than gentle birth lived from three to five in a room, while the rich were given private rooms, as in ordinary inns. Women, who had never resided in Solovki before, were accommodated separately. A stay lasted three days, and pilgrims enjoyed free board: meat was never served, but fresh fish was a welcome substitute. For a longer sojourn, a permit from the monastery authorities was required.

Such brisk activity lasted from May to October, when the Solovki opened its doors wide to the world and kept in touch with it. During the autumnal storms and the silence of winter, the monastery closed its doors and worked for itself, in preparation for the next spring.

As in any complex association of different people, the monastic community concealed within itself a good deal of contention and friction. Although a community of monks, 'staying together in name and at table, and ever more so in unanimity, for the sake of salvation', genuine unanimity remained an ideal. However, the monastery's inner life was barely revealed to outsiders, at least to a casual glance.

Nemirovich-Danchenko recalled a conversation with a gardener monk: 'Literacy is not required. Fewer temptations; our ways here are simple'. Of course, the monks were taught to read and write, but still 'there is little idle talk here, but many hard-working and knowledgeable people'.

In his heart the writer felt sorry for the youth, smothered by monastic life: 'What a wonderful abode of love these islands could be.... Side by side with nature, fascinating and brimming with life, asceticism becomes formidable and horrifying.'

On their return trip to Archangel, Nemirovich-Danchenko and his fellow travellers discussed the peculiar nature of the Solovetsky Monastery. The writer came to the conclusion that the principle sustaining 'this ascetic working commune' was that 'nobody should be idle'. His companions saw the monastery as a smoothly running establishment; for some this was good, for others a dangerous deviation, as cupidity and stinginess, material calculation, overcome spirituality. The argument closed with the question whether such a community could have existed in other than monastic form. 'None of us found the answer. Up till now all working communities have proved durable only when based on religious principles.'[11]

Absorbed in their day-to-day chores, the Solovetsky elders were unable, perhaps, to keep pace with the stormy revival of Russian religious thought, which marked the beginning of the twentieth century. Solovki managed to inspire visiting painters. M.V. Nesterov, who gave all his sympathies to the Russian North, was convinced in the 1920s, that one should not be afraid of staying in a concentration camp – don't be afraid of the Solovki, one feels closer to God there.

This is how, goaded on, now sluggishly, now swiftly, by the centuries sweeping past, life in the Solovetsky Monastery took shape. Labour sanctified by religion, pilgrimage and its own accumulated assets (more than half a million in capital), could have sustained the monastery for a very long time indeed – had it not encountered Soviet government!

The latter ushered in tragedies about which art, within the boundaries of Russia, had no way of telling the world. *Russia of the Past*, a requiem by Pavel Korin, a pupil of Nesterov, is perhaps the only work whose characters hint at the depth of the dramas that played themselves out behind the walls of many a monastery. But Korin was summoned by the secret police, and from the mid-1930s he had to abandon painting and take up restoration work; among his portraits from life he was even compelled to draw Henrich Yagoda himself, the head of that service.

Through the first years of the civil war some of the Solovki monks may have cherished hopes of the return of the former life and made attempts to find a common language with the Soviet authorities. But in the summer of 1920 nationalization of church property took place in Solovki, which had already suffered during the revolutionary years; now the demise of the monastery could be clearly discerned.

Alexeyev, appointed to manage the monastery's economy, reported, not without compassion, to Kem:

> Residing in the monastery are 566 persons. They are all engaged in field and domestic work. There are no shirkers. All are working quite willingly without any nudging and compulsion. They rise at three in the morning, and finish at six in the evening. Here are people already seasoned in an ongoing effort to sustain themselves by fighting nature, who are not daunted by work.

This is the latest available evidence about the existence of that very worker commune in which nobody showed the slightest interest.

Solovetsky property was filched in the most outrageous manner, stripping the monks of their own provisions, without which they were bound to perish. Archimandrite Benjamin, the monastery's Father Superior, complained to Kem that on the orders of political commissar S. Abakumov large quantities of stores had been taken away from the monastery and asked for their return to the fraternity. However, the commissions, which arrived at Solovki in the summer of 1920 one after another, were quite indifferent. Alexeyev wrote in despair:

> In view of the chaotic situation that has taken shape on the Solovetsky Islands, where numerous and diverse authorities arrive from every quarter and take this and that without my permission, one doesn't know who to obey.... Considering all the above, and having no power to resist this, I beg you to relieve me of my post immediately.[12]

In 1921 a state farm was set up on the islands, but the newly arrived bosses had no intention of properly managing it. The system of the Solovki collapsed. And when in 1922 the monastery was abolished, some of the physically sturdy monks left for the island of Balaam, which remained in Finland, together with the Father Superior, while others dispersed over the mainland, leaving in the cells about 150 rather old monks who entrusted their fate to God. They managed to eke out some sort of existence on the farms.

It was at this time that the secret police brought to Solovki the dying inmates of the Pertominsk Monastery and set up a summer camp. Later on it was thought that the Bolsheviks were tipped off about the island as a place of exile by the émigré Socialist-Revolutionary B. Burtsov in 1921. However, the idea could also have occurred to the Bolsheviks themselves.

The disintegration of the Solovetsky Monastery and its well-run economy culminated in an unprecedented fire in its kremlin during the night of 25–26 May 1923. A resolution had already been passed to establish a permanent camp and the first prisoner transports were about to leave the Pertominsk, Archangel and Kholmogory northern camps. Later, this gave grounds for imputing arson, first to fanatical monks, then to White Guards. The cause of the calamity was never established with certainty. According to an article by Zorin, who arrived on the island soon after the fire, neither arson by state farm administrators aimed at covering up utter mismanagement nor sheer negligence leading to inflammable rubbish being kept in the attic of the treasury building could be ruled out. Moreover, the head of the office, who had the key, could not be found and the alarm bell was sounded too late, when the flames had already reached the roof.[13]

The fire raged for three days. The monastery's main buildings were connected by galleries, so that, apart from the domes, the interiors of nearly all the churches were burned out as well. Luckily, the Cathedral of the Transfiguration suffered least and its iconostasis survived. The tower clock, which operated the bell chimes, perished. The huge bell, whose voice on a calm day reached as far as Kem, cracked, and the 35 smaller bells melted. The library was burnt down and only its double iron doors and shutters saved the sacristy. The monastery was destroyed, seemingly forever.

Meanwhile, history was about to stage a great experiment on the island. The time had come for putting to the test ideas which the life of the Solovetsky Monastery had evoked in the minds of progressives in the nineteenth century.

Could a labour commune exist there unblessed by religious and spiritual unity? What would happen to the ascetic Solovki if women were admitted to the island? Is man's social nature at all amenable to change and, if so, in what measure?

The unprecedented experiment that took place yielded convincing and unequivocal answers.

2 The Solovetsky Special Purpose Camp – SLON

> *He's being sent to an island…. It's lucky that there*
> *are such a lot of islands in the world. I don't know*
> *what we should do without them. Put you all in the*
> *lethal chamber, I suppose.*
>
> Aldous Huxley, *Brave New World* (1932)

The more thoughtful Russian intellectuals, upon recovering from their initial dismay, very soon realized that fighting the Bolsheviks, whose slogan 'expropriate the expropriators!' delivered their followers of moral scruples, was, perhaps, hopeless.

Mikhail Prishvin, the writer, taken hostage together with the editorial board of *The People's Will* in January 1918, visualized his time as a huge boiling cauldron:

> It is now becoming clear that to come out against the Bolsheviks on behalf of the individual is impossible: the cauldron is bubbling and will go on bubbling to the end…. All the dust of the earth, all the rubbish and filth is being swept up into the tail of Lenin's comet.[1]

Zinaida Gippius expressed in the pages of her diary feelings of horror and wrath:

> The unheard-of absurdity of what's happening…defies imagination…Assyrian slavery. Oh, no, not even Assyrian, nor penal servitude in Siberia, it is something beyond compare. People are herded to do unnecessary, hard work, without proper clothing and swaying with hunger, herded under snow and rain, in cold and darkness…. Whoever heard of anything like that?[2]

Vladimir Korolenko confided to his wife in March 1919: 'Bolshevism is a sickness that has to be experienced organically. No medicine, not even surgery, can help. The catchword for the masses is rather attractive. In the past you were under oppression, but now you become masters. And masters they want to be'.[3] In letters to A. Lunacharsky, People's Commissar for Education, the old writer reproached the

Bolsheviks for reviving the medieval institution of hostage-taking and for the unheard-of brutality of the Secret Police.

The theme of the absurd, the trampling upon organic forms of life for the sake of a schema of social depersonalization and a sweeping recoil of society backwards was developed with unexpected force in *We*, Zamiatin's anti-Utopia published in 1921. Art promptly penetrated to the core of the experiment, of which even many of its organizers had a rather hazy idea.

Leo Trotsky was not alone in seeing compulsory labour as the main force in building socialism and labour armies as the best form of workers' and Red Army men's organization. Trotsky, again, held that 'terror is a most powerful political instrument', while 'the question of the form or degree of repression is, of course, by no means one of "principle". It's a matter of expediency.'[4]

It was all the more easier to transpose the experience of a life of militarized labour into camp projects. Forced labour was just the natural punishment for social adversaries.

Actually, documents about the Solovki camp have not yet been released from the archives. We can speak, therefore, about the idea of setting up a special-purpose camp there only tentatively.

The northern camps of Pertominsk, Kholmogory and Archangel had the same designation. Their special purpose was the physical extermination of the new government's political adversaries: the White Guards, the socialist–revolutionaries and the anarchists. The method of destruction consisted in either provoking a wrathful outburst on the part of the inmates, to be suppressed by force of arms, as was the case at Kholmogory, or letting things take their natural course of survival through deprivation of light, warmth and medical care and only a bare minimum of food.

Naturally, one ought to remember that in the north in those years, practically anyone was exposed to the most severe conditions, for there was nothing to make up for the break-down of social ties (everything had to be imported): when drugs or kerosene, bread or soap were lacking, they were lacking for virtually everyone. Such circumstances led to death, as was very accurately depicted in the complaints of the socialist–revolutionaries at the Pertominsk camp (1923).[5]

Physical extermination by inhuman conditions of existence was practised widely on the Solovki, where northern camp prisoners from Moscow and Petrograd were brought together.[6] Yet the design, apparently, was different. With the country's rapidly changing foreign policy, in a bid for European recognition the camp was called upon to demonstrate capabilities less for extermination than for reforming social and political enemies.

The editors of *SLON* magazine endeavoured to convince its readers that even the most die-hard criminal could be reformed. An article by V. Belavin, 'A scientific study of the criminal world in pre-war Europe' (*SLON*, 1924, Nos. 7–8), which maintained that any prison was but a half-measure, was promptly amended by the editorial board: on the contrary, the Soviet prison was capable of changing man. The camp received every kind of human material for recasting. The circumstances of that recasting beggar the imagination to this day.

A prisoner who arrived at a transit prison under the jurisdiction of the Northern Camps Board (Kemperpunkt, Popov-Ostrov) was exposed to unpredictable physical and moral abuses, invented by the wardens and former secret policemen: people from every strata of society, punished for service misdemeanours and glaring corruption, including heavy drinking, debauchery and bribe-taking.

Fiodor Dostoyevsky, who well remembered his period of penal servitude, wrote: 'Blood and power intoxicate; a craving for crude vulgarity, for debauchery evolves; the satisfaction of the most weird perversions comes within reach, eventually becoming enjoyable to the mind and senses.... There are two kinds of executioners: some are willing, others are subordinate, duty-bound'.[7] In the camps both kinds abounded; in the atmosphere of all-pervading ferocious cruelty and denial of personality, they differed not so much in quality, as in the degree of cruelty.

These were the people who made up the camp's service personnel from top to bottom, who wielded power, and who, in the main, committed the worst atrocities they were capable of. Demoted secret policemen swaggered about in sealskin jackets, the guards in long, black-cuffed greatcoats, yet without the star on their caps. While to the authorities 'socially' still 'their own', and even politically of kindred spirit, they were expected to mend their ways in the process of correcting the inmates. This is how it went. Kemperpunkt, Popov-ostrov:

Yu. Bessonov. A large barracks, 10 paces long, 20 wide. The frost notwithstanding, the door is open, and despite the open door the air is horrible.... Near the floor it's freezing, yet it's suffocating. The stink of unwashed bodies, stench of cod, clothing, tobacco, dampness – all fused in a thick haze, through which faintly glimmer two ten-watt bulbs.... Four rows of bunks stretching the length of the barrack thickly strewn with lying and sitting bodies.... Emaciated, tired faces.... A clump of naked figures stand under the bulbs holding underwear and clothes – squashing lice.... Behind a partition at one end of the barracks the 'aristocracy' – the 'commanding officers'. At the other end near a window a small table, the best place, and also for 'aristocrats', but this time the moneyed.... The barracks is patched up in many places with rags. So this is where one is to live.... A bell sounded.... A platoon commander strode out into the middle of the barracks and yelled at the top of his voice: 'Line up for prisoner count!'.... Reluctantly, exhausted people climb off the bunks.... For about an hour we just stand there, waiting.... At long last the guards arrive. The door opens sharply and several secret police, spurs ringing, burst in. 'Why on earth spurs?' I ask myself.... The platoon orderly jumps to attention to report to the station officer on duty.... All this was so out of keeping with their semi-civilian clothes, and the general entourage of half-naked people, that everything seemed utterly inane, like a kind of farce, were it not so tragic.... For on this small bunch of people, outside any legality whatever, depended the life of every one of us.[8]

When, at the end of May, the sea cleared of ice and the first ship steamed up to Solovki pier, the prisoners who had withstood the trial of dirt, filth and abuse were again taken to task. Solovki, B. Shiriayev:

The acceptance begins. The chief, rather the lord of the island, Comrade Nogtev, makes his appearance in front of the lined-up new arrivals. Here was the man who throughout the first year of our sojourn on the Solovki, was to play a special, exceptional role in the life of every one of us. On him, or rather, on the twists of his drunken fantasy, not only every step of ours, but our very life depended....

'Hi, you rooks!' the boss welcomed us. By every token he is in a state of strong intoxication and in an ironical, benevolent mood. Nogtev's hands were stuck in the pockets of a stylish sealskin jacket – the ultimate of ostentation on the Solovki, as we eventually learned. His cap is worn low over the eyes. For some time, rocking from heel to toe, he observes sceptically our questionable line-up and then delivers himself of a welcoming speech.

'Well, it behoves you to know, that the authority here is not Soviet (a pause for effect, amazement among the rows) but Soloviet! (This formula is now widespread throughout all prison camps.) Well, now! All laws should be now well forgotten, for here we have laws of our own.' Then we are given an exposition of the law here, in expressions if not too clear, at least using the filthiest language, and surely boding us nothing pleasant.... The welcoming speech over, they get down to business – accepting the party. Nogtev lazily walks away and disappears behind the door of the guard box, his head instantly popping up in its window.

We are confronted with Vaskov, the Head of the Administrative Section of the Solovetsky Special Purpose Camps, a gorilla of a man, no forehead, no neck, just a huge, long, heavy, unshaven jaw and a drooping lip. The gorilla is as fat as a hog. Red, shiny cheeks come up to the bloated, weak-sighted eyes and hang down over the collar. In his hand Vaskov holds the rolls containing the prisoners' names. As he calls them out, he looks them up and down and makes some notations. First called out are the priesthood.... Observing the clergy pass by obviously gives Nogtev a good deal of satisfaction.

'What term?' he asks a white-haired bishop who trundles along with great difficulty against the wind, hindered by the folds of his cassock. 'Ten years.' 'Well, see to it that you make it, don't kick the bucket before term! The Soviet government, all the same, will pull you out of paradise by the beard!'

The counting of the priesthood is over. Now it is the turn of the counter-revolutionaries.[9]

The Solovki population lived in an atmosphere of 'everyone fighting everyone', but national and clan solidarity provided protection from utter peril. Predominating in numbers were the scum, the criminals, those indicated for thieving, prostitution, swindling, robbery, fights and murder, gambling and other crimes. The bosses played on the inner contradictions of the camp and put together in the same barracks criminals and counter-revolutionaries, disrupting unity and denying them any chance of uniting or the peace of an individual existence.

That everybody was always tense suited the warders very well. The rabble were reluctant to work and pulling the harness for them were the counter-revolutionaries, yet the thieves were ready at the first opportunity to strip their neighbours and make short shrift of them.

The counter-revolutionaries, though fewer in numbers, made up a quite significant group, comprising former army officers, repatriated émigré intellectuals, wives of aristocrats and relatives of courtiers, lawyers, historians, scholars of every shade and the priesthood (Russian Orthodox, as well as of other creeds).

The supervising staff, while mistrusting the counter-revolutionaries, still depended on them for decency and honesty. For the camp, having started with 2,000 inmates, received every year prison transports of many hundreds, and so reached towards the late 1920s the dangerous figure of 25,000.

All these thousands had to be maintained in relative order, so that the rabble should not wrench power from the bosses' weak hands. With these thousands demanding at least a minimum of food and other supplies, they could hardly do without help from the counter-revolutionaries: no sooner did they attempt to clear the kremlin of the priests (who handed out parcels, foodstuffs, etc.) than the criminals immediately pilfered everything and the old men had to be brought back.

The camp maintained a precarious equilibrium through the intricate interaction of the social groups of which it was made up. It was at them that the avalanche of corrective measures was hurled, aimed at turning erstwhile enemies and criminals into the country's conscientious citizens – builders of a socialist society. Keeping aloof of the camp's everyday squabbles and controversies was the relatively small group (up to 450 strong) of 'politicians', political prisoners kept on the Solovki for two years from the summer of 1923 to the summer of 1925, when they were shipped to the mainland. They were made up of socialist–revolutionaries, Mensheviks, anarchists and Zionists, who in fact enjoyed the rights of political exiles. They were quartered in the secluded Savvatievo chapel, some ten kilometres from the kremlin, and also on the Muksolma and Anzer islands. The 'politicians' were free to move within a territory separated by wire, lived in rooms at their own discretion, even in families, with children and received substantial rations and also books from the political Red Cross. They were spared re-education.

E. Olitskaya recollected the handwritten journal *Spolokhi* (*Northern Lights*), a copy of which was found in 1955 by seamen, who turned it over to the secret police. She also took part in a drama circle:

> Though we lacked talented actors, we had gifted directors,
> stage designers and musicians. An orchestra was organized
> by Yasha Rubinstein. It is hard to imagine of what the in-
> struments were made! The humorous numbers were subtle
> in content and brilliant in form. They were filled with politi-
> cal satire based on chapel events.[10]

The political prisoners' special status set them distinctly apart from all the other inmates; indeed, they, who believed themselves to be true socialists, had nobody to unite with. The ridiculous shooting of six people on 19 December 1923, stemming from a tightening of camp rules (proscription of night walks), evoked quite an uproar in the foreign press. The political prisoners' demand for transfer to the mainland was granted, and they were sent off to Verkhneuralsk and other prisons for many, many years.

Vestiges of a 'political regimen' lingered on at Solovki till 1937: certain prisoners (foreigners, party functionaries, eminent scientists) were excused from forced labour, enjoyed a larger ration and received parcels from the International Red Cross.

The rest, though, were always being reminded that 'in view of the fact that the Solovetsky Concentration Camp is a compulsory labour camp, its main and basic provision is compulsory adaptation of the inmate to various labour processes' (*The New Solovki* [N.S.] 1926, No. 12).

Counter-revolutionaries were saved only by their expertise and cooperative aid. Otherwise their lot was general hard labour (timber felling, peat working, etc.), rapid emaciation inevitably followed by chilling, scurvy, typhoid fever and death. The Solovki's true, unvarnished visage, especially during the first years, was that of a gaunt, filthy being crawling with lice, his hands scratched red. At the end of a twelve-hour work day he returns to a huge cathedral (the St. Nicholas Cathedral contained four tiers of bunks!), to filth, dust and stench. Without undressing he wraps himself in his coat and drops off into tormented slumber, to be roused on the morrow at 5 o'clock and start another day.

Such figures failed, of course, to demonstrate any of the benefits of reform. And so, in order to cover up the camp's festering sores it had its own court photographer and its own court painter. Captain Boris Sederholm recalled:

> There was also on the Solovki a 'court photographer', actu-
> ally a secret police agent, and once I happened to witness
> the following scene.

> I had been sent to the hospital on some errand.... I loathed going to the infirmary, for patients were lying even in the corridors right on the floor, and the stench was unbearable. Approaching the hospital, I was amazed to notice small tables covered with white napkins set up in the stunted garden planted in front of the building. On the tables were cups and bottles, and sitting around them were patients dressed uniformly and well. It was devilishly cold, and the men at the tables must have felt frozen in their light clothes.
>
> But to healthy people cold is no peril. As a matter of fact, not a single person among the so-called patients around the tables was sick. All of them were 'extras' from among the KGB servicemen, specially dressed up for picture taking.
>
> My rather unprepossessing figure in a crumpled hat, short sheepskin coat and felt boots must have spoiled the idyllic picture of the happily relaxed patients. For one of the stage-managers shouted at me: 'Hey, you there! The bearded one! Get the hell out of the way!'

The role of Solovki's 'court painter' was assigned in 1924–25 to O.E. Braz, a former Professor at the Imperial Academy of Fine Arts, under whom studied such eminent painters as Z. Serebriakova and A. Rusakov. According to Sederholm, Braz was preparing an album intended to show an image of the flourishing Solovki. 'Every time the Professor came back from his censors, he would start, with a bitter sigh, to restore the churches and embellish camp life... in the pages of his album.'[11]

Boris Solonevich reminisced about the shooting of the film *Solovki*:

> When in 1927 the Solovki were immortalized on film, our sports centre featured as all but the principal argument in proving the inmates' 'happy life'. The Red Army men selected to represent prisoners, 'with joyous smiles', performed exercises and games. Then the camera went on to record all the island's gorgeous natural and historical sights and the smartly dressed camp inmates' beaming, well-fed faces, as, gushing with enthusiasm, they displayed 'high labour productivity'. All of them were dressed-up Red Army and secret service men.[12]

General I.I. Zaitsev recalled with horror: 'The Soviet Film Board made a film about life on the Solovki. My God!...What brazen and vile staging of all the episodes and scenes!'

The film's impact was even excessive. During a discussion at the Moscow Society of Friends of the Soviet Cinema, a woman worker said: 'This film cannot be released. Look at what's going on: at a time when here in Moscow we are lining up at the labour exchange, with our children starving, you are showing all these counter-revolutionaries, these criminals having the time of their lives!' She – and not only she – took what she saw for gospel truth!

But the film *Solovki* hit the screens in 1929 and 1930, when half the inmates were afire with typhoid fever and the ferociousness of the warders knew no bounds. It was then, in response to foreign press accusations of cruelty, that the *Solovki* film was released: there! see for yourselves how it really is!

Excerpts from that picture could be seen in a film by Marina Goldovskaya *Soloviet Power*. No tricks of bygone days could strip the image of a concentration camp of its inherent dreariness. The miserable life can be gleaned from the appearance of people, the cruelty of depersonalization from the movements of the crowd. The furnaces of the secret police, though out of view, are there.

Standing out against the background of ideological fraud, that is, deliberate misrepresentation, are two kinds of activity on the Solovki of the 1920s: publication of the journal *SLON – Solovetsky Islands* and the theatre.

'Much in history repeats itself, but there occur unrepeatable combinations, brief in time and place. Such was our NEP. Such were the early Solovki', remarked Solzhenitsyn.

He explained the 'unrepeatability of the combinations' by the fact that at the time the 'Solovetsky regimen had not yet been tightened by the armour of the system. The impression is that the air of the Solovki was already a mixture of utter cruelty with an all but sublime incomprehension of where it was all heading.'[13]

As he comes to the Solovetsky press and theatre, the historian steps into a realm of topsy-turvy, distorted concepts. A frightening shift of culture, back to the Middle Ages, even to slavery, and a vigorous spurt ahead, self-development and adaptation of old forms to the habits and concepts of the twentieth century.

The outstanding Russian actor Mikhail Chekhov, recalling the calamities of war and the sufferings of its victims, remarked, as if in passing, 'only a dearth of the imagination enables us to go on living'. 'A dearth of the imagination' and self-sufficient rationalism enable us, too, to study camp life. For the majority of the inmates it was like a path of broken glass atop a low dam, the waves instantly licking off the blood. And stepping sprightly along, with a hop and a skip, from afar comes a man....

3 The special purpose press:
The Solovetsky Islands and *The New Solovki*

Letter box
Comrade Kozachenko. In that dispute of yours,
he is right who maintained that annihilation
of life on Earth is possible. If more detailed
explanations are desirable, call at the editorial
office in person.

The New Solovki, 1925, No. 21

This is how the Solovetsky press began: on 8 October 1923 Isaac S. Slepian set foot on the island. Seized for speculation in gold, this man, of quite unprepossessing appearance, had, if we are to believe B. Shiriayev, the cunning of Talleyrand and the staunchness of Fabius Cunctator. By trade a lithographer, he was summoned the next day to the administration where it was found that, after looting and fire, the only thing remaining from the printshop was a lithographic stone the size of a printed sheet.

Nevertheless, the first wall newspaper appeared under the touching title of *An Islet* as early as 29 October as an organ of the party cell of the 95th Northern Camps OGPU Division on guard duty at the camp. And in March 1924 the journal *SLON* was produced (fifteen copies off an Underwood typewriter). From its very first 1925 issue the journal was renamed *The Solovetsky Islands*. The newspaper *The New Solovki* was launched on 11 January of the same year.[1]

The idea of the publication, Shiriayev recalls, orginated with Nikolai Litvin, who had just been discharged from the infirmary after a serious illness and could be seen quietly and silently leaning on a stick and wandering about the kremlin yards.

'The present writer remembers that day. Remembers the first printed copy in the hands of N. Litvin, the first to release it. He also remembers something else. He remembers the sceptical, ironic smiles, the disdainfully curving lips', Shiriayev admits.[2]

The years 1925–26 were marked by the flourishing of both the paper and the journal. They even reached the mainland, the wide world, as a subscription to the general public was announced throughout the USSR, allowing them to be mailed from the island to any address.

However, both the paper and the journal were suddenly dead and gone right on the eve of the New Year, 1927. Then, as suddenly, they reappeared in the autumn of 1929, only to vanish again, this time for good, in May 1930. Such is the sad story. Unravelling its logic is important, as the theatre and the press were created by the same people; both the theatre and the paper, in different forms, aspired to protect the individual, and their existence was closely interwoven.

Against the background of numerous prison newspapers and journals published in the 1920s, the Solovki press stands out as something unusual. It was made by just a few people, hiding behind pen-names: N. Litvin, B. Shiriayev, T. Tverie, B. Glubokovsky, B. Emelianov, Ya. Galkh and Tsvibelfish with, of course, the cooperation of other authors too. This team's professionalism imparted to the press remarkable vigour and literary sparkle. Made up of many fragments, feuilletons and essays, here was a mirror, albeit a rather distorted one, which reflected, nevertheless, the life of the camp. Those crafty intellectuals, obeying the Chekists' orders, were able to wrench from the administration essential concessions for the press, and, thereby, for all the convicts. This was the newspapermen's way of existence, both intentional and beyond their control.

Everything that happened in the camp was unexpected and unprecedented. Whoever took the precarious path of a camp journalist did so fully cognizant of the possible consequences. Everyone decided his own fate. The camp's word for those who took the side of the administration was a hard one, meaning 'turncoat', and it sounded like a slap in the face, like a filthy curse. Journalists on the central paper felt uncomfortable in any case. But they had little choice: if an inmate's case file indicated the occupation of journalist (as was the case with, for example, Litvin) what could he do? Fight Deputy Camp Commander Fiodor Eichmans, himself exiled to be reformed?

One such attempt was described by Major-General I. Zaitsev, who, upon his return from emigration and being forgiven all his sins, was dispatched from Moscow to Solovki. Now, Eichmans wished the journal to publish the general's recollections of the civil war in Central Asia. The general declined the honour and found himself felling timber in a common work gang. In Zaitsev's book the matter seems to have closed there and then – with his will intact.

Yet, leafing through the pages of *The Solovetsky Islands*, we do find his writings: *From Bygone Days (Excerpts from the memoirs of Cossack Hetman Dutov's former chief-of-staff, Major-General I.M. Zaitsev, who Returned from Emigration)*.[3] Cold and hunger must have compelled the general to surrender, something he was most reluctant to recall.

So that making choices was for journalists rather conditional, and we can only speculate about their motives. Quite possibly, there were hidden reasons behind their actions: initially the central papers and information in general reached the island's authorities only, yet the camp as a whole needed them too.

From its very first months, day-to-day infighting for power went on in the *SLON* Editorial Board, and through it, for influence in the camp. Former Chekists and Communists looked on the journal as an organ for Party members, behind bars for the time being but ideologically at one with Soviet power. A banner at a party for the GPU's 7th anniversary proclaimed: 'Wherever a Chekist finds himself, he stays firmly loyal to the end!'.[4]

Having wormed their way into cosy places in the administration and supervisory staff, the exiled Chekists goaded the convicts to undertake a speedy conversion of their outlook and a radical 'mental revolution'. To the authorities they offered their services in every possible way: 'The first step in corrective labour and cultural and political work is to secure leadership in these areas in the hands of trustworthy Communist elements' (*SLON*, 1924, No. 5).

There is no point in condemning the naively sanctimonious ventures of former Party members: sufficient to let them speak for themselves. A performance by the children of the administrative officers was presented as 'Children's Week – a great initiation of the new, Communist Man'. A propaganda evening held at the club* on 1 June was devoted to bringing up children in the spirit of social and labour awareness. The convicts in the audience behaved outrageously, as if they regarded the theme as absolutely irrelevant (*SLON*, 1924, No. 4).

Representing the Chekists on the *SLON* Editorial Board and filling the post of secretary, was the narrow-minded Tobias Tverie (Tveros, pen-name Tiberius), an apologist of anything done by the administration. During the civil war he had been carried away by

---

* A club was maintained by the cultural and educational section as a venue for lectures, meetings and small concerts.

his role as a Bolshevik, YCL agitator. Sent secretly to Germany to carry out revolutionary propaganda, he failed ignominiously and found himself on the Solovki – this is how Shiriayev explained his past.

Tverie had no literary ability whatever, yet called for vigorous reforms: 'Our language is undergoing mechanization, improvement and simplification, its active vocabulary is being condensed, while the concepts defined grow more sophisticated. Man is becoming universal. His mind is becoming synthetic, tending towards generalization and simplification'.[5] A tendency towards simplification marked Tverie himself, and the editorial board sighed with relief when its secretary was transferred to Kem, where he took up guard duty.

The Chekist D.Ya. Koganov took a more flexible stance, adroitly hiding behind the opinion (formulated by himself) of the chief of the administrative section, the obtuse R.I. Vaskov (a penname?). The editorial board's new secretary, P.I. Shenberg, a man of culture and polish, conformed to circumstances.

Litvin went out of his way to avoid hurting the inmates, even going to such lengths as being ironical about the bosses, and enjoying, as it were, the silent approbation of his colleagues. On the whole, the editors proceeded cautiously, learning what they could and could not say, every issue of the journal being a journey into the unknown. And each issue of the journal or the paper was in self-defense of the intellectuals confronted by the Chekists and the criminal world.

Literary exercises by the Chekists and Red Army men themselves proved singularly fruitless. They are commemorated in the pages of the journal by *Ercopia*, a cheap poem composed in 1924 by Ivan Mikhailov, probably a soldier in the guards. Its hotch-potch of stylistic cliches turned it into a parody. Yet the love affair between the GPU and Caeria (counter-revolution) is depicted not without sympathy for the latter.

> Stage instructions: an office room draped in red cloth and containing a desk and a few chairs. Portraits of revolutionary leaders adorn the walls. Door on left and in front, Ercopia, with muscular arms and in a red blouse, represents the might of the R.C.P. (Russian Communist Party).

> Dramatis personae: Ercopia (R.C.P.), Caeria (Counter-revolution), Priest, the People, the USSR, the GPU. A young man in a leather jacket, the GPU, addresses Caeria, a woman, age 45, absolutely lifeless, with long bony fingers.

GPU (to Caeria):   Without mincing words, I say:
                   I love you passionately.
                   You'll perish in my arms, or else
                   Sicken promptly in exile

Caeria: Your love scares me stiff,
                   It's full of nonsense.

USSR: GPU never takes his eyes off you,
                   Drinking his brimming cup of bliss.

Caeria: USSR, I beg you humbly, do relieve me
                   From the GPU's scorching arms,
                   Lest I perish silently
                   In his deadly embrace

USSR: Why so untimely, wait awhile,
                   (For fear has a hundred eyes),
                   Until you tell the world
                   The import of a slave's groans and cries.

                                           (*SLON*, 1924, No. 4)

Neither the newspaper, nor the journal had to be published at the
level of *Ercopia*. The administration had to rely on the counter-
revolutionaries (CRs), inciting the envy of the Chekists and the
hatred of the criminals. Expressed in the pages of the paper was
sympathy, either ironic or bitter:

> The once privileged word 'intelligentsia' has turned on the
> Solovki into a curse. The miserable members of that class
> are being abused by the rabble without qualms, indeed,
> would be gobbled up alive by them. Yet the racketeering in-
> telligentsia' survives. Is it so easy, in fact, to gobble it up? It
> grows pallid and thin doing common labour, yet, however
> 'pale', the poor fellows are off to the club for every perform-
> ance (*N.S.* 1925, No. 36).

I.S. Kamenogradsky wrote: 'Here, on the Solovki, during the last
stage on life's road, we vividly observe that the question of further
"ideological" guidance by the intelligentsia falls by the wayside.
Their future is clear: they left their life behind, with nothing but
merciless death looming ahead' (*S.I.*, 1925, No. 8).

Most of the people who read this were of a ripe age, still, despite defeat, full of spiritual stamina and capable of a range of work
useful to their country. A former priest Alexei Trifiliev, a reckless
champion of the Russian intelligentsia and an outright opponent
of Soviet experiments, when asked about the drawbacks of the

Solovetsky press, replied: 'Party narrow-mindedness and intolerance, and all the shortcomings of the clannishness of old-time intellectuals, but without their merits' (*N.S.* 1925, No. 38).

It did not take long before the Chekists were joined in their attempts to bring the intellectuals to heel by the criminals, those whom the intellectuals were lifting out of the bog of camp life by bringing them art. The Don Cossack Alexei Chekmazov, only recently a gangster, was indignant over *The Solovetsky Islands*:

> Hiding behind twenty five pen-names, we'll see five persons playing the same tune on behalf of the Solovki public.... You, professionals, give way to the masses, which have more of life's problems than you have, and not just superficial ones.... We'll latch onto your literary hairdos and shout ourselves hoarse until you tell us how to write! Why do our items lack interest? Correct our mistakes. Since you cry out so much about the public, and we are no aliens to it, admit us to the pages of the Solovetsky press!
>
> (*N.S.* 1925, No. 30)

A man with a penetrating mind, well read, Chekmazov readily mastered the demagoguery of the time, which he skilfully employed in prisons, promptly turning into a 'model' inmate. The writings of the former gangster and other criminals who made their debuts (Son'ka Glazok, S. Okerman, Denisov-Guliayev, and others), lively and engaging when presented by word of mouth, were of no literary worth: their authors had neither the strength nor the patience to learn to write and offered more or less amusing – but raw – material.[6]

Besieged on every side, the journalists would seem to have had every right to seek support among the CRs. However, the remnants of the Moscow and St. Petersburg aristocracy apparently preferred to evade dangerous ties: some were loath to soil their hands, others disdained compromises and hated the newspapermen for collaborating with the administration. Such people realized that 'annihilation of life on Earth was possible' when the brain's creative energy perished in the camps, yet they did not know how to resist.

At their own peril, a tiny group of journalists engaged in a reckless undertaking – that of creating a public opinion in the camp, within the limits of permitted truth (i.e., lies), in external conflict with thousands of convicts, for the sake of supporting the self-same convicts, for the sake of improving their lot, for the sake of raising their morale. A difficult undertaking!

In the end Nikolai Litvin sighed bitterly: 'They are few, the Solovetsky newspapermen. And still fewer are those who have sympathy for these cranky enthusiasts. Indeed, fighting depersonalization and narrow-mindedness irritates!' (*N.S.* 1926, No. 47).

Litvin put his finger on the principal aim of the Solovetsky press – refuting the depersonalization of man, protecting the individual against being turned into dust. This was a worthy cause.

The journal and the papers retained traces of the infighting mentioned above.

On 11 April 1924 a discussion of Lunacharsky's play *The King's Barber* was held. The speakers (Trifiliev, Krasnoperov) searched for meaning in the scenes of this conventional historical drama and talked about man's moral degradation in the struggle for power.

Tiberius (Tverie) instantly threw himself into a defence of the author and his play: 'The corrupting influence of power is not the issue here. That power corrupts men is a formula that cannot stand up to criticism. Power in the hands of a class-conscious proletariat is a good thing, while in the hands of raving maniacs or degenerate monarchs it is laughable and absurd' (*SLON*, 1924, No. 3).

A year later Litvin responded to the talk of the positive power of the proletariat with the parody *Governor of the Green Island*, using characters from the operettas *The Count of Luxembourg* by Lehar and Lecocq's *Green Islands*.

> All around one sees the attributes and prerogatives of power. At the threshold his loyal sword-bearer:
>
> 'Would you like the tea-urn? Just a moment!'
> 'Polish my boots to a sparkle! To outshine a mirror!'
>
> Nice to slap the thigh of a native actress, concurrently scrubbing the floor in his excellency's rooms. Delightful to pay a visit to the Governor-General's just appointed meditation chamber. Oh, what an institution!...An individual, hereditary and honorary hole in the Governor-General's meditation chamber – the supreme attribute of power.
>
> (*N.S.*, 1925, No. 33)

Bliss in one's own warm toilet (in the absence of a sewage system in the Kremlin) is a rather understandable symbol of self-assertion for the Green Island's latest ruler.

A cook to Litvin about the convicts on Anzer Island: 'Take a hundred of them, for instance. Ninety of them should be sent packing.... Why feed them for nothing? Ten, perhaps, could be kept'.[7] Litvin described the cook as 'a very kind man, indeed'. In essence, though, he did not refute his arithmetic, which would soon appear as the 'voice of the people', an appeal to common sense.

Tutor Yevgeny Semionov from the Isakovo parish (where timber-felling went on) sent in a memorandum in which he politely tells the camp authorities what they ought to be doing.

1. Every measure should be taken to awaken, wherever proper, and develop in the convicts a sense of human dignity. Most resolute measures should be taken against all, not excepting members of the administration, who by their actions abuse and diminish this sense.
2. An institution of tutors should be organized, elected by each specific group of convicts.
3. The convicts' character references should be drawn up by the administration, based on the opinions of their immediate authorities, as well as on those of the tutors.
4. The convicts' correct and stable labour discipline should be encouraged by material incentives, the establishments of percentage quotas entitling to normal sustenance.... No prizes or other distinctions in supplies, which corrupt the inmates.[8]

The editorial board played it safe, adding a footnote: 'While not fully sharing the author's views....it prints it for its topicality'.

Eichmans, the chief of the camp, corrupted by drunkenness and utter irresponsibility, was on the defensive rather than the offensive. He reminded the intellectuals that the camp regimen corresponded to the time of War Communism, 'when domestic life was monopolized by the state and the individual was levelled out and fused with the masses'.[9] To him the mass of criminals were, naturally, not individuals, but a 'workforce'.

The 'workforce' was insistently urged to work. The vogue for didactic posters came in time also to the Solovki, where all the walls of public premises were plastered with them: 'Through work we shall return to society', 'Work redeems guilt' and even, in the theatre, 'Work without art is barbarity'.

Of course, discussing in the pages of the journal the absurdity of 'reforming' a man who, half-starved, slaved away in the winter forest for twelve to fourteen hours, was out of the question. Yet to cast doubt on the great experiment was, as it turned out, possible. The thought, substantiated historically, was suggested to the reader in an article entitled 'The Monastery – a Polar Industrialist', by V.I. Massalsky.

The scholar cited the book *Solovki* by Nemirovich-Danchenko in which he found food for thought: the monastery had all the features of a 'good working community', caring for its labourers who came for a year or two. Work, perceived as a moral, spiritual mission, yielded abundant fruit.

Massalsky gave the reader an insight into the workings of the author's mind: 'seeing the amazing results of such labour, the exponent of the sceptical nineteenth century was bound to ask whether a working community could have existed in some other form, i.e. other than that of a monastery?' And he cited Nemirovich-Danchenko's answer, already known to the present reader: 'Up till now all working communities have only proved durable when based on religious principles'.

The scholar offered no further comment on this thesis. Once again the editorial board was worried: 'without concurring with certain propositions of this author, who looks at economic phenomena from an angle other than that of dialectical materialism....'[10]

There were other ways in which the journal intimated to its readers the fatuity of the hopes of creating a new man: A. Akarevich (Boris Shiriayev's pen-name) wrote a jolly film-script, *Professor Kal's Experiment*, in which a certain professor arrives on the Solovki: 'a luminary, a scholar of world renown. Eventually they calmed down: a charlatan.'

Kal expounds his ideas to Doctor Ognivtsev:

The world is saved. Psychological deformity is a thing of the past. Life forms are rendered healthy, with the development of an average mental type. Genius is permitted as an exception, under a preliminarily authorized plan....

Tomorrow, I, Professor Kal, and you, Dr Ognivtsev, will launch a human experiment, the greatest in history. There can be no failure. A psychic cell, withdrawn from the gland of an individual indicated by me, and transplanted into the organism of another, will doubtlessly in a very short time develop in the new body the mental characteristics of the former one, thus producing an intermediate type.

By varying and combining the mental make-ups, we shall
be able to elaborate the ideal average human type. Crime is
done away with, along with mental illness. The world is
renovated. A bright future is opened up to mankind.[11]

The experiment is carried out on Vas'ka Buzyga, a thief, blasphemer
and pimp, and Father Ferapont, a grey-haired priest in his seventies.
As a result of successful surgery their behaviour undergoes drastic
changes: 'Vas'ka at his cot is praying fervently…. You ask him for tobacco, he answers about the darkness of hell, and aims to pinch
some of yours.' While Father Ferapont steals a ham, uses foul language and keeps a date with Son'ka Knurka, the prostitute. In the
long run both land in a punishment cell – Ferapont for whoring,
Vas'ka Buzyga for religious zeal. The heroes, it would seem, have
simply changed places. But instead of one debauchee, there are now
two. Crime is on the rise and Professor Kal is a charlatan.

Thus, in diverse forms, from a scientific paper to a story, the
writers for *The Solovetsky Islands* expressed their rejection of the re-
formative illusions of the age.

The Solovetsky Islands had other tasks: it provided information
about all the islands (the Muksalma, Anzer, Zayatsky) and about the
camp stations and assignments (temporary seasonal stations) and
took the reader beyond the islands, reporting on life at Kem and in
the Karelian backwoods.

N.G. Neverov, head of the cultural and educational section, a
free, hired employee, a former teacher and a harmless person, coun-
selled the newspapermen: 'Do not fear openness – openness that is
right and unbiased'. And so the writers of *New Solovki* swung back
and forth between right and wrong openness, commended for the
former and reproached for the latter, on occasion doing time in the
punishment cells. The inches of gained openness were measured by
their own skins and fates.

4 Profiles and masques

*...the last thing that becomes
a journalist is sincerity!*

B. Glubokovsky, 1926

An artist has left on the pages of *The Solovetsky Islands* portrait sketches of two of the journal's staff members, Litvin and Shiriayev. Photographs of them are lacking (nor do we have their autobiographies), so that we see them only in thin and broken outline, rather vague, in fact.

Nikolai Litvin was the most active and gifted journalist on the Solovki during those years. Born in 1890 in Mogilev, on the Dnieper, he was, in all probability, of Byelorussian stock. Byelorussians were called for a long time 'Litvins' in Russia and the Ukraine, for their lands were part of the Grand Principality of Lithuania.

Yet he lived and went to college in the southern city of Odessa, apparently beginning his journalistic career at Rostov. During World War I he enrolled at the Odessa School of Ensigns, ending the war with the rank of second lieutenant. The civil war found him as a war correspondent on the Don; in 1918 he appears briefly in Kiev, and then retreats with the Russian troops from the Crimea. The trials and tribulations of camp life at Gallipoli, Turkey, were followed by the none too easy work of editor of the paper *Russkoye Delo* (*The Russian Cause*) in Sofia, and of a journalist in Yugoslavia. None of this lasted. Somehow, Litvin was unable to strike root in the West.

Poetry was clearly not his forte, even though he was born a lyric poet. But in emigration he write prose too: an excerpt, *In the Mikhailov Woods*, and the story *Colonel Komov*, which he published on the Solovki, resemble fragments of some major piece.[1] Yet the mediocre poet promised to become a good, modern prose writer, who combined lyricism with scenes from ordinary life, southern descriptive sparkle and a keen sensitivity. Litvin's stylistic devices are close to the early prose of Bulgakov. (Apart from this temporary stylistic similarity, it would seem that Bulgakov must have read *The Solovetsky Islands* in 1926 and responded to them in his play *The Flight*.[2])

The response came in the image of a church ('In my dream I saw a monastery...'), where people fleeing the Bolsheviks sought refuge. Bulgakov invoked this image of a monastery once again towards the end of *The Flight*: at Istanbul a choir sings a folk ballad, retold in his time by Nekrasov about the great sinner, and robber chief Kudeyar ('Once there were twelve robbers...'). Bulgakov left out the legend's end, for its concluding line, 'this we were told on the Solovki by a monk, the Holy Pitirim', would not have been allowed on the stage. Many at that time remembered it well.

Litvin alludes directly to associations of the images of the Solovki and Istanbul. In the bustling Turkish capital in 1921 he had heard a choir of colonels unexpectedly break into this ballad: 'I remember, remember very well, how strangely that ballad's line about the Solovki struck a chord in my heart'. And later, in the autumn of 1922, on the veranda of the *Rossiya Café* above the Adriatic Sea, émigrés were again singing the same ballad. Later Litvin devoted an article to Chieftain Kudeyar.[3]

Like some of Bulgakov's characters, Litvin had left foreign lands, boisterous Sofia, to return to Russia. Tall and lanky, fair-haired, grey-eyed, straight-nosed, clad in a well-worn officer's greatcoat, he stepped onto the railway platform in Moscow, and there and then, on 13 November 1923, was arrested. He had no residence in Moscow, nor any relatives.

Litvin was indicted for involvement with a counter-revolutionary organization championing the overthrow of the Soviet system, and even of serving with the secret police of Imperial Russia. The investigation dragged on in a stupid, muddled way. Litvin went on hunger strike. A resolution of the All-Russian Central Executive Committee of 6 February on extending his term of detention till 1 March 1924 Litvin signed in the following manner: 'Read on 21 February, on the tenth day of my hunger strike'. Next day he was sentenced to three years in a concentration camp, and on 3 June 1924, he arrived, via Kem, on the Solovki.[4]

While in camp Litvin wrote a good deal. It took him little time to master the role of theatre critic (under the cryptonyms En Lee, N.L., and others). Reflected in scores of his short items and sketches was the amazing rise of the Solovki theatre, for which he himself and his colleagues had prepared the ground, and which was now moving ahead spontaneously and at times even uncontrollably.

Litvin the critic is tolerant and benevolent, not beholden to any special stage theory or specific authors. The product of a southern urban culture, he is likely to have subscribed to the journal *Satiricon* and enjoyed couplets by Agnivtsev and stories by Averchenko. He had loved the smaller theatrical stage: satire and cabaret.

For the Solovetsky troupe *Khlam* (*Trash*) Litvin wrote small dramatic scenes. In his minor comedy *Love is a Golden Book*, which enjoyed a tremendous success, he touched upon a dangerous theme – that of love on the Solovki, something which was punishable by penal exile: the women were transferred to the deserted Zayatsky Island, where the 'sinners' were made to feel miserable and desolate. However, around the 8 March holiday in 1926 the women in the Zayatsky isolator put out a wall-newspaper bearing the slogan: 'Long live world-wide emancipation of women!'. It was not quite clear whether the ladies were visited in their misfortune by a sense of humour, or had lost it.

As for the men, they were dispatched to punishment cells on Sekirnaya Hill, an ordeal not everyone survived, for there one could pay with one's health, and on occasion, with life itself.

The scene of the lovers' joyous rendezvous culminated in the appearance of the camp nemesis – the rough and ready overseer Raiva in a long grey greatcoat and a white bespattered guardsman's cap on his head.

The one-act play *Governor of the Green Island* was done in a keen and engaging manner, its mood being reflected also in Litvin's pamphlet of the same title. Once again there are unexpected parallels with the dramatic pamphlet *The Purple Island*, written a couple of years later by Bulgakov: both pamphleteers utilize as a stylistic key images of the theatre and the motifs and characters of operettas.

Perhaps belonging to Litvin himself are the lyrics of a song in the stage production *A Solovetsky Review*, again a resounding success, a song about the Solovki which spread far beyond the camp. At any rate, for its lyricism, sincerity and mildness of tone, for its message of forgiving mistakes and pain, it is a composition by Litvin alone, rather than a collaboration with Shiriayev, as was later suggested by the latter.

In all his satirical articles and essays Litvin displayed a sensitive heart. Take this instant sketch of camp life. It is spring, convicts are shovelling snow. The Muslim fast of Ramadan is just over. An *effendi* from Bokhara and a crowd of other Muslims in colourful striped gowns have gathered in the yard.

> I stood watching this strange Ramadan on the square of the Solovetsky kremlin, then took a stroll with the striped *effendi*, yearning for his faraway Bokhara. Having stopped in the middle of the square, the *effendi* said to me:
>
> 'Oh, bairam uraza! Why Solovki?'
>
> I responded softly:
>
> 'Such, I take it, was the will of the prophet....'
>
> The *effendi* smiled ruefully.
>
> (*N.S.*, 1926, No. 16)

At times Litvin's eyes and spirit grew tired. At such moments he would recall coloured glass plates, through which the world looked much brighter: 'If only one could find in the wanderers' puny baskets a forgotten coloured plate. How much easier it would be for the eyes to see. To see and wait for life to beckon with a Beethoven sonata: "Come!"' (*N.S.*, 1926, No. 34).

Litvin longed for freedom, yearned to bury 'his damned past'. In the middle of 1926 he grew restless, apprehensive, apparently dreading the pinning of some indictment to him and a new stretch. He was not mistaken.

The Attestation Commission, which assessed the performance of every prisoner, deciding his or her fate (cutting or extending a term, exile, etc.), never forgave Litvin his talent or his independence of mind. His progress report as drafted in the 1st Department was good: useful, hard working, a model for others. Yet the report bore the chagrined postscript of the 1st Department's Chief Barinov: 'Stubborn, capricious, does only that which he fancies himself' (10 November 1925). And two days later the Central Attestation Commission (R. Vaskov, D. Koganov, A. Zapolsky, Secretary M. Piliavsky) records: 'Type of intellectual confused by the revolution. In camp works professionally (man of letters). Being alien to everything new, labour-oriented, is a CR.' So Litvin was buried as incorrigible, the uneducated, dim-witted Vaskov and the intelligent, cultivated Koganov playing the same tune: talent offended them all. He refused to lick their boots, so he was 'stubborn'.

The reports for 1926 are more ambiguous. 'Showed himself on the satisfactory side', the latest, dated 14 September, runs; 'showed himself in every respect on the positive side'. Mended his ways! But it mattered no more.

That is why he was nervous: he foresaw the bosses' revenge. In the sketch *When Gossamer is Flying* he created a pen portrait of the physician Yakov I. Shvarts. Shvarts was released, and having received a 'minus' (prohibition from residing in large cities in the European part of the country), went to Siberia. 'During our last walks together Yakov Isayevich tells me: "If you happen to get a minus, skip over to me. Siberia is a good land, a land of plenty, full of pies and all, complete with a university town' (*N.S.*, 1926, No. 33).

If counted properly, from the day of arrest, Litvin, having been sentenced to a three-year term, should have been released on 13 September 1926. Yet the OGPU in Moscow vengefully robbed him of nearly half a year by counting the sentence from the day of trial, 22 February 1924. And on 12 November 1926, the special board of the OGPU passed a resolution (most probably in a string of hundreds of similar cases) altering the former ruling (sentencing him to three years of prison camp, but without exile) so as to exile Litvin via OGPU bodies to Siberia for three years. On 4 December Litvin left the Solovki and on 20 December at Kem he was handed over to a Leningrad convoy to proceed further.

And then he vanished, dropped from sight without a trace. Shiriayev recalled that much later, noticing his signature in some paper, Litvin sent him a letter from the Yenisei where he was working as a cook for a fishing co-op. There, too, he allegedly felt out of place, just as on the Solovki, there, too, he observed life from outside, as it were, 'until death carried him away...'.

The words of Shiriayev about Litvin's 'alienation' are refuted by the whole body of his publications. Who had written more than anyone else about the life of the Solovki? Of course, Litvin. Who was the kindest of all and most indulgent to man, who valued in him courage and valour? Of course, Litvin. Who most believed in the need for spiritual repentance and hope and that unintentional mistakes could be forgiven and old sins forgotten? Litvin. Who was least inclined to cringe before authority, for which he was to pay with additional exile and death in obscurity? Litvin.

He was condescendingly called a romantic by people thinking of his gullibility and naivety. If one considers a gentle heart, a reluctance to get embroiled in the wrangles of everyday life, to mean romanticism, then Litvin was, indeed, a romantic.

Boris Glubokovsky appeared in the camp in May 1925. His tall, bulky frame at once stood out among the convicts, while his tremendous, rumbling voice, rich in modulation, betrayed an actor, both by profession and by calling. And he played both on stage and in life, coolly and recklessly confusing one with the other, at once attracting and repulsing people.

This gifted man had seen and experienced a lot before a chance incident cast him out, 30 years of age and in the prime of life, onto the cold, chilly Solovki. It seemed fate itself had generously paved his path to success, providing him with material well-being in a cultured milieu (his father was a Moscow professor) and an excellent education (in law at Moscow University).

As a young man he was attracted to the stage. Having tested himself in philosophizing roles in the popular theatre of F. Korsh, he defected to A. Tairov at the Chamber Theatre. The richly musical, refined productions, which exposed that theatre's conventional principles, apparently appealed to Glubokovsky's tastes, though his restless character looked to life for something different.

He was drawn to Moscow's small Bohemian restaurants and was apparently even capable of staking his life as a card in a game of chance. Perhaps, as was the vogue in that milieu, he had also experimented with drugs.

The destructive outbreak of the revolution and civil war expelled Glubokovsky for ever from his customary way of life, sweeping him along in the general whirlwind. In the tale *Journey from Moscow to the Solovki* (printed in *The Solovetsky Islands* but not finished) he describes a character called Boris speaking in 1918 before Red Army men at the Saratov Club of Proletarian Culture. Quite irresponsibly, in the fashion of the time, he denounced bourgeois art, created for drawing-rooms and taverns, and concluded his speech with the fiery appeal: '...you must wreck the obsolete canons and forms of art to create an art of your own! Out, all of you, onto the squares, let's pull down the theatres and the museums.'

The meeting's chairman, the partisan Kolya Kirasov, for whom, as the speaker suspects, there is no barrier between word and deed, calls him aside:

> 'When are we going to wreck the theatre? Tomorrow, or the day after? Well! That'll be fun burning down the anathema!'

> I looked at him to see whether he was joking, but no, he was deadly serious.

> 'What d'you mean – burn down the theatre?' I wondered, shocked.

'But didn't you say so yourself? We must go tomorrow; I'll fetch the boys and off we'll go'.[5]

In 1918 Glubokovsky appeared at Simferopol. In the summer of 1919 he was in the well-fed, already Soviet, Ukraine; in Kharkov and Nikolayev, where he directed the *Red Pepper* satire theatre and, in 1921–22, composed propaganda pieces. He attended the show trial of Slashchev, a criminal general, whose notorious cruelty was still well remembered: 'Torturing Communists. Jewish pogroms. The shooting of the "61". Mass flogging of peasants.'

Having returned in 1922 to Moscow and the Chamber Theatre, Glubokovsky went with it on a foreign tour, and there, as Shiriayev recalls, instead of Berlin, he turned up in Madrid, which probably alerted the OGPU. However, he would have been caught anyway, for the habits of a bohemian life made him conspicuous, while all the stir and din created by the Imaginists group around Sergei Yesenin annoyed many.

Two articles by Glubokovsky appeared in the pages of the journal *An Inn for Travellers into the Beautiful* (1922–24), surrounded by the names of Yesenin, Osip Mandelshtam, Nikolai Erdman and Anatoly Marienhoff. Yet Glubokovsky never became a theoretician or a prophet, for his interpretation of the dawn of the Russian renaissance was too abstract: 'What, then, are the mysterious main features of the Russian renaissance? We are certain of the following ones. Theme, nationality, polytechnology'.[6]

After leaving the stage, Glubokovsky often contributed in 1924 to the journal *The New Footlights*, as nearly every issue carried items on Moscow's theatrical life.

Yet his literary pursuits stemmed from his cultural interests and erudition rather than constituting a calling. Despite his passionate temperament, his writing was permeated with a spiritual coolness and detachment. Concealed behind them was bewilderment and lack of moral inspiration.

Glubokovsky was arrested, it seems, for alleged involvement in the 'Union of Russian Fascists' and on 27 March 1925 a Collegium of the OGPU condemned him to 10 years in camp.[7]

Thus, the actor became a political prisoner for the second time, but this time not merely on the stage.

In camp Glubokovsky was assigned to the theatre of the 1st Department and at the same time, as a journalist, contributed to *The Solovetsky Islands*. In his very first publication, 'Songs of the Rabble'

(1925, Nos. 4–5), he hit upon a theme that was close to him – the life of the city slums, a subject of interest to him during the revolutionary years when he was still in Moscow. The artist V. Komardenkov recalled the time when, with Glubokovsky, he went down into the cellars of the still unfinished building of the Central Telegraph on the corner of Tverskaya street, at the time a den of prostitutes and the homeless.

> Boris was trusted by the waifs. He intended to write a book about them and suggested that I do the illustrations. We found the nooks of the cellars furnished with a degree of comfort, with an occasional gilt armchair, vases, carpets, paintings. There were even stoves laid of brick, on which a dinner was cooking in nickel-plated pans from a restaurant. A game of cards was in progress.[8]

Former knowledge, unexpectedly refreshed, came in handy. From separate articles a single and unique book was born, published on the Solovki: *The 49th* (1926, two printings). It represents the caste culture of the criminal world, the entertainments and predilections of thieves, and the title is derived from the number of the Criminal Code article dealing with nonprofessional offenses. Glubokovsky was not the only one to concern himself with a study of the lore and ways of criminals: the language of thieves attracted the attention of men of letters (N. Vinogradov, D. Likhachev). Yet he is the only one who managed to complete his work and get it published. *The 49th* has a special section, 'Their Theatre' – a generalized description of the theatrical tastes of the rabble.

Pondering on 'their theatre', Glubokovsky regards himself as a follower of Dostoyevsky, who, in *Notes from the House of the Dead*, was the first to recreate the theatrical performances of penal labourers in Siberia. The artist drew attention to the remarkable fact that in the short plays presented by the convicts (*Kedril the Glutton* by an unknown writer, *The Rivals Filatka and Miroshka* by P. Grigoriev) a certain, rather strong tradition could be felt. The writer suggested a search for its roots as a vestige of folk theatre.

Dostoyevsky noticed also that on performance days the convicts, a touchy and morose lot, became more animated and 'better': there were fewer rows and fights, less swearing. The theatre infused a fresh spirit into the moral atmosphere of the barracks.

Dostoyevsky was not only the prison theatre's first historian, but also in certain measure, as recalled by Polish revolutionaries who witnessed the preparation of a play, a stage director.

Life confirmed how sharp Dostoyevsky's observations were. Glubokovsky's little book demonstrated a strong tradition of prison pastimes and cruel games, which was, indeed, carried by the criminals from one prison to another.

The first postrevolutionary years introduced fundamentally new features into the traditions of the rabble, associated with the idea of reforming criminals as elements socially akin to the new power, and of involving them in politics. But the old foundations survived. The explosive mix of the new and the traditional gave birth to a peculiar theatre of 'our own'*, and it was precisely this that Glubokovsky's articles were about.

He also made an attempt, appealing to the convicts, to collect material on all the Solovetsky and other prison theatres (*N.S.*, 1926, No. 20).

Two responded: Alexei Chekmazov wrote an article about his stage experiments in corrective labour homes, and an intellectual thief, Vladimir Bedrut, read notes on the Solovetsky theatre during a literary soirée.

Glubokovsky himself published the report *Solovetsky Theatre*, mentioned earlier in the preface. In it, using the very minimum of political rhetoric, he gave a list of plays and the number of performances and presented general thoughts on the nature of stagecraft. He believed that, on the Solovki, in the performances by the rabble, the acting principle came prominently to the fore.

Glubokovsky's story 'Journey from Moscow to Solovki' (*S.I.*, 1925, Nos. 10–12; 1926, Nos. 1–4) strongly engages the reader not just because it is the only major work in the journal's pages. Glubokovsky realized how ephemeral was his success and explained in the preface, which appeared after part of the story had been printed, that the 'author is apprehensive lest a casual stop is mistaken by the reader for the last station'. The story ended abruptly with the words: 'Everything got jumpled up in the whirlwind of the post-war muddle. Scores, hundreds, thousands of white faces flashed by, and we were given a brief respite as we stopped at a new, strangely understandable, curt word: NEP.'

Glubokovsky warned that his opus was 'by no means an autobiography, but the milieu passing in front of the reader is familiar and known to the author'. He had known many people and in the

---

* 'Our own' in the thieves' jargon, meant a professional criminal as compared to a casual one, a 'sucker' or 'chump'.

fleetingly outlined characters one recognizes Kamensky, Vertinsky, Yesenin and other figures, fashionable in 1917–18, bringing back to life scenes from literary bohemia.

The purpose of the story was to show bohemianism as an internal emigration (while the 'Solovki' are conceived by the author as an image of redemption) – a purpose which, apparently, determined the starkly sarcastic, vicious characterizations and apparent coolness of presentation. Glubokovsky could never bring the reader to either repentance or thoughts about 'just' redemption, because he himself never thought along those lines. A chasm separated his face from his mask.

In 1926 Glubokovsky was appointed the chief stage director of the theatre of the 1st Department. But next year both the paper and the journal disappeared, denying us the opportunity to follow his work. It is clear that he devoted himself to the theatre, but, just as before, he knew the camp, and he, too, was known to many. Likhachev recalls:

> Before the camp's administration moved to Kem, Boris Glubokovsky played a tremendous (I am not afraid of using this word) role in the life of the Solovki.... Tall, comparatively young, vigorous, easily forming links with many people, from thieves and camp officers to intellectuals, he actually stood at the head of the theatre and the camp's cultural life, which still glimmered amidst all kinds of misrepresentation.[10]

Glubokovsky was apparently finding it more and more difficult to live and work. There was nobody left of the group of creative personalities with whom he had in previous years raised the theatre and the press – some were home, some in exile, some had died. And Glubokovsky's 'tenner', despite the reduction of his term by two years, somehow never ended. He seemed doomed to stay in the Solovetsky hell for ever. Hope glimmered at long last only in 1930.

Unlike the mild Litvin, his colleague Boris Shiriayev gives the impression of a stern personality, far more persistent in attaining his goals and capable of great concessions to circumstances to achieve them. He is the only Solovki journalist who lived to write a book about his friends in misfortune: *The Inextinguishable Lantern*. The stories about the Solovetsky theatre make up a considerable and most interesting part of it.

Stylistically, Shiriayev's book has more similarities with *belles-lettres* than memoirs, its facts scattered through time and space rather haphazardly. Perhaps they did happen, but when? Quite often in Shiriayev's book we come across that confusion of frames about which Likhachev had complained, and this requires the checking and rechecking of his text.[11]

Entitled, even duty bound to speak of the departed, Shiriayev, as one can now see, made far from the best use of them. He understood Glubokovsky well and spoke of him quite explicitly:

> He had an excellent analytical and critical mind, but was absolutely inept when it came to synthesis, and even more so in the realm of constructive, creative mental work. 'Making short shrift' was his forte, and this he did boldly, strikingly and engagingly, of whomsoever and whatever.

> Did he possess any inherent ideological backbone or, at least, some definite immutable ideological aspirations? I knew him intimately, and venture to state – no. None whatever. He was nothing but an acid, perhaps a rust, that would eat into anything he touched.[12]

In this verdict, probably, Shiriayev could be trusted. However, in the case of Glubokovsky, just as in that of Litvin, he is not being altogether delicate: he is posing as the co-author of the little book *The 49th* ('our work', 'Glubokovsky and I', and so forth). Meanwhile, *The 49th* was published in 1926 and there was nothing, it would seem, to prevent the putting of a second name on the title-page. But this could not be done: the book was actually made up of Glubokovsky's own articles that had appeared in *The Solovetsky Islands*.

Having been associated with Litvin for two years, Shiriayev certainly knew him. Yet they were never close, and towards the end of his stay in the camp, their ways all but parted.

Shiriayev wrote little about his spiritual life on the Solovki, and nothing at all about his past. He was probably reluctant to speak of the concessions he had made, not merely to survive, but to get away from the Solovki.

Whereas Litvin, returning to Russia from emigration, was sent to a prison camp, the Muscovite Shiriayev (1889–1959) was given a term for his wish to leave Soviet Russia and go abroad. After an attempt to do so in 1918 he barely escaped from being shot and for a second try in 1922 he was awarded a 'tenner'. He arrived in the camp on 17 November 1923.

Publishing in both the journal and the paper under different pen-names (S. Akarsky, Akarevich, and others), he gave the theatre ardent support. As a person with a higher philological education and a literary gift, he fitted in very well, showing a knack for light elaborations and combinations of existing themes, stylistic devices and characterizations. He wrote not only poetry, but even his travelling notes *Moscow to Solovki*, in stanzaic form, which looked rather amusing, if not strange.

A certain dryness of style in Shiriayev's journalistic publications reflects the circumspection of his mind: he is observant, but restrained, feeling at ease, apparently, with only a few people not beset with complexes. The most pleasant portrait sketched in his book is that of Mikhail Yegorov, 'the Parisian', a director of the Solovetsky theatre.

> I saw him for the first time in a common cell of the Butyrka prison, where Misha was brought ... direct from Paris.
>
> The door slammed, and as always, everyone stared at the 'new boy'. He was, indeed, something to behold!
>
> Facing us stood a splendidly attired young man, holding in one hand a yellow suitcase of foreign make, stuck all over with bright hotel labels, and in the other a huge sky-blue bonbonnière. Hooked on the same arm was an elegant walking stick, and flowing from the shoulder was a stylish, long, modish striped silk scarf.
>
> Struck dumb by his appearance, so unusual for the Butyrka, the cell fell silent. The newcomer cast his eyes over us in amazement, slowly said: 'Well, well...' and suddenly smiled broadly:
>
> 'Bonjour, my worthy friends!'
>
> Within an hour we all knew Misha's tragicomic epic. His father was an upper-middle-class Moscow merchant, which did not prevent the son from joining the Communists as early as 1917. Following the October revolution he was sent, as one not ignorant of commerce, to the Trade Mission in Paris.
>
> 'I've had the time of my life, lads! And what a good life it was, dammit!' Misha related, smiling dreamily. 'Paris, you know, is a far cry from ... Khamovniky!'

Misha's sojourn in Paris was brought to an abrupt end by an urgent summons to Moscow. He went, filled, as usual, with the most radiant optimism, having even fetched a huge box of chocolates for his sweetheart. And this is how, with his yellow suitcases stuffed with fashionable clothes, the box of sweets and all, he landed in the Butyrka prison, arrested upon stepping down from the carriage of the Paris–Moscow express. The charm acquired in Paris never left him even on the Solovki, where Misha wangled a soft job and walked about the monastery courtyards flourishing the same fancy walking stick, the same silk scarf and a felt hat set at a precarious angle.[13]

His Parisian chic and dapper checked jacket made Yegorov a desirable performer in some of the plays, while his directorship also nudged the Solovki westward. Carried on the crest of NEP, he became the director of a profit-making canteen for the camp administration – two light halls, stylish curtains at the windows and doors, a sparkling parquet floor. White tablecloths and flowers on the tables. Attractive waitresses in brown uniforms.

The fantastic luxury of the hall can only be appreciated, if we recall that even the Red Army guards never took off their overcoats in the camp canteen, and the entertainment there was on occasion like this:

> At lunch time Comrade I.Kh. likes to amuse himself by hurling bits of bread at others. The other day, a piece of bread thrown at Comrade Diachkov landed in the plate of soup the latter was carrying. Without a moment's hesitation Diachkov approached I.Kh. and poured the soup over his head.
>
> (*N.S.* 1926, No. 2)

Quite possibly it was due to Yegorov's efforts that a Solovetsky tradition struck root in the camp – that of celebrating the New Year by holding a gala concert, for which the camp élite gathered. Gradually the convicts were denied all this, but even the New Year of 1937, its last year, was celebrated by the camp with a tremendous concert.

Shiriayev was involved in all such initiatives to a greater or lesser degree. For the theatre he wrote small satirical scenes, which still crop up unexpectedly in some unknown folder from the KGB archives.

As an author of essays, sketches and *feuilletons* for *The New Solovky*, Shiriayev is interesting, rather professional, but hardly measures up to Litvin and Glubokovsky: he lacks a theme of his own and a kind of averageness, of thought, feeling and image, predominates. But Shiriayev's publications and diverse work set the overall tone of Solovetsky life, though at difficult moments he lacked stamina and made a sharp turnabout towards the administration, scorning the camp's moral code and concepts.

He slipped up on literary and theatrical servility, so much despised in the camp. Of course, for a creative personality on the Solovki, sincerity was a hazardous trait, and seemingly a stupid one, not just unnecessary, but capable of putting one in mortal danger. Yet deliberate falsehood and frank toadyism, along with papers for preterm release, could pry open the tall gates of the Kem transit prison and the doors of the fast Murmansk trains.

Everyone was compelled by circumstances to make his or her choice. However, even the Solovetsky press could not exist without sincerity, without at least professional zeal for its cause. This is also true of the theatre, 'that true friend of those extraordinary years. An immediate extension of the entire phantasmagoria called Solovki' (Litvin).

PART TWO

5 The Theatre of the 1st Department

Life is harsh, art is without sorrow.

F. Schiller

The scene that unfolded before the Chekists and convicts who arrived on 6 June 1923 at Solovki from Archangel on the steamship *Yamal* shook everybody. The mighty cathedrals stood stripped of roofs and doors, contorted pieces of iron lay scattered about on the ground, their once white, now soot-blackened walls held neither clock nor bells. A burnt-out site exposed to the elements. A miserable bunch of Soviet officials, apprehensive of being called to account. The black cassocks of the old monks....

The enormity of the calamity became apparent gradually. Life depended on how quickly the camp could manage to prepare for winter and put the power plant back in order, for new convicts were already on their way by land and by sea. Existence, it seemed, could never get away from the rigid schedule of the 'work–sleep' cycle.

And still, on 23 September of the same year a theatre gave its first performance on the island, of Miasnitsky's comedy *The Treasure*.

In *The Inextinguishable Lantern*, Shiriayev vividly described the outstanding role of the provincial actor Sergey (Ivan Andreyevich) Armanov in the creation of the theatre.

To this tall and lanky fanatical art lover, whose passion for the stage knew no bounds, everything seemed possible. 'Even while still under investigation in the Butyrka prison, in an overcrowded common cell, he managed to knock together something like a Chinese conjuror.'[1]

Shiriayev went on to reproduce not only the birth pangs of the theatre, but even its first poster. Some discrepancy sets in when we look at dates only now coming to light: Shiriayev arrived on the Solovki on 17 November, while Armanov's two-year term started on 16 November 1923, when he was still in Moscow, and he could have arrived on the island in December at the earliest.

In fact, the theatre was created by another person, G.I. Nikitin, who initially adopted the stage name Vecherin, though later he played under his own. We may guess that he was either an amateur

with experience, or a modest, no longer young professional actor. On
1 July 1924 the theatre gave a benefit peformance for 'Nikitin – the
first stage director, one of the theatre's founders'. The director staged
P. Nevezhin's melodrama *The Abused One* and played the central role
in it.[2]

During his first year Nikitin produced more than ten tradi-
tionally realistic plays, but also demonstrated a capacity for development. A reviewer later lauded him for his production of a little
comedy, *Deviltry*, with simplified staging and the wide use of
motion-picture-like dynamism in moving from scene to scene. 'He
cast aside routine, and presented the Solovki audiences with an interesting, new production, well received by the public' (*N.S.*, 1925,
No. 17).

In *Sivolapin Comedy* by D. Chizhevsky, staged by Nikitin 'in
the tone of a cheap popular poster', the director's 'profoundly
thought-out' work was largely undermined by the still inexperi-
enced performers, unable to cope with fast-moving action based on
trick effects (*N.S.*, 1925, No. 26). As an actor Nikitin tended towards
the prerevolutionary type of the 'philosophizer' (a dramatic actor of
imposing physique, with a knack for reasoning on the stage). He
had a pleasant voice, a sincere, soulful tone, according to a critic
who saw him play the part of Ivan Kaliayev, a poet–terrorist and
hero of the 1905 revolution.

Another founder of the theatre was V.E. Liubokhonsky. It was
of him, perhaps, that Litvin wrote: 'a tall, thin, redhead with long
hair, a Chekist stage director who looked like a decadent poet. Thin
as a rail and consumptive…'.[3] Liubokhonsky staged several plays; in
concerts he recited verses by Severianin. He never got on with
Armanov, yet both reconciled themselves when the company was
joined in the summer of 1924 by Makar Borin.

Nikitin, Liubokhonsky, Armanov, Stankevich, Nikitina,
Osinovsky, Shuman and many others made an enthusiastic contribu-
tion to the establishment of the theatre. They would come out of the
pitch-dark winter nights into prison cells poorly illuminated with
candle stumps 'looking for talent' – people capable of playing on the
stage. They rehearsed after a 12-hour, hard working day. Only a few
could stand it, the ones who made up the backbone of the theatre
which acquired the name of the Theatre of the 1st Department, or of
the cultural and educational sector.

The stage was in the vestry of the Assumption Cathedral, for
the flames had failed to penetrate its double iron doors and shutters.

Benches seating about 250 people were set up in the elongated audi-torium, and a curtain bearing the emblem of a white seagull was hung up. Later on this inspired someone to write that the seagull of the Moscow Art Theatre had been displayed on the Solovki, allegedly a sign of the artistic bond linking the two theatres.

In fact, the Solovki's silvery seagull, for half a year never leaving the camp inmates at peace, was perceived as a symbol of spring. The seagulls' first appearance in April, followed by their mass arrival in May, signified an end to icebound captivity, the arrival of letters and parcels. The seagulls, according to the inmates, rather ugly on land and magnificent in flight, brought with them the hope of freedom. It was not for nothing that convicts on the island used to sing:

> Away from the blizzards and storms,
> We shall fly, like the seagulls, south,
> And leave behind the twinkling lights
> Of the islands called Solovki....

The theatre's first productions were popular comedies and melodra-mas of the turn of the century: *The Treasure* by Miasnitsky, *The Abused One* by Nevezhin, *Let Down by the Batman* by Turbin and Chekhov's *Uncle Vanya*. The library at the time held just a few hundred books and many of the classics were present in a single copy, so the actors performed whatever they could recall from the past.

Nevertheless, opening the theatre with a comedy was not just something customary for the theatre's first company, but also a matter of principle. In this way Armanov stated the tasks and conditions of a people's theatre, setting forth the ideas of Romain Rolland as interpreted by P. Kerzhentsev, author of a then popular book *Creative Theatre*:

> Condition one.... The theatre must serve as a place of moral and physical relief for the convict, tired by a day of hard work.

> The second condition for a theatre is to serve as a source of energy. The theatre should avoid anything that depresses or belittles, and should boost spiritual strength and energy.

> Third, the theatre should serve to develop the mind. Joy, good cheer and knowledge are the three props of a people's theatre.[4]

Ya. Ginesin, an old theatre lover, wrote in the pages of *SLON* of the traditions of humanism, recalling the succour found by spectators in the cheery productions of the prerevolutionary theatre: 'Laughter at that time went hand in hand with daily sorrow. Why is it, then, that today we have buried real, gusty laughter, which we recall so seldom.... Why not try to revive it, make it more bracing.'[5]

Armanov would have liked to see the theatre brimming with high spirit and health, yet he himself lacked the gift of a comedian, leaning, rather, towards dramatic and melodramatic characters – Svengali (in G. Ghe's play of the same title after Du Maurier's novel *Trilby*) and Tikhon (in Ostrovsky's *The Storm*). He never learned his parts properly, relying more on intuition and a spontaneous response, which at times produced quite unexpected effects.

> We were presenting an adaptation of Zola's *Paris*. Vanya [Armanov], clad in a priest's soutane, having realized the sacredness of labour and the suffering of the workers crowded around the scaffold (behind the scenes), was supposed to prostrate himself. Suddenly filled with adoration for Matisse, the hero, he fell down on his knees before him, clasped his hands and, covering them with kisses, pathetically exclaimed – I kiss your hands, Matisse!....
>
> The audience was puzzled, Matisse was stunned, the prompter was in a rage.[6]

Such escapades and outbursts by Armanov, who had no systematic experience and was incapable of sharing it with others, could have set a bad precedent to amateurs, had the actor persisted in them; fortunately, though, his work from 1925 to 1926 showed him capable of doing better. The theatre survived its first season.

The repertoire also depended on current events and clearly reflected didactic and educational bias. This is how it looked in March 1924. 2 March – *Days of Our Life* by L. Andreyev, produced by Armanov; 4 March – to mark the anniversary of the death of the Russian classical writer, N.V. Gogol, his comedy *The Marriage*, staged by Vecherin; 8 March – to mark Women-Workers' Day, *The Fiery Serpent* by Vecherin; 12 March – anniversary of the overthrow of autocracy in Russia, *Slaves*, a drama in three acts by M. Krinitsky, staged by Liubokhonsky; 18 March – Day of the Paris Commune, *A Revolutionary Wedding* by Zet, a three-act play, staged by Vecherin and Stankevich; 26 March – anniversary of the deaths of the French actress Sarah Bernhardt and the anarchist poet Walt Whitman, soirée dedicated to them. A dramatization of Whitman's poem *Europe*.[7]

Many wished to get to the theatre. However, the administration was quick to appropriate this creation of the counter-revolutionaries (CRs) for their own pleasure. In fact, whatever differences between Chekists and CRs, they were contemporaries, their enthusiasm for the stage reflecting the sparkling, burgeoning art of the turn of the century and the hypertrophy of the theatre that marked the years of the civil war. Nogtev's deputy, the better educated Eichmans, loved theatre and the other camp officers tried to keep up with him.

A cultural and educational sector was established and charged with supervising the theatre. The bulk of the tickets were reserved for the administration. The audience would patiently wait, at times for an hour, for 'someone' to appear and give the signal to begin.

But those who slept on bare plank-beds in the huge cathedrals that stank with sweat and filth, who were slowly dying of scurvy and injuries while doing hard labour, all those doomed ones could never have made it to a performance – they simply lacked the strength. Circumstances also prevented the theatre, created by the convicts for their own kind, for CRs, from giving them any support.

So it was compelled to cater to the lucky ones, those who managed to escape common labour – the tally clerks, the secretaries, the economists and other camp servants. M.Z. Nikonov-Smorodin wrote of this: 'The proletariat was barred entry.... Chekists of every ilk, a few people with special skills who managed to get off the work gangs, those lucky enough to have curried some sort of favour, overseers and guards, these were the ones who filled the theatre, had access to the library, to bathhouse No. 1 and other camp blessings.'[8]

An angered Tiberius wrote with malice:

Some mangerial 'twerp' deemed it especially chic to be seated where everybody could see him, right before his bosses' eyes. And the closer to the big shots he could squirm, the more arrogant he would get in grabbing the best front-row seats. (Another detestable tradition was) the excessive zeal of the commanding officers in disciplining their charges... as, when having gained access to the cherished auditorium, you looked around in vain for a spare seat, only to see the best already taken by the 'chosen'

members of the public, and to hear a threatening hiss –
'Quiet!', 'Enough of that!', 'Silence!' after every cough (and
nearly everyone was coughing, for the harsh autumnal season made itself strongly felt).[9]

The spectators who had 'reserved' the best seats, knew, of course,
the rules of behaviour in a theatre, which could hardly be said of the
hardened criminals condemned under Article 49 (gambling and
similar sins). Occasionally the peace had to be kept by an order of
the day, such as appeared on the Solovetsky Island's 'Black Board' in
1924: 'For disturbing the peace in the Kultprosvet Theatre on September 7 the inmates listed below shall be placed under arrest for 15
days each, and subsequently be barred from the theatre for a period
of two months'. A list of seven names followed.

Even when, in later years, the theatre became a fixture, ad-
missions were valued and tickets were regarded as cherished gifts
for 'the ladies'. Ruffians were no longer put through the drill in the
auditorium and women, who had been segregated, were eventually
admitted to seats side-by-side with men. A hardened criminal could
be overhead whispering into his female companion's ear witticisms
that would have made even walls blush.

As the actors gained experience, the theatre grew more and
more professional. Theatrical critics, reviewers, and later on, memoir
writers made their appearance, thanks to whom we can form some
idea of the productions themselves.

In July 1924 Makar Borin (1871–1938),[10] an actor with a 30-
year stage career in the theatrical companies of major Russian cities
behind him, arrived on the Solovki to serve a three-year sentence.
His first appearance was on 10 and 11 August in *Krechinsky's Wedding* by A. Sukhovo-Kobylin (Shiriayev mistakenly refers to *The
Forest*), in which Borin played the key role of Raspliuyev, a part he
had polished to perfection, having excelled in it in the past, unfailingly evoking cheers and applause for every sparkling repartee,
every gesture. Counting the Solovetsky performances, he had played
it 127 times. Armanov, as Krechinsky, 'struck just the right, consist-
ently self-possessed tone', Liubokhonsky as Muromsky seemed
somewhat young and Nikitina (as Auntie) and Shuman (as
Lidochka) rendered their parts quite well, so that Borin's triumph
both as actor and stage director was unqualified.

The play evoked loud acclaim, shouts of 'bravo' and an ova-
tion. The reviewer Ya. Ginesin wrote: 'Raspliuyev ... is a most accomplished figure'. Borin was appointed the theatre's leader.

Quick on the uptake and not entirely without cunning, he promptly took stock of the situation and according to Shiriayev, 'on the sly, laid brick upon brick in building up his own edifice: for a start he cajoled from the authorities the release from the work gangs of several leading actors, then a few score more and had some backstage staff assigned to the theatre, such as a tailor, a hairdresser, a props manager, a couple of carpenters'.

Both as actor and stage director, Borin held his finger on the pulse of his audience and was able to see the real Solovetsky spectator and do his best to please him – he bewitched, amused, and enlightened, but had no intention of reforming or, still less, fighting him.

Borin started off with light plays from the Russian classical repertoire. He staged a great number of short comedies from the prerevolutionary farce and miniature repertoire (*The Governor Underground*, *A Well-Made Tailcoat*), with which he was familiar, having produced these plays in Odessa in the early 1920s. Some critics (one, 'Spectator', has so far defied identification) voiced concern over the introduction of philistine ideology and the decline of the theatre. Of course the stage director did make concessions to NEP, and NEP men and presented old-time works lacking ideological content. The theatre gave its audience relaxation and recreation; after a good laugh, there was time to discuss ideological purity.

Borin's favourite roles were in the Russian classical repertoire, which he knew how to stage and loved to play. He touched and bemused his audience with the charming, carefree Respliuyev (*Krechinsky's Wedding*), the crude buffoonery of Arkashka Schastlivtsev (*The Forest*) and his convincing psychological portrait of Shmaga, deprived of his share of happiness (*Guilty Without Guilt* by Ostrovsky). He confidently performed the part of Ferdyshchenko in a dramatization of Dostoyevsky's *The Idiot*. Litvin lauded Borin for his performance as Ivan Nikiforovich (*How Ivan Ivanovich Quarrelled with Ivan Nikiforovich*, after Gogol). Many scenes in the play were done 'boldly and enchantingly', and were vividly picturesque. Appearing with Borin were both professionals and dilettanti: the reviews retain the names of Osinovsky, Zemliantsev, Golgoer, Gromov, Stankevich, Telnov, Panin, Nikitina and many others.

Since the repertoire was boundless, from *Anna Christie* by Eugene O'Neill to *The Storm* by Ostrovsky and *The Lower Depths* by Gorki, suitable roles were found for everybody: Borin was concerned not so much with ideas (these, being an old hand, he somehow sorted out), as with keeping the actors happy, and he managed to stage plays with touching care both for himself and for them.

One of the pen portraits left us by Shiriayev is of Lev Kondratiev (b. 1889), actor and stage director, brought up in the Alexander Lyceum, a former civil servant on the staff of the Senate, sent to the Solovki in the summer of 1925 with a group of 'lyceum graduates'.[11]

> Clad in a tar-besmirched sheepskin jacket, and a horrid cap with earflaps, he, nevertheless, remained himself, an elegant, worldly Petersburger, neither a Muscovite nor a Parisian, but most pointedly a Petersburger. A fir stick in his hand turned into the walking cane of an idling dandy, and the huge and clumsy blunt-toed boots could not, it would seem, alter his gait, cultivated on polished parquet floors.

> But he was no snob. His looks were no less refined and sensitive than the strings of his heart.... He was a born artist. In St. Petersburg he studied stagecraft under Varlamov, and the grand old man counted him among his best pupils ... in *Three Thieves*, a most trite, translated comedy, he contrived to create so vividly the banal role of a gentleman-crook, who would steal as a labour of love, for the sake of an emotive thrill, and invest it with so much unfeigned grace, that an old diplomatist almost of the times of Chancellor Prince Gorchakov, who happened to see the 'Bolshevist' spectacle, shed genuine tears: 'The tails, just see how he wears that tailcoat.... It's something we'll never see again ... never ... never....' And the expansive small thief Fomka Ruliok exclaimed as he was leaving the auditorium, gesticulating wildly: 'There goes the most real "Urka"! A smashing, lucky devil! Now, just what are we, after that?'[12]

He reached his true peak as Tsar Feodor in A. Tolstoy's *Tsar Feodor Ioannovich*. The drama was drastically cut, not for reasons of censorship though, but for shortage of actors; the part of the tsar became all the more striking.

After the play Shiriayev and Kondratiev went for a stroll along the bank of the Holy Lake. They paused at one of the numerous votive crosses raised by the monks, one that had a figure of Christ carved on it.

'While working on the role of Tsar Feodor, I would come here, quietly, lest I disturb the peace of the purple dusk,' Kondratiev murmured. 'It was from Him that I sought a profound, complete understanding of that role … just from this one, only from Him, not from any other.'

'Why from this one? And from him only?'

'Look at Him carefully. Does He resemble those that you saw under the dome of St. Isaac's, or the canvasses in the Hermitage? No. This one is quite different. Look at those prominent cheek-bones. At the eyes – small, slightly squinting, and the beard, sparse, tufty…. For here is a puny little peasant from some village of Terpigorevo, locked in the marches. Just have Him don a tattered, homespun coat, put a knapsack on his back – and off He would go, trudging along the meandering, snowswept roads… .'

Among the great number of huge votive crosses raised by pilgrims 'for the veneration of every Christian' (they thickly studded the bank, reinforcing it at the monastery), some were quite striking for their skilful carving. N. Vinogradov encountered a similar one along the Savvatievo road: 'On the cross was a crucified Christ, whose face and whose drooping body nailed to it, were rendered with stark realism'.

The cross that attracted Kondratiev's attention perhaps seemed to him a link in the chain of Russian culture, rising from the Nekrasov tradition (the peasant–Christ from Terpigorevo) and the soul-searchings of Dostoyevsky himself.

By sheer chance no famous actresses were sent to the Solovki. Till the autumn of 1926 the leading dramatic performer was L. Rakhman, a professional actress, with a striking, nervous manner of performance. This trait ruined her Katerina (in *The Storm* by Ostrovsky), where the woman went into tantrums that were quite out of character, but beautifully fitted the role of Esther (*Overseas* by Ya. Gordin), when the audience was 'captivated by moments of profound drama, a most refined sense of measure throughout and the beautiful crescendo of moods' (Litvin).

Appearing with invariable success in comedies, Goltgoer, the wife of a general and commander of a guards regiment proved on stage to be a most expressive comic old woman. Quite attractive were the beauty and elegant plasticity of Khomutova-Hamilton, a former landowner, called 'Lady' in camp. Vysotskaya, coming from a family of prominent Moscow tea merchants, also proved a rather good actress. Unfortunately, no concrete information on their fates has so far been found, but memoir writers have singled out these names from among the women who sought the stage as an escape from the common work gang. The path of an actress was fraught with great hazards: God forbid being fancied by the camp bosses!

Among Borin's definite contributions to the camp's cultural life was his firm support for concerts. In winter the theatre produced, more or less regularly, at first one and then two plays monthly, repeating performances two or three times. Free evenings were given to musicians of whom the camp had quite a number, from modest professionals to brilliant dilettanti.

A brass band was formed (conducted by I.S. Levkassi-Lieberman), which played operatic music by Verdi, Gounod, Bizet and Chaikovsky during intermissions. In summer the band gave concerts in one of the kremlin's courtyards.

A symphony orchestra also took shape. Quite popular with music lovers was the trio: Levkassi – piano, Struckhoff – cello and Gorodetsky – violin. The vocal trio of Kuzmin, Gorodetsky and Rodnov also gave concerts.

Competitions between the Solovetsky choruses (Russian, conducted by Ravtopulla, and Ukrainian, conducted by Romashchenko) were usually won by the Ukrainians. The choruses were short of female voices, yet the male ones were truly phenomenal: everybody remembered the magnificent, even if quite uncultivated, voice of the Moscow dentist Hans Milovanov. Following the closure of the American Relief Administration,* which he had served as an interpreter, he was sent to the Solovki as a spy.

In 1926, having replaced the excessively temperamental Levkassi, S.D. Korobovsky became the theatre's musical director. As a result, by the middle of that year the concert program included Act Two of Rimsky-Korsakov's opera *Sadko* (Sadko – Yadrov, merchants – Kuzmin, Asatiani, Osnova) and a performance of Rakhmaninov's one-act opera *Aleko* was promised.

Thus, filled with activity, Borin's term neared its end: of his three-year sentence he had served two. Bidding him farewell, Shiriayev wrote:

> Borin united us all ... captivated everybody by his love for the theatre, and put together one play after another.... He produced more than sixty different plays.... He is now leaving to give guest performances at Kem. What shall we add to our thanks to Borin for all he has done on the Solovki? Let us wish him success at Kem!"
>
> (*N.S.*, 1926, No. 22)

---

* ARA (active 1919–23); in 1921 the Soviet government permitted it to help the famine-stricken population of the Volga area.

The assessment of what Borin had achieved goes wider to embrace the role of the theatre in the life of the camps in those years and, despite what one might think, it was far from unanimous. Today, as we gather views of the comedians and dramatic actors who entertained the 'honourable public' in those years, it is evident that opinions vary strikingly.

Points of view in the camp were poles apart. The Solovetsky memoir writer A. Klinger was undoubtedly not alone.

> These supervised culture workers were no different in their rights and duties from the serf actors before emancipation.... Toadies also turned up among the actor prisoners, who curried favours with the administration by exploiting the labour and talent of other actors, forced under threat of repression to entertain the Chekists by genuine acting and laughter through tears. They included, for example, the dramatic actor Borin, a person not without theatrical skills, but morally depraved, a drunkard and rascal, and Armanov, a charlatan without any talent at all, which however, did not prevent him from posing as an actor of the well-known Korsh theatre in Moscow.... The great majority of convict intellectuals did not attend the 'Kultprosvet' plays and concerts. I will never forget the bitter remark of a fellow-member of my work-gang, a noted Russian professor: 'Go to the "Kultprosvet"? But why? Just to realize ever more profoundly all the horror of one's situation? So that this travesty of the theatre, of art, can remind you once again that you are nothing but a mute beast? Let them all go to hell!'[13]

Such a stand had supporters throughout the theatre's existence. It is quite understandable, and hardly anyone would condemn the noble rejection of coercion. Respect for art and a person's self-respect precluded the acceptance of the prison camp theatre.

Another view on the problem, shared by many, also gave expression to the sense of self-respect, finding support for it in the very possibility of going to a theatre. It was voiced by Gennady Andreyev (G.A. Khomiakov), who served his term from 1927 to 1929, a time when many of the theatrical initiatives had been hopelessly destroyed. And still....

He named two pleasures of the long polar night: a trip to the bath-house, and a visit to the theatre.

> The latter carries one away into a mirage, into another world. It's balm for the soul, the Solovetsky theatre.... One

sees there the same platoon commanders and monitors pushing us around, dressed in their grey peajackets or greatcoats, with black collars and stripes on the sleeves; the same Solovetsky lords, those hired officers who hold in the palm of their hands our life or death; friends, acquaintances; yet, invisible to the eye, there reigns a different atmosphere in which the shell of captivity choking your heart somehow melts away.

Even the very fact that downstairs at the box office you are on your own, buying a ticket, holds a grain of freedom. Upstairs, at the entrance to the foyer, your ticket is torn, just as in all theatres round the world. In the foyer people are strolling, sitting along the walls, and from the auditorium come the sounds of the orchestra; you feel quite differently from the way you feel in the platoon. Walking about and conversing with the men are women: this is the only place on the Solovki where one can casually, freely, without fear, talk to a woman. If one meets a woman on the road or in the kremlin, if one exchanges a few words with her in view of everybody, it could be construed as an illicit date, for which one, as well as the woman, could be sent to a punishment cell or a penalty prison. But in the theatre one can speak freely to a woman.

The bell goes, the music dies down, the lights go out; the curtain swings open, and another world unfolds before your eyes. At this moment, if you focus attention on the stage, if you warm to the play so as to feel that you're one of the characters, you may completely forget about the Solovki, forget altogether that you're a convict.[14]

In fact, both attitudes confused aesthetic with non-aesthetic motives, as happens in any life, yet in camp life the confusion is perforce one-sided, and, therefore, painful.

In discussions of camp and serf theatres, an important factor is omitted: whereas a barrier existed between the patrician spectators and the actors, on the Solovki, the spectators (those beyond the front rows, of course) identified with the actors as regards both their fates and their aspirations. And this proved a tangible buttress both for the stage and the audience.

Of course, in its confrontation with the camp system the theatre always stood to lose. It lost its actors and its spectators, as they succumbed to typhoid fever, heart attacks or tuberculosis or were quietly shot after supper. On the morrow, pretending nothing had happened – and how is a convict expected to respond? – the theatre resumed its fight for humanity.

Was the theatre expected to rise up heroically and, thereby, suicidally? On the theoretical level, any answer would be right. However, let us heed what life itself had to say on this score. For it came up with an answer of its own.

6 The smaller theatres – 'Trash' and the group of 'Our Own'

> *We, actors, therefore, are called upon to bring people the joy of gambling against the fatality of death.*
>
> M. Prishvin, 1930

Unusual enthusiasm for the theatre in the camp's centre, the kremlin, relieved the winter months of 1924–25. Neither did it abate with the coming of spring. On the contrary, it spread over the islands, where theatres were built or premises were adapted for them at Savvatievo and at the brick kiln on Anzer and the Greater Muksalma. The crest of the wave was nearing its peak, yet its impetus was still strong. Theatrical freedom reached its highest point in 1925, when it was marked by something inconceivable: the birth of another two theatrical companies. This would have looked fantastic, were it not for the new companies' billboards, which appeared one after another near the canteen and in other places.

Tiberius (Tverie) was spiteful: 'Large billboards well in advance alerted the patient Solovki public for an evening with *"Trash"**.'[1] And the brightly coloured billboards were, indeed, quite artistic, for the camp held plenty of people handy with a brush: N. Kachalin, the stage designer of the Theatre of the 1st Department, gifted professionals and young beginners.

The Solovetsky reviewers Litvin, Shiriayev, Glubokovsky, Tverie and Galkh all wrote about the new companies. And still, one gets a feeling that neither at that time, in the heat of the struggle, nor a little later, in Glubokovsky's 1927 report, nor many years afterwards, in Shiriayev's *The Inextinguishable Lantern*, were the details of those initiatives, so important for the camp, ever revealed. Shiriayev's book merely confuses the reader who puts his trust in it. The author maintains a mere semblance of truth, while distorting circumstances.

The birth of two theatrical companies within a short period of time (*Trash* on 28 February, the theatre of *Our Own* in April) were

---

* *Trash* – theatre of artists, writers, actors and musicians.

evidence that the intelligentsia, cowed, battered and bruised during the first eighteen months by the indescribably harsh life, was just getting back on its feet again. And since the theatre, their own creation, was taken away from them for the general needs of the camp and for the entertainment of the administration and camp keepers, they built it up again, this time for themselves. The *Trash* programme kept alive the memory of a different, prerevolutionary epoch – a demonstrative memory, not spat upon just to please the new powers that be. The actors also presented scenes of camp life and the authorities sustained quite caustic criticism, though the text of the couplets looked quite harmless. In a word, the actors were having fun, and entertaining the public, as if they feared neither their commanders nor the camp.

The *Trash* performance, according to Shiriayev, began with a scene called *Fireflies*:

> The opening of the curtain can be neither heard nor seen. The stage is dark.... But lo! Out of the darkness come voices, reciting sadly:

> The winter snowstorm tucks us in
> For half a year, for half a year.
> Till spring brings back the fishermen
> To Solovki, to Solovki....

> Coloured lanterns light up one after another.... They flicker out, then flare up again, more and more of them.... In the darkness one discerns rhythmically swaying female figures, the lights swirl round and round, dancing through the haze, dispersing the darkness. The rhythm of the song grows livelier, the sounds now seem caressing, to offer vague hope.

As if it was, indeed

> So good to gaze with childish glee
> Upon the distant world.
> No matter where you glance, you see
> Folks leaping up with joy....
> And, when old, on some calm winter day
> We'll all crowd together again,
> To renew, without rancour, fond memories
> Of our own, our beloved Solovki.

What a truly innocuous text! How could it be forbidden – what for? Yet Glubokovsky, in connection with this ditty by Litvin and Shiriayev, recalls 'satirical couplets', which caught on in the camps' platoons.

Indeed, the secret of their impact was in the performance, in the ironic tinge the inoffensive lyrics took on.

Staged by N.M. Krasovsky, a young Moscow stage-director, the song turned into a kind of hymn of the Solovki inmates, and, with various lyrics, lived on for many years, travelling together with convicts into exile to the Vorkuta and Central Asia. From the stage it bore a subterranean resemblance to the song of the *Letuchaya Mysh* (*Bat*), the prerevolutionary cabaret–theatre of George Baliyev. The *Fireflies* imparted a measure of sadness, of ridicule and pitiful merriment which in the circumstances satisfied all and left a 'loophole' into the future.

Trash also put on Litvin's risky playlet *Love is a Golden Book*, the lampoon *Governor of the Green Island*, Shiriayev's sketches *Island of the New Code* and *Oleum Ricini* and other work.

A popular hit of those years, *At Night Marseilles is All Astir*, enjoyed great success. 'Nikolai Erdman', recalled the actress Rina Zelionaya, 'composed the lyrics of a song (music by Yu. Miliutin) for my night shows in the *Nerydai* (*Don't weep*) tavern. It was a bit of a burlesque in the apache dance style ... I sang, and everything I sang was shown on stage.'[2] The 'bit of a burlesque' was presented in the same style on the Solovki.

The *Trash* programme borrowed some of its dancing numbers from the repertoire of the *Bat* and the *Crooked Mirror*, the best prerevolutionary cabarets.

During the civil war actors clung to traditions, and in the ensuing chaos both entertained and rescued themselves, appearing at night in artistic cabarets; this included the *Trash* in Kiev (1919), Odessa and other cities. Mime, short satirical scenes, recitations to musical accompaniment, topical couplets – everything was quite lively and easily combined. People were attracted to the *Trash* soirées by the performers' high artistry, their unexpected responses and free and unrestrained forms of presentation.

Baliyev and his *Bat* emigrated, while the Petersburg *Crooked Mirror* of A. Kugel and the *Crooked Jimmy* (established in Kiev, later moved to Moscow) remained, nourishing the revived cabarets and small theatres of comedy.

Small companies still held out, though their days were already numbered: they were attacked for the banality of responses and couplets, for low artistic standards, for indulging the tastes of the bourgeois spectator.

Such reproaches may have been fully deserved. Yet the decisive argument was never voiced: the theatres of miniatures, of satire and the like, were not amenable to control, even though the texts were checked before performance. It was impossible to predict a compère's responses, the behaviour of the actors and the reaction of the audience; all this aroused suspicion.

On the Solovki a somewhat bewildered Tiberius wrote:

> The soirée's moods shift throughout, opening with a musical bagatelle 'And So, Let's Start', followed by Lunacharsky's comedy *The 'Internationale' According to Duncan* and moving next to cabaret imitations on Solovetsky motifs. One should recognize as very apt the popular pieces *Evening, Late Out of the Wood, The Cards* and the propaganda piece *The Confession*. The evening's hit, *At Night Marseilles is All Astir*, is done very well technically.... The adaptation for the stage of *How Lovely, How Fresh had been the Roses* introduced a discordant elegiac note into the recklessly hilarious pace of the evening. Generally speaking, *Trash* justified, if only partially, in the sphere of entertainment, the hopes pinned on it.

> But this is not enough. What's needed is a statement of its ideological credo!
>
> (*N.S.*, 1925, No. 10)

One might think that the show's 'ideological credo' was evident in the overall benevolent atmosphere of the aestheticized spectacle, in the ironic abstraction of the little scenes and the steadfast desire to develop the specifically Solovetsky camp theme, something about which Tiberius keeps absolutely silent.

Wonderment over the *Trash* program was still alive when criminal offenders lined up on the stage of the theatre to assail the audience with their own songs, scenes and couplets. Of their second programme (23 May) the *Zritel* (*Spectator*) reported:

> The audience, strongly differing from the usual public, received each number with enthusiasm. Predominant in the auditorium were members of the work gangs, the riff-raff of the camp, with only a few intellectuals.... Whether it was

the lament of a shackled convict in Moscow's Central Prison or the hymn of escaped prisoner in the taiga, 'Baikal the Sacred, Our Glorious Sea' or a wild, reckless round-dance, the audience, as one man, vociferously acclaimed them.[3]

The CRs and the camp's 'riff-raff' began talking, in the language permitted, about their life and their past, bluntly, by allusion and suggestion or by intonation.

The camp's two main forces gained an expressive aesthetic voice. Behind them were thousands of convicts, indifferent, disillusioned, despairing, embittered with the whole world. How they received the appearance of the smaller theatres was not all that important, for the majority never saw a single programme. Never saw them, but might have wanted to see. Never knew, but might they not, all of a sudden, want to know?

Even the fleeting, flimsy emergence on the level of entertainment of a common language between the upper crust of active intellectuals and members of the rabble threatened the administration with dire consequences. For the camp's mainstay was the build-up of hostility between the various groups of convicts. In everyday life an intellectual and a ruffian existed side by side, but differently, and in the case of reciprocal hatred one of them would seek other neighbours, even though the chiefs of the divisions indulged in devising unthinkable combinations and would put side by side a baron and a gangster. But the very thought of a possible union of former enemies, was, to the Chekists, something horrible to contemplate.

Moreover, the appearance of the *Trash* undermined the foundations of the popular propaganda theatre, which persisted in the barracks and the overseers' club. The art of the CRs proved too seductive and vivid compared to the drab spectacles put on by the Solovetsky Special Regiment. And so, waving the banner of ideological principle and of opposition to vulgar buffoonery, the degraded Chekists and Communists purged from the Party rushed into the fray.

Tiberius, ever spiteful, wrote: 'What does it matter, if on the eve of March a miscarriage takes place'.[4] Shiriayev was scared, and immediately announced that, 'being concerned for his professional reputation', his work in *Trash* was over and he would have nothing to do with the group (*N.S.*, 1925, No. 14).

In fact, we do not even know who directed the *Trash* and was responsible for its destiny. In *The Inextinguishable Lantern* Shiriayev describes a collective decision to create a theatre of miniatures. Litvin, Shiriayev, Glubokovsky, Yegorov and Emelianov were all directly involved; they were also co-authors of the scenes and couplets.

However, when the authors came up against the unfavourable reaction of the camp authorities, they renounced their connections with *Trash* and chose a stance of opposition to the theatre's deviation.

Suddenly Shiriayev discovered at the theatre a dictatorship of those 'who adhere to a literary trend diametrically opposed to my own' (*N.S.*, 1925, No. 16); he was 'offended' by the sway held by old art in the *Trash*. If one makes an effort to decipher the generalities (Shiriayev's 'opponents' at the head of the theatre have never been identified in print), only two figures can be meant – Litvin and Glubokovsky. Whether at that time Shiriayev was their earnest opponent, or donned this mask perforce, we do not know.

A general meeting of the troupe was attended by the chief of the 1st Department, Barinov. Speakers eagerly persuaded the *Trash* leaders that they had deviated from their intended target of 'collective revolutionary art'. A commission to define 'more rational forms' for the theatre was set up: Bodukhin, Koganov, Raisky, Nedzvedsky, Roganova, Yegorov, Litvin and Akarsky-Shiriayev, who joined *Trash* once again.

The New Solovki set forth the immediate educative tasks: 'Philistine, petty-bourgeois deviations should be resolutely cast away; the repertoire should be permeated by new revolutionary life, reflecting the everyday existence of the worker and peasant...' (*N.S.*, 1925, No. 17).

A meeting of the company on 22 April dragged on into the small hours of the morning 'as *Trash*'s two main groupings were sharply divided on how to realize collectivist principles'.

This was how a living theatre was destroyed by untalented Chekists under the pretext of concern for 'rational forms'. True, in *The Inextinguishable Lantern* Shiriayev wrote that the theatre existed until 1927. However, the absence of any mention of *Trash* in the pages of *The New Solovki*, which reported in detail the productions of all the theatres, makes one question the above date. More probably, the company fell apart as soon as people turned away from it. Inner disarray facilitated the hand of its adversaries in destroying the *Trash*.

Perusal today of issues of *The Solovetsky Islands* and *The New Solovki* suggests the conclusion that Litvin, who also had to beat a retreat, suffered most in the affair although he never stooped to indicting his own creation, for which, in all probability, he was denied the Party's thanks on *The New Solovki*'s anniversary in January 1926. True, it was later disclosed that it was 'the scribe' who was to blame for omitting his name.

In 1927 Glubokovsky wrote quite justly of the theatre that it was:

> the first to hurl from the Solovetsky stage into the auditorium the sparkle of Solovkian satire, topical smiles and grins of the day…. The *Trash* repertoire is the topical satire and lyricism of a bad theatre of miniatures. Of course, its repertoire is no model of creative boldness, of course, its aesthetic form is, at best, a Baliyev-type *Bat* on the prewar Kievan scale, but still, it is the freshness of youthful fervour; from the inmates' chorus in the Solovetsky theatre came a breath of everlasting life.[5]

The 'everlasting life' lifted the spectator up from his knees, gave him strength. The camp had organically to survive, had to overcome through spiritual resistance.

The energy of a general upsurge on the Solovki impelled even the most unorganized camp inmates – criminals, the rabble – toward competition and joint creative endeavour.

Before the revolution, prisons in Russia knew no theatre, but this was not the case in labour camps, whose productions were described by Dostoyevsky in *Notes from the House of the Dead*. One, watched by Dostoyevsky around Christmas in 1852, was presented once a year, during the Christmas celebrations, though the impression it left was that of a firm, time-hallowed tradition.

M. Gernet, who studied prison life and prison psychology, wrote: 'Purely theatrical productions were extremely rare in the prerevolutionary prison. Yet the prison was unwilling to reject them altogether … it created amusements out of spectacles, which only very remotely resemble theatrical productions.'[6]

For many years the most widespread and 'innocent' diversions were 'rehearsals of a trial' when actors for the relevant parts (members of the court, of the jury, counsel for the prosecution, counsels for the defense) were chosen from among the prisoners in the cell, and a sitting of the court was conducted according to the rules, the performers competing in witty repartee and cunning self-defence.

Gernet found the spectacle, *The Wedding*, as described by a person who saw it in a Siberian prison, a diversion that was far from innocent.

> The purpose of the spectacle, complete with make-up, dressing up and even with props, was not the staging of some play; in an extremely crude and cynical form it reproduced a wedding scene and, especially, all the wedding rites. It is evoked at once by sexual starvation and a lusting ear and eye. The spectacle of *The Wedding* turns into a peculiar divertissement, it has everything – singing, music, dancing.[7]

At the beginning of the twentieth century, at the Zerentui prison in Siberia political prisoners, who enjoyed relative freedom, put on plays. They removed the bunks in the cell and made a platform and a prompt box. Blankets sewn together and suspended from the ceiling formed a room, and a curtain was made of bed sheets. They staged a play by an anonymous author – *The Clandestine Meeting*, and *The Marriage* by Gogol. During World War I prisoners staged many plays: Gogol's *The Inspector General*, *The Lower Depths* by Gorky, comedies by Ostrovsky and Chekhov's vaudevilles; a few of the plays were Ukrainian.

E. Makhlin, a participant, wrote: 'The theatre afforded us the opportunity to get away from the prison for a few hours, to cease being a convict for a time, to feel, to experience, to weep, to laugh…. Generally speaking, the theatre relaxed the regulations'.[8]

Gernet rejoiced that under the new historical conditions prisoners were allowed to arrange plays themselves, and the theatrical rush that had swept through Russia did not bypass the prisons: 'in places of confinement accounting for two-thirds of the total prison population, 3,650 plays, soirées, concerts, etc., were held in 1922'.

All these streams met on the Solovki: the popular, farcical principle from the theatre of the labour camps, the numerous small amusements and games of a rather cruel nature and the new tradition of the Soviet prison. All this resulted in the swift birth of a company called *Our Own*.

The ideas of competition and self-assertion in art were nourished in *Our Own* by rich prison folklore. The first spring report is indicative: '… the inmates of the 2nd platoon decided to prepare an evening of prison songs without the help of professional performers' (*N.S.*, 1925, No. 14). Winter was over, April softly glowed in the last ice and it seemed there was no need any more to escape from winter's boredom.

However, adapting songs to the stage not as a mere pastime, but rather as a token of a spiritual need, attracted both spectators and performers. A group of felons persisted in repeating soirées of song, then performed playlets and ditties.

The chorus of *Our Own* began with 25 members, growing in half a year to 80 people; given greater scope, it might have grown still more. The choir became the firm foundation of the group's performances, invariably evoking admiration from both spectators and listeners. But *Our Own* claimed something bigger – a stage production touching on current life. And this proved the reason for both their sparkling success and their very quick undoing.

Zritel (*Spectator*) wrote of the show: 'The first part was devoted to reflections on social and political life.... Noteworthy was a satirical presentation of the international scene. *Our Own* showed deep feeling for the tragic events in Bulgaria, and was able to reflect them in an awe-inspiring propaganda piece.'

After the intermission came the dramatization *At the Prison Gates*, which made a strong impression. The programme ended with scenes from camp life and a lot of humour. '"Heroines" from the women's barracks, "*Trash*men", limericks, couplets about everyday life, satire, a polemic. Gay and merry, all to the point, topical' (*N.S.*, 1925, No. 24).

The theatre's new programme, presented on 13 and 14 October, won approbation for a very good dramatization of *The Solovetsky Public*, as well as of *Having Heard – Resolved* and a short play *Within Monastery Chambers*.

On 28 October, in honor of a KGB 'relief' commission (Bokii, Katanian, Feldman, Yakovlev), a joint programme was put on by all the groups. *Our Own* opened the concert with *The Solovetsky Public* and a cycle of especially well-loved prison songs (*N.S.*, 1925, No. 44).

Boris Glubokovsky wrote more than anybody else of the folklore and theatre of the rabble. It was also he who singled out the personalities making up the backbone of *Our Own*, of whom he has left us brief pen portraits.

The tall, snub-nosed, slightly eccentric Panin, who had started, as Glubokovsky wrote, back in 1918, at the Butyrka prison, on the 'Red Corridor' stage, was one of the founders of the theatre in the Ordynka camp in Moscow. An extraordinary personality. The

circumstances that made him part company with the law are unknown; it is clear, though, that he, a professional pickpocket, was a
victim of circumstances and harsh times. Further, there was the iron
mechanism whereby Moscow and other major cities were cleared of
socially harmful elements. Whoever was caught in a round-up and
started serving his first term was henceforth provided for to the end
of his life.

Panin, too, after his release from the Solovki, was returned to
the islands again. He could well have come out on the stage with
the very couplets that Glubokovsky cites:

> Hallo,
> Though recently I bade farewell,
> I'm here with you, my friends, again.
> For, as a pest most dangerous,
> From Moscow – the Red capital
> They sent me packing into exile,
> Back to this here ancient cloister.
> And so, hallo, hallo, hallo![9]

> In his invariable red necktie, cap set on his head at a pre-
> carious angle, he would come out onto the stage welcomed
> by loud cries of 'bravo' and read from a crumpled slip of
> paper his Solovki-inspired couplets. The life reflected in *Our
> Own*'s satire was that of a concentration camp, a life not at
> all distinguished by variety. The performers monotonously
> castigated chiefs, deputy chiefs and commanders, poked
> fun at an unlucky fellow prisoner caught in some mis-
> demeanour, lashed out at the prices in the 'Rozmag' store
> opened for the inmates on the ground floor of the adminis-
> tration building. The cellar beneath it held punishment cells
> intended for those arrested for crimes in camp. Hence, the
> camp phrase 'to go under the Rozmag'.[10]

Panin's talent, poetic and as a performer, was doomed to follow the
roundelay of narrow camp motifs. People loved him and sympa-
thized with him, but of his fate we know nothing; yet, being an
artistic personality, he could never stop writing and singing. Therefore, he must have got into trouble, for eventually he disappeared.

Alexei Chekmazov, a Don Cossack, who took to banditry
during the Civil War, was of stronger, more tenacious stuff. He
engaged in creative pursuits only in prison and camp; when free
he indulged other interests. For him writing and drama were a form

of adaptation to prison and camp circumstances, rather than an inherent need. His thoughts and feelings lived freely within a system of clichés drawn from his reading; as a writer he is of no interest. But as a representative of the seething popular sea, trying to adjust to the new conditions, Chekmazov excites curiosity. He is one of the few who justified the hopes of the 'man-reforming' ideologists, for he eventually became the direcotor of a small factory of musical instruments in the White Sea–Baltic Canal zone.

Glubokovsky introduced also another curious personality, an actor of *Our Own*, Vladimir Bedrut, an intellectual burglar and poet.

> This felon is not a former 'homeless child' from the Khitrov market-place; hailing from elegant drawing rooms, a scion of a rather 'proper' lawyer's family, he joined the criminal world in search of adventure and thrills. Bedrut is a brilliant product of cheap aestheticism of the prewar vulgar-decadent kind. He carries his profile as if he were made entirely of Dresden china, a poseur to the core. Though not entirely without culture, he is vulgarized by the trivial life he led. Posing through life, playing the role of a ruffian raised on decadent yeast, he is stilted, stuck-up and false, a far cry from Chekmazov's rustic mediocrity. In a typological classification he would occupy a very special place. N.N. Yevreinov with his 'theatre-for-oneself' theory, would have found in him worthwhile material.[11]

Bedrut's talent for the stage, if any, failed to manifest itself in his parts: reviewers more often mention his consistent inhibition and stiffness. Nevertheless, even Bedrut imparted some colour to *Our Own*'s performances.

Among the actresses in this group Glubokovsky singled out one, T. Timokhina. 'Before imprisonment – a dyed-in-the-wool prostitute, a dweller of the Khitrov market-place, cocaine addict. Semiliterate. Under 30. Having begun with a crowd scene, two years later she was playing Nast'ka in *The Warrant* and Yefrosinia in *Prince Alexis*.'

In the article 'A Solovetsky Lunatic' Glubokovsky presented Marusia Yegorova, another prostitute turned actress. 'Her eyes were blue and as large as saucers, her lips bright crimson, youth just throbbed in her rosy cheeks; yet her smile was pitiful.' And she was known in the camp by her nick-name 'Marusia the Doggie'. What made her recover her name and a concept of dignity was the theatre, which revealed in her both a temperament and a strong voice.[12]

What remained a riddle was the road Marusia would choose on her release from camp: to go on to an intelligent life, such as opened before her at Solovki, or back to her former profession.

In the summer of 1925 the *Our Own* group went to Savvatievo, giving several performances at the timber-felling sites, and appeared in Kem, invariably enjoying great success. They tried to defend themselves against Glubokovsky, author of the article 'Songs of the Rabble' (*S.I.*, 1925, Nos. 4 & 5). A debate was arranged and the theatre appointed official opponents to the criticism. Generally speaking, *Our Own* were energetic and vigorous. Their stand helped the Ukrainian drama circle and the remarkable chorus, as well as a newly established Byelorussian group, to defend their right to exist.

But the controversy, far from abating, flared up anew.

> Dispute about the groups. Heated debates galvanize the audience. A major question of the camp's public life is posed: Are the groups to be or not?.... Vasiliev's introductory remarks. At a time when they ought to have engaged in raising their cultural standards, in self-education, the full strength of three groups, uniting only 200 people, was directed at the easiest, demonstrative work – theatricals, though lacking the materials for it. The purpose of the dispute is to find out what the groups have done, and whether they are needed at all.
>
> (*N.S.*, 1925, No. 51)

The chairmen of the groups, the Ukrainian (Savitsky), Byelorussian (Skuratov) and *Our Own* (Chekmazov), continued to insist that the groups be allowed to exist.

The discussion was opened by Glubokovsky, who reiterated the charges of the theatres' opponents. Why, he asked, did the groups engage in theatricals, rather than in serious work? Because it was much easier to smear one's face with paint and utter from the stage other people's words, than seriously to work towards raising one's standards.

Vasiliev, associated with the theatrical group of the Solovetsky Special Regiment, made the concluding remarks: 'The period of the groups' independent existence is over. The time has come for regular general-education work under the firm guidance of the culture and education section.... Off to school! Pick up your books! Down to work!' (*N.S.*, 1925. No. 52).

Members of *Our Own* tried to hold out. They promptly examined all the performers for literacy and a smattering of historical materialism. Sixteen persons, led by Chekmazov, began grinding through the proletarian catechism, N. Bukharin's question-and-answer manual *The ABC of Communism*.

Yakov Galkh stood up for *Our Own*:

> An artistic group of criminals is needed, its usefulness is obvious: during its existence not a few natural talents have been discovered among the felons before our very eyes.... Moreover, a criminal joining the group drops such deplorable habits as gambling, using foul language, etc., not to mention the benefit of his or her involvement in cultural pursuits.
>
> The existence of the group does no harm. What needs to be done is to reinforce it.
>
> (*N.S.*, 1926, No. 1)

K. Vasiliev responded to the champions of the independent groups, asserting that all the three of them were barren. The Ukrainian and Byelorussian groups were 'stillborn creations', since it was folly to unite on the nationality principle. The *Our Own* group needed not reinforcement, but unqualified liquidation. 'Nothing but the cultivation of criminal ethics and traditions, laying the ground for all kinds of violations of camp regulations, could have come, nor does come, from this group.'

Vasiliev's programme was to set up at the club a small group of the 'Blue Blouse' type, a newspaper–literary circle and a joint chorus (*N.S.*, 1926, No. 4).

A theatrical and art council was now in power. In this the camp was obviously ahead of the mainland, where similar councils appeared only a few years later. Stanislavsky at once viewed them as an enemy. The council on the Solovki was headed by the new division chief, the former warder Yu. Blumberg. The repertoire was examined closely and numbers lacking artistic merit discarded. Glubokovsky assured readers that setting up a group of the 'Blue Blouse' type would not detract from the topicality of scenes of camp life on stage.

Shiriayev proclaimed the intention of organizing a Solovetsky working-class theatre under the name of *Solovetsky Farce*, disowned any form of 'intelligentsia-oriented' theatre and immediately won the council's support.

The group of the Solovetsky Special Regiment was now called the Aesthetic Propaganda Group and two dilettanti staged its plays: K. Vasiliev and the club's director V. Golubev, a former doctor's assistant.

In April the first results of the theatrical reforms were summed up. Shiriayev failed. There was no working-class theatre. Nor could he select an appropriate repertoire, even for the actors' circle. A reviewer wrote of boredom and anachronistic revolutionism (*N.S.*, 1926, No. 31).

The Aesthetic Propaganda Group (APG) gave three performances in January – the antireligious propaganda piece *The Holy Devil*, a small play about events in China, *Zone of Influence*, and another about the 1905 revolution, *Spare No Bullets*. In February they produced another play, and in March none. As Vasiliev explained, circle members were reluctant to work. Thus, the Chekists failed, too.

The failed reformers were saved by the well-known coupletwriter and accomplished professional, George Leon, who presented at the club the 'Red Blouse' ensemble with a variety programme. The spectators were in raptures: the performers were rhythmical, lively and excelled in dancing and singing. George Leon's group was nicknamed 'Zhivprofsolgaz', a horrible acronym for 'Living Trade-Union Solovetsky Gazette'. But in summer the ensemble dissolved and the actors scattered. True, in the autumn they got together again, but by this time George Leon, having served a year of his three-year sentence, had returned to Moscow.

The kremlin, as before, retained two theatres: the Red Army amateur theatre of the Special Solovetsky Regiment, which was losing its spectators, and the still vigorous Theatre of the 1st Department, headed after Borin's departure by Glubokovsky (succeeded as stage director by N. Krasovsky, Akarsky [Shiriayev] and Kondratiev).

The new living theatres were destroyed. Publically the responsible camp authorities kept out of the controversy over *Trash* and *Our Own*, relying on the efforts of intermediary elements. Nor were they disappointed. The motivation for closing down the *Our Own* company was indicative: the education sector had allegedly banked 'on the criminal elements as the camp's proletarian mass', but the latter 'kept cultivating their own habits, jargon and ethics', thereby corrupting the actors and the spectators.

The explanation offered by P. Shenberg, secretary of *The Solovetsky Islands*, is laughable, though understandable: the rabble could not be permitted to go on singing knife-edged, bristling couplets about camp life from the stage. And *Our Own* was eliminated.

It should be noted in conclusion that Solzhenitsyn's remark about the 'silent, cruel Solovki' was due to a lack of newspapers and journals. The Solovki of the 1920s, with their press, local history society and theatre, were anything but silent. After all, Solzhenitsyn himself acknowledged the existence of improbable combinations, brief in time and place. 'Such also are the early Solovki.'

Cruel and unpredictable, indeed. Fantastic...

In the autumn of 1926 the theatre opened in specially rebuilt premises seating 500. Despite a delay in laying the pipes, the theatre and the library were provided with central heating. The troupe was joined by newly arrived actors, and the season opened on 3 October with N. Erdman's comedy *The Warrant*, rendered in strident tones. The theatre was preparing to brighten up the inmates' morale through the dreary winter months, when there were no letters or parcels and no sun. But everything turned out differently.

7   The end of the early Solovki

Living in the cell with me during the last three months was an old actor, now already freed. And every day, upon returning from the theatre, he would reach with slow, age-tired movements for his pencil and, taking his time, steadily cross out on the wall calendar another, vanishing date.

B. Emelianov, *In the Quarries of a Term* (1926)

From 1926 imperceptible currents and obscure thrusts altered the steady flow of Solovetsky life.

Shiriayev attributed the overall crisis in camp life to typhus, and also to the appearance on the island of the prisoner Naftaly Frenkel, events that were, indeed, important. In fact, the Solovki in those years were doomed to perish from typhus and cholera. The very word 'insanitary' was utterly inadequate to describe the standards of daily existence that had become a norm at the camp. A convict's only chance of escaping death was appointment as a petty chief, assistant, tally clerk, book-keeper, cleaner or watchman – anything but the common work gang. For only this made life, however precarious and uncertain, more or less humanized: a cell for four or five, a wooden sofa, dim illumination and warmth, facilities to wash and dry out.

For the majority, life took a different shape: wooden bunks stretching across former cathedrals (four tiers high in St. Nicholas'); cold; bedbugs; filthy, damp clothes. Visits to the monastic bathhouse, which had room for only a few score at a time and where one was handed a single basin of tepid water, evoked visions of Dante's inferno. In fact, this was noted by Dostoyevsky during his spell of penal service: 'It struck me that if we ever happened to be together in hellfire, it would resemble this place very much'.[1]

It was only by some amazing chance that the camp survived for over two years without a devastating epidemic. But suddenly an obituary in the pages of *The New Solovki* (5 March 1926) announced the death 'after a brief illness' of E.V. Vlasova-Zapolskaya of the medical unit. Then came a modest report of the death of N.S. Vasin, supervisor of the Golgotha work site on Anzer Island. On 14 March there was another death 'following a sudden and brief illness', that of E.A. Polozova. Judging by these unusual publications, February 1926 marked the arrival of the typhus louse on the Solovki. For their fatal lack of preparedness medics paid with their lives.

Never once, though, did the newspaper use the word 'typhus'. On the contrary, as a diversion, in April, medical assistant V. Golubev appealed (in verse!) to readers to step up the fight against scurvy: sleep less, eat more and take up sports.

That same April saw the establishment of a disinfection facility at Kem on the mainland. By that time the epidemic was already sweeping through Solovki and persisted for several years (1926–30). Racked by typhus, the convicts in the infirmary and in the barracks lay on floors strewn with shavings and sawdust in their own excrement, which was raked out in the morning by women's hands. The nurses perished together with the sick. This is how Baroness Natalia Modestovna Friederix died, a profoundly religious person, who went to the typhus wards voluntarily. Her example was emulated by the elegant Sonka-Glazok, a Moscow prostitute, and author of the merry limerick:

> After heaving hefty logs,
> Trubnaya's forgotten.*
> When its raining cats and dogs,
> Clubwork is a godsend.

She collapsed on the sawdust-sprinkled floor.

We have no official data for the epidemic's casualties, but memoirists agree that half the camp's population was affected.

Now, concerning Frenkel. Born in Turkey in 1883, he appeared on the island long before the typhus louse. A secret GPU agent, he was sentenced in 1924 to a 10-year stretch, either for disobeying the 'organs' when organizing an Odessa–Istanbul–Rumania smuggling chain and preferring to work for himself or to protect their secret agent against exposure, but with a promise of early release.

In June 1924 Frenkel was probably already on the Solovki, and next year was commanding a separate timber-felling brigade. In February 1925 he was given the following character reference: 'Acquitted himself as an exceptionally outstanding worker, thereby enjoying the trust of the SLON administration'. And half a year later: 'One of the few responsible workers at SLON. Head of the Economics Division.' At last a review of the case resulted in 'preterm re-

---

* Trubnaya ploshchad' (Trubnaya Square) in Moscow, a customary place for prostitutes to ply their trade.

lease'. In June 1927 Frenkel left for Kem as Chief of the Camps Board Economics Department.[2]

Frenkel was an accomplished type of international adventurer, a man with an iron will and rare resourcefulness, possessing a phenomenal mathematical memory. Like many 'phenomena', he was of small stature and quite ordinary appearance. His face would have been rather attractive had it not a chilling, tenacious stare.

The Solovki typhus epidemic demonstrated the inadvisability of holding a great number of convicts on a remote island. Frenkel managed to prove how unproductively they were utilized, how the inept, obtuse camp authorities were destroying 'manpower' in pointless, antiquated ways, by exhaustion, starvation, and exposure. Frenkel's active, purposeful mind sought ways of attaining power, and promptly found them in shaping the work of the convicts by threat of repression and penalties into a single mechanism of rigorously organized slave labour yielding the GPU maximum profit. Unlike other administrators, who operated intuitively and not infrequently while drunk, Frenkel developed a precise system based on knowing the limits of human endurance. Under Frenkel the laws of the Mafia – fear and total submission – become Soviet laws.

He made the Solovki serve the mainland: on 16 December 1925, virtually by the last steamship, a detachment of 500 workers was despatched for timber felling. In the summer of 1926 the sawmill at Bab-Guba near Kem operated round the clock; the prisoners, whose labour was sold to the exporting Karelian Timber Trust, earned the camp up to 2 roubles a day each, while being paid 20 kopecks.

These are the economics not merely of serfdom, but of slavery. *The New Solovki* perpetuated the image of the SLON slaves: about the beginning of May, batch after batch, filthy, faces raw from smoke and wind, lips all chapped, sloshing in their boots through melting snow for 80–100 km, the 'foresters' come back from winter work (*N.S.*, 1926, No. 18). Naturally, nothing was said of those who remained in the forest for ever.

Both typhus and the appearance of Frenkel were the results of changing external circumstances. We can now see how important the international scandal was which raged for several years over the Solovki. Moscow's brazen response, as well as that of the GPU, only succeeded in raising the pitch of accusations in the foreign press.

In the summer of 1925, after two years of condemnation following the shooting of six 'politicians' at Savvatievo, the campaign in the socialist press seemed to be abating. The politicians were transferred to the mainland and the democratic press sighed with compassion over the fate of the inmates.

Probably the Solovetsky journalists were assigned the task of upholding the camp's honour. Responding to a French assertion that 'Solovki is a deadly place for the convicts held there', Shiriayev-Akarevich wrote the pamphlet *The Cheka's Bloody Atrocities (Deadly Solovki)*. The eager defender recognized no bounds in lauding life 'under the Polar night skies': during the day there were newspapers and games of chess and draughts and at night debates, lectures and concerts. And theatre all over the place, everywhere music and a singer, touched by her welcome, 'exhausted, points to her throat'. Outdoors there were sports, a skating rink, and a brass band (*N.S.*, 1925, No. 51).

It seems improbable, but the facts, as such, were no lie, though the piece left the impression of unparalleled, shameless deception, which it was. For the ordinary mind could not conceive of brutality and musical concerts, freezing punishment cells in a former church and a fiery operetta like *The Count of Luxembourg* coexisting on the island side by side. Yet the absurdity of such a blend actually presented a natural aspect of the camp's life, of which Litvin had written repeatedly.

Having depicted women with children in barracks on the second floor of the church on Golgotha Hill (Anzer), he was amazed once again: 'One reached them up a narrow staircase. As one comes up, there is a very large painting above the cots which could be of Jerusalem or Jericho. In a word, a kind of hazy Galilee, with a dash of Hoffmann. A Solovetsky phantasmagoria.... One can hardly forget Golgotha, that surprising, strange 'kindergarten' and the nappies hung up on the walls of Jericho'.[3]

'Many were the miracles in the concentration camp in the late 1920s', exclaimed the usually restrained historian of the area, N.P. Antsiferov.

'A fantastic world!' Solzhenitsyn muses of the GULAG.

Shiriayev's *The Cheka's Bloody Atrocities* shocked everybody. Perhaps even Moscow dealt with the matter. Glubokovsky attempted to save the situation.

> I read the witty pamphlet. But I did not laugh. I was saddened. Does a forced labour camp consist of loud theatricals and merry skating rinks? It is not the task of our press to

create prison camp rabbits kissing the hand that punishes them. It ought to help foster citizens of the USSR. Windows in the republic are not obscured by iron bars and it is no secret that the road towards the goal is strewn not with the roses of 'aesthetic pleasures' alone, but also the thorns of harsh labour. The path towards freedom is hard.

(N.S., 1926, No. 3)

Soon a fresh scandal broke: in Riga the White Emigré paper *Sevodnia (Today)* published excerpts from the notes of S.A. Malsagoff, a former officer, an Ingush, who escaped in 1925 from Kem on his way to the Solovki. Malsagoff's notes, 'An Island Hell', which evoked special interest as the first evidence by a convict, was published in English.[4]

The Chekists were fooled: the image of the camp according to Malsagoff and in the pages of *The New Solovki* differed strikingly. Obviously, someone was lying.

This time the émigrés were answered by an unruffled Glubokovsky. His trump card was the fact that Malsagoff had never been on the island. And the journalist went out of his way to acquit the administration, alleging that it fought drunkenness, women's enforced cohabitation, etc. (*N.S.*, 1926, No. 13).

Circumstances compelled Litvin to speak out, too. Since mention of typhus was not permitted, he used the word 'scurvy' and explained away the difficulties – the shortage of cod liver oil, the early onset of spring. Rather than condemn his adversaries, he devoted the item to a defense of the Solovetsky medics. 'Nor let us forget that five of our comrades, having donned white coats this winter, fell victim to duty and rest for ever under the pine trees in the cemetery.' (*N.S.*, 1926, No. 18).

In the realm of the absurd, Litvin relied on his readers' discernment. Yet in 1926 the administration no longer needed Litvin's services or perhaps, even those of Glubokovsky. More flexible and unscrupulous reporters had made their appearance, prepared to go to any lengths to show their loyalty – for example Tsvibelfish and B. Emelianov (pen-name Rado).

Tsvibelfish, a journalist from the Moscow rag *Rampa (Footlights)*, where, stepping into the shoes of the exiled Glubokovsky, he was head of the Weekly Chronicle column, showed the way. He incautiously started on the Solovki with the pamphlets *Writing to the Press* (*N.S.*, 1926, No. 6) and *Bisons* (*N.S.*, 1926, No. 8). The target of his vicious sarcasm were intellectuals from the old nobility.

Since the inmates would not stand for undisguised fawning, and most were unanimous on this point, a scandal broke out.

Tsvibelfish defended himself: 'I wrote *Writing to the Press* and a score of people stopped speaking to me: You're a scoundrel, Tsvibelfish. After *Bisons* I couldn't venture into the passage, so glum were the faces I encountered.' (*N.S.*, 1926, No. 11)

The camp never forgave Tsvibelfish. And in a further pamphlet, *The Turncoat*, he squirmed under the guise of the little man: 'I know. They will read the title of my pamphlet and start squealing: He's writing of himself. Ha-ha. Well, pride is not for Tsvibelfish. Tsvibelfish is humble. He will endure this trial too, just as he endured many others. He is that tough'. (*N.S.*, 1926, No. 18)

Nevertheless, the journalist appealed for the protection of the head of the administration, who ordered an end to the baiting. This was a better safeguard than toughness.

Interest in the Solovetsky press waned both in the USSR and beyond. Mikhail Koltsov attempted to save the situation by printing the article 'SLON Writes' (*Pravda*, 1926, No. 75). *The New Solovki* reprinted it and Shiriayev publicized it. However, interference by Koltsov, regarded as an odious figure abroad, did nothing but raise passions: many were watching as Friedland, the son of a Kiev footwear merchant, built up his journalistic career.

But Koltsov did not matter. Following Dzerzhinsky's death in July 1926, power in the OGPU devolved to V. Menzhinsky, a person rather remote from practical initiatives. His neutral name obscured the power struggle waged by his deputies G. Bokii, G. Yagoda, and others. A regrouping of teams and changes in direction were under way.

Changes were imminent. September saw the departure from the Solovki of I. Sukhov, secretary of the camp's Party cell, virtually the island's censor, who even appeared on the stage as General Barklayev in *A Hornets' Nest*. In November R. Vaskov, whom the journalists had learned to control to some extent, took his leave, wishing the newspaper men 'happy and peaceful work'. And on 12 December 1926, with its 50th issue, *The New Solovki* comes to an end. *The Solovetsky Islands* disappeared, too. As was later explained, it 'merged' with the journal *The Karelian–Murmansk Territory*.

Thus the camp's sharp and slippery tongue was curbed.

It would be quite fitting now to return to a question asked at the beginning of the book: was it possible to avoid participation in the camp's press?

No doubt an individual could reject (at a price) a path the hazards of which nobody really knew. But the camp could ill afford to neglect the least opportunity to project itself, albeit in an utterly distorted way, and make the outside world aware of it. The press extended a helping hand to camp inmates simply by being there.

And since it was run vigorously and skilfully, it was able to tell at least something about the camp. Who could count on more, at that time, in that place?

The summer and autumn of 1926 were marked by many departures: those sentenced to two or three years, who in the past years had maintained the ever quicker, fuller rhythm of the camp's evening life, were reaching the end of their terms. Other people replaced the inmates of the first years: that community of definite sociopolitical types.

The New Solovki, then still alive, all but started a special column, 'Farewell Parties', although it continued announcing them for half a year.

On 1 June Borin's party was held. The inmates took leave of the 'grand old man' affectionately, well realizing the importance of his zeal, talent and experience in consolidating the theatre, D. Kuzmin, the possessor of a soft tenor in the bel canto manner, gave his last concert. At the party for L. Rakhman the audience took leave of a professional artiste of profound temperament, a champion of striking contemporary forms. The comedy *Not a Minute of Rest* rounded out two years of stage appearances by the actor A. Orlov. Among the departing dramatic actors were the hard-working, charming Andriyanov and Osinovsky.

Leaving Solovki for the second time was the camp's favourite, Ivan Panin. Of this event Alm wrote:

> The cunning Solovetsky wit, a well loved versifier, whose satirical limericks were on the lips of an enlivened camp, how can he forget the Solovetsky theatre? Dear stage friends! Today I am in a lyrical frame of mind. And since you are leaving the Solovetsky stage, this gives me license to feel blue. For autumn is with us, the bleak, hapless Solovetsky autumn.
>
> (*N.S.*, 1926, No. 24)

Litvin also responded to Panin's departure:

> His is a vigorous, sturdy rhyme; his couplets are the terror
> of work assigners, shop-assistants, all those whom the camp

may and ought to poke fun at, occasionally.... He was loved by our camp in the sad years of exile. I mention his name with warmth and affection.

(*N.S.*, 1926, No. 47)

Boris Emelianov said farewell to the actor and stage director S.M. Stanislavsky*, who

> in his non-Solovetsky past had never been near the footlights. Nor was he even an amateur: his life was spent behind the control column of an aircraft. Stanislavsky, a beginner, was able to score off past masters of the stage.... Not only did he reveal an actor's soul, but even staged several plays.

(*N.S.*, 1926, No. 47)

Also leaving were George Leon, who gave the Solovki a professionally accomplished operetta and a jazz band, the correspondent 'X', real name Yakov Galkh, compositor of the camp newspaper and I. Slepian, the veteran head of the island's printing press.

The time came for the chief newspapermen, Litvin and Shiriayev. Litvin left the island a fortnight before *The New Solovki's* last number. It is likely that he knew what lay in store for his creation; at any rate, he summed up the efforts of the 'special purpose' newspaper, which in hundreds of issues had reflected a whole epoch of camp life. (*N.S.*, 1926, No. 47)

This, in fact, was his way of saying goodbye to the camp, his work, his friends and his manuscripts.

For once forgetting caution, Shiriayev took strident leave of the camp in advance. 'In a month I shall be leaving,' he wrote, blurting out that his heart was aching with sorrow for the god-forsaken 'island of torture and death'. 'I can already hear the virulent hissing of the Solovetsky "beau monde", as they read my anguish. Sorry? Sorry for the pulpwood, the shock-workers, the peat, the bricks? Height of perversion!' But Shiriayev, impatient, had already counted the days. 'In a month and four days I'll embrace the streets of Moscow, and greet its good old Kremlin!' (*N.S.*, 1926, No. 40)

We do not know what happened, but a month later he was still on the Solovki. By that time, of his 10-year term he had served

---

* No relation to the famous stage director Konstantin Stanislavsky.

four. Counting on the camp administration's gratitude may have misfired. At any rate, the last steamship in December 1926 did not bear Shiriayev away and his hopes of a smooth return to Moscow were dashed.

Shiriayev left the camp in 1927. We do not know why he was additionally sentenced to exile in Central Asia, which he had not anticipated. His file was never found. But, having shown a dogged persistence in staying free, he managed during the war years to flee abroad, and it was in Italy that he wrote his book and ended his days.

While forgetting and confusing much, Shiriayev preserved in *The Inextinguishable Lantern* an echo of the specific physical and spiritual tension of the Solovki prison camp in the first years of its existence, when everything was so new, unfamiliar, brutal and awful. The strange, wild enthusiasm for the theatre proved a means of self-preservation, of restoring a semblance of balance, at least for those to whom the theatre was accessible.

Boris Shiriayev confirmed that sense of a return to normal human existence by the very presence of actors and an audience: 'A theatre in a forced labour camp was a test of the right to deem oneself *human*. A restoration of that right.' In his words, the footlights transformed the 'ordinary actor Armanov into the most powerful billionaire Deterdinger, while he changed the audience into the human beings they had despaired of ever being again'.

To Shiriayev, just as to Glubokovsky, a play's impact was much more important than its artistic merits and was due to elements other than aesthetic that at the time had a special weight. Even if it was a matter of saving one solitary soul languishing in the loneliness of the camp.

1. Pilgrimage to Solovki.
Caricature by Ver. *SLON*, 1924.

2. From Our Aphorisms
(a) The Solovetsky ordeal is like tightrope walking: one wrong step and you can hurt yourself.
(b) Beginning of term… (c) Mount Sekirnaya. (d) Punishment cell. (e) Extension of term.
(f) End of term – FREEDOM!
Caricature by Ver. *SLON*, 1924.

3. Felling Logs – Our Shock Workers. (Dedicated to the 10th platoon)
(a) 5 a.m. – Hey, you, come out! (b) 6–8 a.m. morning roll call.
(c) Day – felling logs. (d) Late evening – getting back.
Caricature by Ver. *SLON*, 1924.

4. Caricature of I.S. Levkassi. Persecution, calamities, going from platoon to platoon, drums and percussion (irons and logs) in no way impaired his skills and energy, to the joy of all Solovkians. Caricature by Ver. SLON, 1924.

5. Organizers of the theatre.
I.A. Armanov as Krechinsky in
the play *Krechinsky's Wedding*.

6. Organizers of the theatre.
M.S. Borin as Raspliuyev in
Krechinsky's Wedding.

7. Organizers of the theatre.
I.S. Panin.

8. Organizers of the theatre.
N.K. Litvin.

9. Organizers of the theatre.
   B.N. Shiriayev.

10. Organizers of the theatre.
    B. Glubokovsky with actors on the Solovki (at Kem?).

11. Front page of *The New Solovki* newspaper, 7 June 1925, with portraits of A. Nogtev, Solovetsky Camp Chief, G. Bokii, OGPU Collegium Member, and F. Eichmans, Camp Chief Deputy.

В Ы П И С К А
ИЗ ПРОТОКОЛА Ц. А. К. УСЛОН
от 12/IX-1925 г. № 22

Председатель: Р. И. Васьков.

Присутствовали: Члены: { Д. Я. Когнов.
                              А. С. Запольский.

Секретарь: М. Х. Пилявский.

7.

Слушали:
ЛИТВИН Николай Кириллович
фоуж. Ком. НКВД по 60, 62
и 67. ст.ст. УК на 3 [illegible]
22/II-24 г. СЛОН [illegible] У-24г.

Постановили:
§ 19. Тип интелегента, обитого с
толку революцией. В лагере
работает по эпециальности
/литератор/. К.Р. постолько,
поскольку чужд всего ново-
го трудового.

Выписка верна. Зав. [illegible]

12. Character reference of N. Litvin, from the minutes of the USLON
Central Attestation Commission, 12 September 1925.

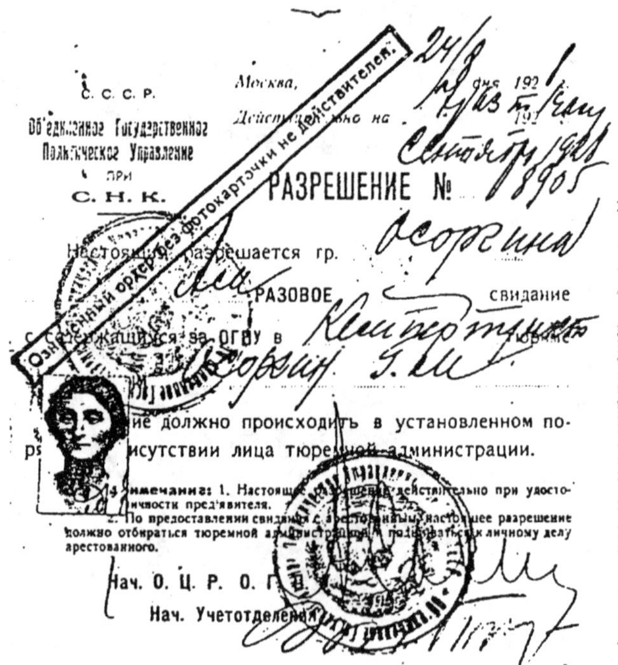

13. Permit of G.M. Osorgin's wife to visit her husband, issued 24 August
1928.

14. Plays of the 1st Department Theatre.
The Decembrists by N. Lerner, Director Borin (?), 1926.

15. Plays of the 1st Department Theatre.
The Warrant by N. Erdman, director Glubokovsky, 1926.

16. Plays of the 1st Department Theatre.
Masquerade by M. Lermontov, director I. Kalugin, 1929.

17. Plays of the 1st Department Theatre.
A Lyre for Hire, 1932 (?).

18. I. Terentiev. Self-Caricature. *Teatr (Theatre)*, 1987, No. 5.

19. The Povenets Propaganda Brigade named after Firin. Singing verses on a good attitude to horses. In: *The Stalin Canal*, 1934, 313.

20. Theatre at Tuloma. General view. Banner says 'Welcome'.

21. Jazz-band in the Tuloma theatre.

22. Final scene of Griboyedov's comedy *Woe from Wit*. Tuloma theatre, 1934.

23. Scene from play by unknown playwright, Tuloma theatre, 1934–35 (?).

24. Scene from comedy by unknown playwright. Tuloma theatre, 1934–36 (?).

25. Theatre at Medvezhiegorsk. Destroyed by fire during World War II.

26. Leading figures at the Central WSBC Theatre. Right to left: D.M. Person, I.I. Vovk, S.A. Taneyev, Misha (lighting engineer), A.G. Alexeyev, and (in armchair) B.S. Pshibyshevsky. 1936.

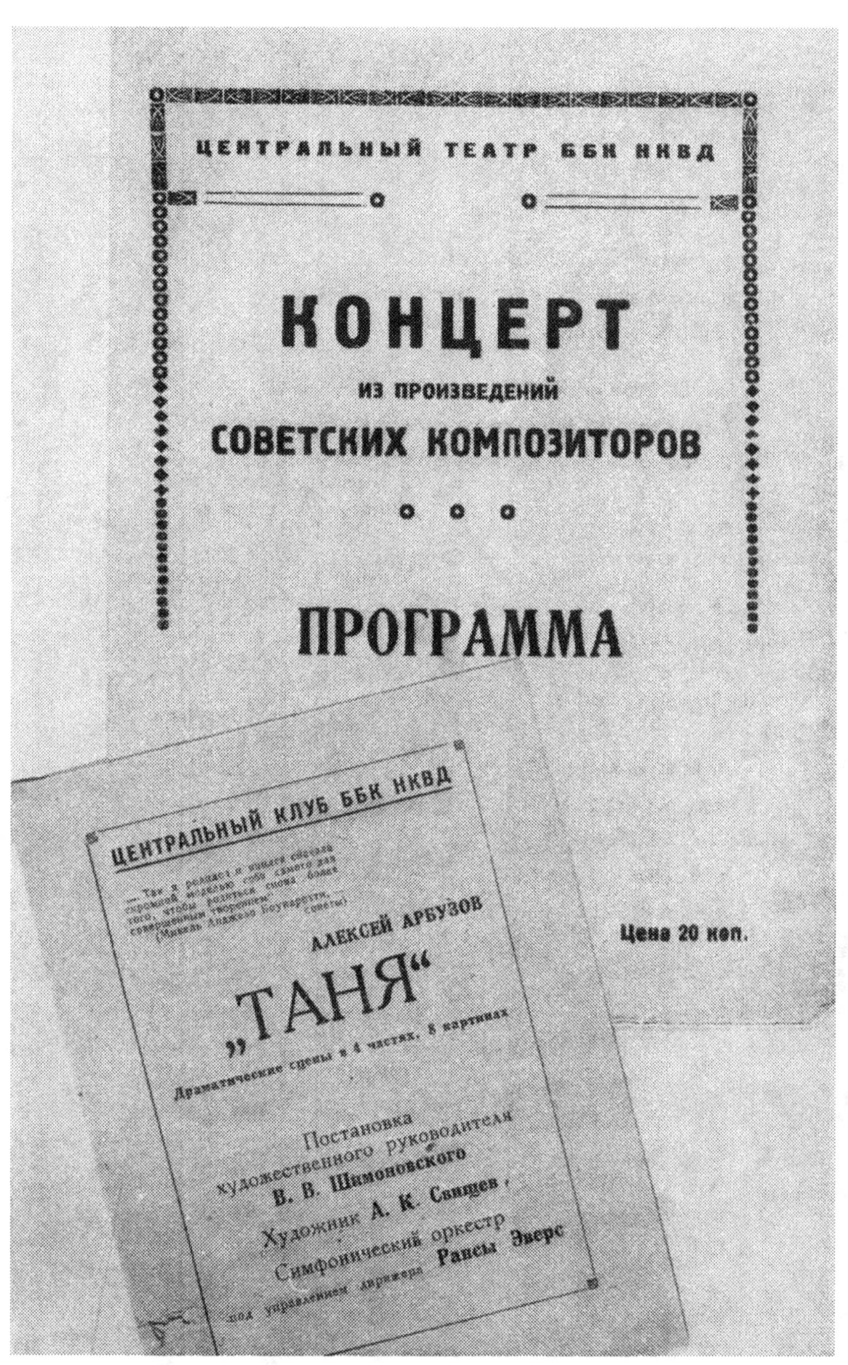

27. Concert programme and bill for A. Arbuzov's play *Tania*. 1939.

28. Barracks on Anzer Island. Photograph by Yu. Brodsky.

29. Stage director A. Kurbas. Photograph from camp case file.

30. Bill for N. Pogodin's play *Aristocrats*. Director A. Kurbas, Solovki theatre, season of 1936–37.

8   At the crossroads

*If a sign over the prison gates reads: Country Park
Livadia*, do not believe your eyes.*

Solovetsky aphorism

Theatrical life did not cease on the Solovki in 1927. To overcome its
impetus, years of persistent, ruthless breaking down and denial of
the concessions won by the prisoners, of searching by the super-
visors for additional means of oppression and invention by the convicts of new forms of self-protection were required.

We cannot resurrect with any measure of veracity the theatre
of those years, for there was no press. Camp recollections of the time
are dominated by an overall picture rather than particulars.[1]

In his book *In the Claws of the GPU*, the Byelorussian playwright Frantishek Alekhnovich wrote of a dreadful octopus on the
body of the Soviet Union's hapless peoples, its tentacles 'stretching
over a sixth of the globe and further – across borders, seas and
oceans'.[2] That monster was a prototype of the cancerous GULAG
country, later the subject of a study by Solzhenitsyn.

This mysterious country expanded to the tunes of swishing
northern winds and crackling frosts, in the fever of typhoid de-
lirium. As General Zaitsev saw it, the camp's high mortality rate was
due to the deliberate destruction of inmates already exhausted by
starvation rations and denied clothing giving adequate protection
against the elements. There was also the Solovki's rapidly growing
population, which started at 2,000. Memoir writers quote different
numbers of convicts: Zaitsev reckoned that, early in 1928, all the
camp's divisions held about 30,000, after which the figure was dou-
bled by the arrival of peasants. Bessonov mentions around 25,000
and Nikonov-Morozov also estimates the number of prisoners in
January 1930 at 25,000.

This is close to the truth. Ivan Chukhin, referring to still un-
published data, gives the total number of camp inmates in 1929 at

---

* In pre-revolutionary Moscow and St. Petersburg 'country parks' were
gardens containing restaurants offering customers stage performances or
cabaret.

28,000, 44 percent of whom had had typhus. A perilous leap to 71,000 (?) inmates was observed in 1930–31.

Typhus was on the rampage. In recollections it appears to have had two peaks, in the terrible winter of 1928 and the no less awful winter of 1929–30. Of all methods of disease control the administration failed, apparently, to resort in time to the most radical – prompt closure of the camp. Between typhus in winter and dysentery in summer, the Solovki floundered on for several years.

In the absence of even the most stringently controlled publicity and left completely to their own devices, the guards indulged in the most outrageous brutality and torture. The findings of the Shanin Commission (the name of the OGPU officer who headed it), which investigated the performance of the supervisory staff in 1928–29, plunge one into horror and despair.[3]

The savagery of the camp authorities required a cover-up, especially since passions abroad had never abated. *The Solovetsky Hard Labour Camp*, the reminiscences of A. Klinger, a Finn, written in 1926, were published two years later; unlike Malgasoff and Bessonov, he had been not only in Kem, but on the island as well.

The crisis over the Solovki reached a climax in 1929–30, when, in response to mass repressions of the clergy in the USSR, the Pope called for an anticommunist crusade. Ironically, the same year of 1929 marked the quincentenary of the Solovetsky Monastery's foundation.

The foreign press condemned the Soviet government for exploitation of convict slave labour and appealed for a boycott of Soviet timber exports.

Solovki no longer countered the accusations in newspaper articles. The camp's 3rd Sector (GPU, the investigation unit, which had stool pigeons everywhere) set in motion a carefully thought-out provocation.

Agent provocateurs among former officers, seamen and well-meaning intellectuals inspired the idea of an uprising aimed at annihilating the island's administration, followed by an escape to Finland. This is how the 'Kremlin Conspiracy' case mentioned in the preface was concocted.

The camp was rife with rumours and misinformation. The legend, nurtured by the Chekists, lurked as a possibility in the camp's subconscious. So enticing was the belief that there were, after all, some forces of resistance, that most memoir writers were convinced that the conspiracy had been real, but unsuccessful. Special interest in the circumstances was evoked in the summer of 1929 by rumours of the imminent arrival on the Solovki of Maxim Gorky, whose visit aroused in the convicts many hopes.

Actually, as shown by L.Ya. Reznikov, Gorky's journey came as a surprise even to himself. On arriving on 30 May 1929, from Sorrento, the writer told those who welcomed him at the Negoreloye border station that he intended to make trips to familiar places in the Orlov Region and 'visit oil fields discovered in the Urals'.[4]

Circumstances unknown to us made Gorky alter his plans and spend two days – 20 to 22 June – on the Solovki. Members of Gorky's party: G. Bokii, a deputy of Menzhinsky, Matvey Bogrebinsky, chief of the Bolshevo labour colony near Moscow, and Gorky's son Maxim Peshkov, took a lot of photos that have survived in the archives. They could well have made up an album — *The Solovki Shown to Gorky*....

Standing out conspicuously in the group of Chekists accompanying Gorky was an attractive young woman clad from head to toe in brand-new black leather: jacket, breeches, high boots – the works. The Solovki campers were impressed. Today, we would have been struck by the resemblance to the SS uniform! It was Nadezhda Peshkov, wife of Maxim, apparently already enjoying the GPU's special and favourable attention.

Gorky's jolly company were also taken to a concert.

> A small symphony orchestra performed the overture to the *Barber of Seville*, a violinist rendered Wieniawski's *Mazurka* and Rakhmaninov's *Spring Waters*; the prologue from *Pagliacci* and some Russian songs were sung, there were cowboy and eccentric dances and someone brilliantly read *The Accordion* by Zharov to the accompaniment of an accordion and a piano. Quite amazing was a troupe of acrobats – five men and a woman, performing feats that could seldom be seen in a regular circus. During intermissions a brass band brilliantly played Rossini, Verdi, and Beethoven's overture *Egmont*; without question, the conductor must have been a talented person.

> I didn't see the plays, but was shown photographs of productions of *The Decembrists, The Break, The Rails are Humming, Secrets of the Harem* and *Trotsky Abroad*.[5]

Gorky was extremely cautious. When addressing the convicts in public he made no promises. On the contrary, in the article 'Solovki', published in the journal *Nashi dostizhenia* (*Our Accomplishments*), he stated: 'The conclusion, it seems to me, is clear: such camps as the Solovki, and labour communes as Bolshevo are necessary. This is the way in which the state will quickly attain one of its purposes – the abolition of prisons'.

In November the passions aroused by Gorky's statement calmed and Petrashko, Verbitsky, Chekhovskoy, Grobovskoy..., 36 persons in all, arrested in the 'Kremlin Conspiracy' case, were shot. Quite nearby, behind the women's barracks, in the light of lanterns.[6]

A dark period ensued in the life of the camp. The supervisory staff were all depraved individuals, mostly those who, having renounced their past, had long been associated with the Cheka and in some way found wanting. Therefore, when it is stated that riding roughshod at Solovki was the responsibility of White Guards and felons, this is not so: those responsible were former Chekists (from diverse strata) and felons.

For all the disappointment of Gorky's visit to the Solovki, it was not quite barren. In anticipation of foreign missions straining to reach the Solovki (only one got as far as Kem, where its car 'broke down'), publication of *The Solovetsky Islands* and *The New Solovki* was unexpectedly resumed.[7]

The thinned journal and narrowed paper, published at Kem, suited the times. They were short-lived: the journal came out from 1 August 1929 until May 1930, the paper from 1 January to 25 July 1930.[8]

The voice of the revived Solovetsky press had a strange ring: like the deep, hollow voice of Big Bad Wolf, licking his chops upon gulping down Grandmother and now eyeing lovely Little Red Riding Hood. Forcing a smile, the beast tried to sing in a small voice, waiting for the moment when he could gobble up the gullible granddaughter.

On its front page the paper reported:

Events on the KVZhD* evoked the just indignation of the Solovki camp inmates. An order of the day by the Chief Administrator noted the inmates' ardent desire to respond to the Chinese events by a voluntary collection for the 'Solovkians' Response' Foundation; hundreds of convicts at the Kovda worksite (sawmills 45 and 46) signed a collective appeal for permission to organize a Shock-Labour Day. The request was granted.[9]

(*N.S.*, 1930, No. 1)

---

* Chinese Oriental Railway.

Formerly a day-off was simply announced as a 'shock-work' day. Yet now, suddenly, 'hundreds of signatures' were required for the convicts to work an extra day! That was Big Bad Wolf with a big sly wink at those foreign journalists.

And now (grinning from ear to ear): at the Sekirnaya punishment prison 'the convicts in a body were carried away by the idea of helping to build an airplane, 'The Solovkians' Response', and contributed the sum of 21 Rb., 92 kop.'. (*N.S.*, 1939, No. 2)

Furthermore, in the past year USLON (the Northern Special Purpose Camps Board) had received 'some 60,000 money orders to the tune of 1,000,000 Rb and 30,000 parcels estimated in value at about 900,000 Rb,' addressed to the Solovki (*N.S.* 1930, No. 1). How touching when a people maintains its own prisoners!

Of course information of another kind also found its way into the first issues: meals were wretched at the kremlin's canteen, the bread bad and there was no water in the bath-house and people covered in soap had to wait for hours. Boiled water for tea 'is often tepid, only slightly warmed up ... the place where the water is drawn is slippery and filthy ... people often fall...'. The barracks lack washing facilities and many, having risen at 5 a.m., leave for work without having washed their eyes. 'And this goes on day after day, year after year...'.

The administration seemed to have no intention of bothering with the camp, but planned to move to the mainland where new buildings were going up for USLON.

O.V. Sinakevich-Yafa recollected that, as if to console the inmates, the camp painters drew on the cathedral's white outer walls 'the gigantic silhouette of a contemporary city with smoke-belching factory chimneys and cranes and aircraft soaring above, and still higher a huge five-pointed red star. A runner beneath the city, also in red, proclaimed: "Long Live May 1st! Long Live Free and Joyous Labour!"'.

But what of the theatre? Available material suggests that in 1927–28 it functioned, with intervals for the waves of typhus. The photographs of plays shown to Gorky therefore kept alive the memory of productions long past (*The Decembrists, Secrets of the Harem*). *Trotsky Abroad* was a new production, possibly not a play in the proper sense, but part of a political review, *A European Tavern*, seen by the Solovki radioman A.N. Kuznetsov in 1929, a photograph of which is presented in L. Reznikov's book.

It is quite probable that by the autumn of 1929 the theatre was headed by Ivan Kalugin, a former Leningrad actor, whose recitation of *The Accordion* had appealed to Gorky.

Reporting in its first 1929 issue (i.e., in August) that the 'theatre has settled down', *The Solovetsky Islands* named three productions: Lermontov's *Masquerade*, A. Afinogenov's *Raspberry Jam* and V. Kirshon's *The Rails are Humming*.

Audiences received the plays with interest. The *Ivan Voznesensky* dredger team (50 men), who were granted a visit to the theatre and the museum, left an entry in the visitors' book: 'The play *The Rails are Humming* exceeded all our expectations, few of us had ever happened to see actors perform so brilliantly' (*S.I.*, 1929, No. 1).

However, the journal carried few items on the theatre. A report described the opening of a theatre on the second floor of the church on Anzer Island. Work was completed in 23 days and the initial repertory comprised two plays: *At the Frontier* and *Moon on the Left* by V. Bill-Belotserkovsky. A.A. Kenel, a piano player from Leningrad, devoted an item to the music in *Masquerade*. Kenel, who for several years was the Solovki theatre's musical director, recalls play titles from the past: *Teacher Bubus, Moon on the Left, Harmful Element, A Lyre for Hire*. Mention was also made of the reviews, which apparently were of particular interest: *General Roll Call* and *Disinfection Chamber*.[10]

Memoirs by Solovkians brought to light the names of actors and stage directors of those years. In 1928 Ya. Shneyerson produced I. Utkin's play *The Party Secretary*; I. Girniak relates that after seven years in the camps he found himself at Chib'yu, where he staged the same play. Oleg Volkov tells us about his Solovki companion of 1928, the Georgian prince and Russian officer Piotr Asatiani-Eristov, who had a pleasant baritone and successfully appeared in concerts and operetta. The prince would promenade leisurely along the cobblestone Solovetsky sidewalks, as if along the Golovinsky Prospect in Tbilisi. 'A broad Caucasian shirt was girded with a fancy belt, a tall golden fur cap was tilted low, right down to his eyebrows.'[11] In the autumn of 1929, just a month before the 'conspirators' were shot, Asatiani was, fortunately, exiled to Archangel, where he became a carrier.

In 1928 the Byelorussian Alekhnovich worked in the theatre as an actor and play-copier. He recalled a play that was invariably presented to the OGPU 'unloading' commission that usually arrived in October. It was the review *General Roll Call*, the text of which, as he remembered it, was written by a talented man of letters (Glubokovsky?).

> Though the main theme of the author's witticisms was self-praise, which means depicting his mates, the political prisoners, in a favourable light, he managed to smuggle in a few couplets ironically lauding some of the camp customs. The important guests, sitting in the front rows, enjoyed the witty limericks and roared with laughter…. The actors sang, and laughed … through tears. One could sense the impotent despair of a bondsman, ordered by his master to amuse him.[12]

Meanwhile, in Moscow new legislation was being prepared for the country and in April 1930 the Council of People's Commissars authorized the Statutes on the OGPU's Corrective Labour Camps. The purpose of the camps was to isolate from society especially dangerous lawbreakers, who had been removed from working communities for a term defined by a court sentence or a decree of the OGPU, and adapt them to the conditions of such a community on the basis of cultural and educative measures, combined with socially useful work.

Those subject to dispatch to the camps were persons not more than 60 years of age, sentenced by a court to deprivation of freedom for not less than three years, and also all those condemned by the OGPU.[13] Since the latter included more than enough old and sick people, everyone was subject to dispatch from the age of 12 years, as a special resolution spelled out in 1932.

The decree of the Council of People's Commissars, ostensibly putting certain limits to punitive measures, actually gave a license for arbitrariness. Limiting the term (not less than 3 years) meant that very soon 5-, 8- and 10-year sentences were meted out for any sin from drunkenness and homosexuality to involvement with Trotskyism. The convicts used to joke that all the stamps at the Lubianka had been lost, except the 5-year one.

Looming behind the stern words about the 'principle of paying one's own way' was the demand that work be done quickly and cheaply. It proved a delayed action mine laid under many a project in those years. Exhausted by unbearable work quotas, emaciated by lack of nourishment and essential facilities, the convicts frequently handed in false reports, creating only the semblance of meeting planned targets. The lumbermen simply hovered on the brink of survival.

> On 21 and 22 December there was no bread at the Yuma timber felling work-site, Panozersk section.... The hungry workers went to the accountant Merkulov's office. 'So, you want bread? Here's bread for you, eat!' and Merkulov tossed a bread crust that was lying on the desk to the workers. 'If that's too little, here's more, eat it'. He pointed to an axe.... For two days the inmates refused to work. 'He treated us like dogs', they told the investigators. The case is to be heard in the people's court at Kem.
>
> (*N.S.*, 1930, No. 11)

Since collective refusal of work carried a stiff term for the defendants, and considerable trouble for the authorities, the incident went before the court. On another occasion, when the lumbermen twice threw away 300 kg of bread containing pieces of brick, old rags and even black rats, it was not turned into a 'case', for there would have been too many of them in those hungry years.

The USLON held sway over a vast territory, on both the mainland (Kem, Pertominsk, Kin-Ukht, Parandovo) and White Sea islands (Miag, Kond, the Solovki). The staff of the board drew up plans for reorganization, dividing the territory under USLON into 12 divisions accounting for a total of 60,000 people (Solovki, the fourth, had only 6,185).[14]

In December 1929 the board, the print shop and other services completed their transfer to Kem. The main part of the Solovetsky troupe was moved there, too, to become the ULSON's Central Theatre.

Yet theatrical life on the Solovki did not wane. Upholding with difficulty the 'Solovetskians' rights and traditions in the face of inexorable time, the Solovkians supported amateur dramatics and a propaganda brigade. Once again a professional theatre was created only to perish, this time for good.

9   The theatre at Kem

> *The clown and the gravedigger are equally*
> *important to life. The clown is even more so, for*
> *he brings us into the true realm of laughter.*
>
> Yu. Kazarnovsky, 1930

The musings of the poet Yuri Kazarnovsky, another Solovki inmate, were inspired, perhaps, by the characters of Shakespeare's *Hamlet*, though neither a clown nor a jester are listed among the tragedy's dramatis personae. Actually, the role of madman is played deliberately by Hamlet. Involuntarily, the players unfold in front of Claudius a picture of his heinous crime. Prince Hamlet in the churchyard picks up the skull of the King's jester Yorick: 'Alas, poor Yorick!'.

We may agree that a skull as a plaything is authentic enough. Out of a group of 300 Solovki inmates set in November 1928 'on a rock'*, 150 had their hands and feet frostbitten; what could be more intolerably authentic?[1] Yet, both aphorisms and epigrams by Kazarnovsky himself in the pages of the camp's press in 1930 were also of irrefutable authenticity, for they represented the last effort to uphold the thread of continuity in culture, preventing it from breaking for ever.

At Kem the fragility of the invisible thread was felt especially keenly. The theatre found itself in extremely unfavourable circumstances, much worse than on the Solovki, where it had excellent premises, a diversified choice of artistic personalities, and its own special audience, well-known though each time different.

Kem, a dreary township of Old Believer coastal dwellers, with wooden sidewalks and sturdy grey houses, was a place of exile even before the revolution. A. Voronsky, a future editor of the Soviet journal *Red Virgin Soil*, recalled in his story *Fetching the Water of Life and Death*, that there were only 70 exiles then, of whom two-thirds were political and the rest criminals.

---

* To 'set on a rock' meant to have a naked, barefoot prisoner stand motionless in the frost for several hours.

The coastal dwellers and the exiles tolerated each other in the midst of a 'wordless sea, monk-like forests, dead tundra, vast, empty spaces and the indifferent, placid skies'.[2]

Flat-bottomed boats moored at the flat beach with fish and seals, an occasional foreign merchantman called for timber.

The 1920s broke the back of free life on the coast. The men were deprived of guns and boats, while the town found itself serving the needs of the burgeoning lands of ULSON. Watch-towers, barracks, whining saw-mills sprang up everywhere. The convicts knew only one life cycle: work – sleep – work. Not a single kind word about Kem can be found in their recollections.

The townlet had never had a building for a theatre nor any theatregoers. The streets were unlighted, the plank sidewalks sagged under one's feet. Could it be that the former Kuban Cossack and petty tyrant A. Nogtev transferred the theatre from the Solovki just for his own pleasure, like part of his luggage? That was part of the story: prestige required something for the amusement of the big-shots arriving from Moscow and Leningrad. But there were weightier considerations: the veteran chief felt his place threatened by the winds of change. Eichmans had already moved from the Solovki and some fresh action was expected from Nogtev. At a meeting of Kem workers he explained to them the benefits of the ULSON system for the growing North!

In 1924, at a plenary session of the Russian Communist Party's Central Committee, Leo Kamenev had reported that the country's export plan for 1925 was based 'on the maximum expansion of oil and timber exports'.[3] This trend steadily strengthened. In 1929 the Soviet Trade Mission in Norway sold 60 shiploads of timber from Leningrad and Archangel: ten times more than in 1928.[4] An ULSON order of the day, signed in Moscow in October 1929 by OGPU Collegium member and Special Department Chief G. Bokii, demanded a 300 percent increase in timber felling compared with 1929. 'The Karelian–Murmansk timber-felling plan is our export plan, our hard currency revenues', was repeated again and again (*N.S.*, 1930, No. 2).

The timber export plan – and the entire colonization of the North – were accomplished by the forced labour of convicts. Hundreds of thousands of prisoners were sent north and north-east along new routes (principally Kem–Ukhta) to extract grey-black apatite and coal, fell timber and build new camps.

A conference at Kem discussed, among other topics, the theatre. Its failings were pronounced capable of correction and it 'was noted as unquestionably valuable and needed by the working people of Kem'. A resolution stated that 'while the plays and concerts produced by the USLON troupe should be subject to rigid control, their growth in number in workers' clubs should be promoted in every way, and the method of prohibiting them out of hand rejected as harmful'.[5]

Concealed behind opaque words like 'failings' and 'prohibiting' concerts are the circumstances, unknown to us, surrounding the theatre's efforts to retain the remnants of 'freedom' in its choice and execution of repertory. The struggle was indirectly reflected in the pages of *The New Solovki*. The convict Yu. Kazarnovsky in his article 'The Face of a Philistine' came out in defense of the theatre, which had been criticized in the newspaper *Red Karelia* as 'anti-educational and ideologically unacceptable'. The trouble stemmed from the singing by the actress Loskutova, during a tour of the theatre, of the jesting folk songs *Mishenka under a Cherry Tree* and *Little Magpie*, the humour of which seemed too fresh to the reviewer (*N.S.*, 1930, No. 2).

In 1930 *The New Solovki* carried information on various stage productions as the theatrical wave subsided slowly, unexpectedly halting at some remote backwoods camp or work-site and restoring the severed ties.

A Ukrainian drama circle appeared on the Solovki once again (led by Mily) and put on *Fighters for an Idea*, a play by I. Gogobochny, promptly followed by *Vanity* by I. Karpenko-Karii. The circle made a seemingly sudden appearance, but this was not accidental, as since 1929 there had been an increasing number of Ukrainians on the northern prison transports.[6] A Ukrainian choir also sprang up at the Raznovoloka work-site.

On Miag-Ostrov, an island in the White Sea, the logger prisoners built a wooden summer stage covered with sacking painted with blackberry dye, later building winter premises. 'Somehow the work-site "suddenly" discovered a host of talented people: good actors, readers, dancers, musicians (a strong orchestra!). The only shortcoming is too few plays' (*N.S.*, 1939, No. 1).

Pul-Ozero: The drama circle staged *The Ninth Wave*, repeating the play at the Taibola settlement for the local population (Lapps). 'It was perhaps the first ever stage production in that forest' (*N.S.*, No. 3).

Sawmill No. 45 (Kovda): *Live Not the Way You Like* by Ostrovsky, *On the Frontier* and *October*.

Sawmill No. 4 (Kandalaksha): *The Lower Depths* by Gorky, a Chekhov soirée (usually *The Bear* and *The Proposal*), *Scum* by Speshnev, *The Treasure* (?) and *Squaring the Circle* by V. Katayev.

Savvin-Ozero: 'This is not a production site. They repair sick workers here … and a drama circle has been organized – 25 prisoners. They staged the play *A Wedding on a Gallows* about the French Revolution. At present they are rehearsing a play by Ostrovsky' (*N.S.*, No. 4).

Kolvitsa Distance 3rd camp: *Young Fir Grove, An American Comedy* and *Editor of an Agricultural Newspaper* (after Mark Twain).

Trav-Guba: *I'm Dead, A Living Corpse* and *The Crooked Mirror.*

Kolvitsa village: *The Bear* and *The Proposal* by Chekhov, followed by a concert.

Savvin-Ozero: Camp inmates made excellent wicker furniture for the stage, such as 'heavy armchairs', sofas, a piano.

The type of production presented by the drama circles depended on the availability of professionals: at Kandalaksha the circle presented big plays involving many actors, while in the backwoods a drama circle would play small scenes and short pieces. The drama circle at Trav-Guba, 'cut off during the log-rafting and left without a repertory, restored the text of the play *The Red Eaglet* from memory and staged it' (*N.S.* , No. 33).

The artistic merits of the amateur productions varied, of course. On the whole, this peculiar hybrid (folk and literary) theatre tended towards social masques. On Letnaya Rechka, outside Kem, Olga Sinakevich-Yafa marked the New Year of 1931 with rhymed prose:

> On the last days of the thirtieth year
> They handed out to us a premium ration:
> Some bread, a few sweets, and even some cookies,
> And of sugar (what luxury!) two hundred grams…
> On New Year's Eve we staged a play
> About Communists and the Women's Question,
> About a young underling and debauchee.[7]

A preference for masques can also be seen in the productions of larger companies as reported in the press.

The stage of the 1st Department at Solovki was left without professionals, and a troupe had to be put together again. On 1 March twelve actors presented the satirical review *The Smidgen* (directors

Derevshinov and Kolosov, designer Lovtsov). 'The overall impression is quite pleasing', Wrote reviewer 'B' (Boris Emelianov?), who found the text of some of the scenes wanting from the literary point of view and protested against the use of 'immobile masques in all the numbers' as concealing the actors' mimicry.

How long *The Smidgen* survived we do not know. It sought, apparently, to carry on the tradition of satirical reviews, which invariably enjoyed a success among the Solovkians, but their time was over.

USLON's Central Theatre at Kem was to cultivate the tastes of a new audience, the clerks and officers of the board's expanding administrative offices and the town's free population. Filling in gaps in the repertory, the theatre offered a concert performance of Chaikovsky's *Eugene Onegin* to the accompaniment of a symphony orchestra under the baton of A. Kenel and the scene between the Pretender and Marina from Pushkin's *Boris Godunov*. Recited with verve and élan by I. Kalugin and O. Drozdova, the scene won every heart by 'the superb rendition of Pushkin's verses, which wholly appealed to the audience' (*N.S.*, No. 9).

The theatre confidently produced satirical plays: *The Inspector General* by Gogol, *The Swindler* by V. Shkvarkin and *Soufflé* by B. Romashov. In anticipation of Gogol's comedy, reviewer Ya. Valin reassured spectators: 'Yes, indeed, we are going to have a laugh, but not at our own expense. It is not our generation, not our churning contemporary life, that comes under the scathing lashes of the smart metropolitan clerk, but only that which is a thing of the past' (*N.S.*, No. 12).

Such stark separation of Gogol's satire from contemporaneity is evidence of the extreme caution of the theatre, which resorted to an all but museum-like stagecraft. Nevertheless, the paper found praise for the brazenly sober Khlestakov (Ya. Shkuratovsky) with his dash of stupidity, the cunning mayor (Mostepan) with his Ukrainian accent, who was reminiscent of the tragic actor Rychalov of 'Crooked Mirror' fame, Anna Andreyevna (Polianskaya) and Maria Antonovna (A. Zalesskaya).

The Swindler by Shkvarkin was positively reviewed by Kazarnovsky, who believed that 'traditions of contemporary Russian vaudeville approach those of old-time Italian comedy, through the substitution of Soviet everyday masques for traditional ones'. He supported the new vaudeville, although he clearly saw that 'the play of masques in a parody of the preceding action is borrowed entirely from *The Princess Turandot*, as staged at the Vakhtangov Theatre'. The customes came in for censure: 'If the designer was unable to think of something sufficiently spicy, he ought to have used traditional costumes'.

'Is this play necessary?' Kazarnovsky asked. 'Yes, it is! It is as necessary as laughter, as spring, as necessary as bright colours and fireworks' (*N.S.*, No. 17). As to fireworks, that, perhaps, was a thoughtless slip of the pen....

'M.I.' defined the theatre's general status thus: 'Many actors, and not inferior, either. Yet its productions do not go beyond the mediocre. What's wrong? Our stage direction is not quite up to the mark. One feels a kind of tiredness, a fatigue and as a consequence the staging is not thought out well enough' (*N.S.*, No. 4). The reviewer's judgement was probably right. Kalugin, a disciple of the well-known actor M. Yuriev, a gifted pupil of the Alexander Theatre in St. Petersburg and the possessor of attractive looks and a good voice was quite agreeable in the parts of dramatic heroes. His recitals of Pushkin, as well as of contemporary poetry, were expressive. Yet there was no verve, and his indifference in managing the affairs of the theatre betrayed a bitter despair. G. Ramensky attributed his woes above all to the fact, that, having submitted in 1926 to Trotsky's secretary a memorandum on bettering life, all he received for his pains was a 'tenner' in the camps.[8] Kalugin had no motive for showing zeal, while abject servility was, apparently, not for him. Moreover, the example of Boris Glubokovsky, whose conspicuous activity earned him no tangible reduction in sentence from the Chekists, left no hope. Even Glubokovsky had tired of the squirrel-cage camp milieu. In 1925 he responded to Yesenin's death with a commemorative soirée dedicated to the great national poet. Now, in 1930, he could still summon enough energy for an evening to commemorate Vladimir Mayakovsky. Something, he felt, had to be done to oppose the official commission's policy of playing down the poet's funeral by making a despicable and false-hearted appeal 'to remit all monies, rather than for a wreath, to the newly established Mayakovsky Young Writers' Relief Foundation'.

Glubokovsky arranged a soirée and published an article about the poet, although with a measure of caution. Perhaps, having recalled the recent success of George Leon's "Red Blouses", he gathered from among civilians at Kem a "Red Blouse" propaganda brigade.

At last, in September 1930, Glubokovsky was freed. When Nadezhda Mandelshtam saw him in Leningrad in the studio of the painter Osmiorkin, her impression was that the camps had taught him nothing. Her judgement was unfair. The camps had left their imprint. In Moscow the former prisoner found himself in another life, without a home, without family, without his former friends, most of whom had been scattered or died or were avoiding dangerous connections. According to Shiriayev, Glubokovsky soon died in hospital after taking an overdose of morphine, either deliberately or inadvertently. According to another version, Glubokovsky was sent into exile in Siberia and committed suicide in 1937.[9] His case file was not found.

Glubokovsky left behind the stage directors Shkuratovsky, who produced *The Swindler* and L. Korsakov, who staged *Fury* by E. Yanovsky in an absolutely realistic manner. However, for lack of material we cannot evaluate their professional merits.

The troupe needed a firm and very energetic leader capable of protecting the theatre from those who favoured its irresponsible break up. Time was rooting out living theatre and confining stage-craft to narrow, utilitarian tasks: 'Above all, leaders of drama circles ought to know that drama circles are neither professional troupes, nor studios or experimental workshops, but a means of organized club work and useful recreation for the masses' (*N.S.*, 1930, No. 33). This had been repeated on the Solovki without let-up since 1925, but at that time it had not been possible to do away with the theatre for good. Now the time of the wretched dogmatists had come, and again the cry of 'club work among the masses' of convicts went up; theatrical joys were to be exclusively for USLON's chief officers.

At this crucial moment a new convict appeared at Kem – David Person, a theatre lover and, without doubt, an artistic personality by nature. In the 1920s his keen mind and business acumen had led him to the cinema, where he became the commercial manager of a successful film studio.

Arrested in 1930 after the playwright V. Kirshon had accused him of reluctance to support contemporary Soviet cinema, i.e. to produce films of his, Kirshon's, scripts, Person was sentenced to a term of 10 years and sent to Kem. He maintained an independent stance, but was well aware of the tastes of the bosses.

Officially appointed managing director under director N. Kakhidze, Person's energy and experience served the theatre well in the new period of restructuring. Ahead was the move to Medvezhya Gora, where the Board for the Construction of the White Sea–Baltic Canal was being established.

10 The 'court' and 'vulgar' theatres of the White Sea–Baltic Canal

> *I am firmly convinced that the laws of Shakespearean drama, rather than the court conventions of Racine's tragedies, are suitable for our theatre.... Drama has left the square and, at the demand of enlightened and chosen society, moved to the palaces. Poets have settled at the court. Meanwhile, drama remains loyal to its primary purpose of impressing the crowd, the multitude, of entertaining its curiosity.*
>
> Alexander Pushkin

The idea of a waterway linking the White and Baltic Seas was born in the times of Peter I. Its realization, however, would have demanded tremendous means and human effort, for the route of the canal would stretch across the poorest lands of Russia's North. 'Wild is Karelia, wild indeed!' sighed the Russian poet Feodor Glinka in 1830 and in the century since, life there had hardly become easier.

The small Karelian villages of ten or twenty houses with tiny allotments along a single street, (of five tithes on the average), surrounded by impenetrable forests, barely sustained themselves. Far wealthier were the settlements of Russian Old-Believers on the banks of Lake Vyg and the river of the same name, yet even they were unable to afford additional labour and horses for the development of the area, where civilization extended as far as the road: a step to the right or left met only rocks or bogs.

Scholars persistently anticipated the next stage in the territory's colonization. Selfless explorers of the Leningrad Institute of Northern Studies, oblivious to the hazards of hunger, cold and sickness, ventured forth to explore the wealth of the Kola peninsula, the Pechora and the distant islands (Novaya Zemlia, Franz-Joseph Land). Fifty published reports of expeditions between 1920 and 1931! The enthusiasts had no inkling that some of them were destined to implement their own recommendations as prisoners.

A Solovetsky newspaper mentions the expedition of one Professor Sovietov (pseudonym?), who in 1926 started prospecting work: 'This new northern waterway will pass from the White Sea along the route of Lake Onega–Povenets Bay and beyond via the Svir river' (*N.S.*, 1926, No. 31).

The idea, once revived, was gradually instilled into the proper heads, in which sprang up bold plans of a future world war. 'Long live an International Socialist Revolution!' proclaimed a slogan on the building of the OGPU Board at Medvezhiegorsk. The canal could help move a submarine fleet between the White and Baltic Seas, and fortify the frontier with Finland.

A resolution of the USSR Labour and Defense Council (18 February 1931) and Stalin's order to build a 227 km canal in 20 months and without a cent of foreign exchange, though not quite unexpected, proved premature, for the draft project was issued only in July 1931, but excavations along the route were already under way.

That summer the chain of camps along the future canal was convulsed by the news that some British people visiting the USSR wished to learn about the methods used to build socialism. They were Bernard Shaw, Lady Astor and their party.

On 22 July they were taken to the corrective labour camp at Bolshevo, which had already been converted into a model demonstration NKVD utility.[1] Perhaps Shaw's more serious interests were under scrutiny by the NKVD. Nikonov-Smorodin and Vera Nikitina recall the sudden feverish activity in the camps: convicts were marched and driven along the entire Parandovsky highway into the backwoods and watchtowers were removed.

The alarm proved false. Shaw, after spending a couple of days in Leningrad, returned to Moscow. The elderly eccentric saw little of Russian life. The Russian villages he was shown appeared to him so terrible as to exonerate the Communists, 'who burnt them down as soon as they prevailed upon the peasants to join collective farms and live as human beings'.[2] Persecution of intellectuals, he believed, had not lasted for long.

Asked by an American journalist about forced labour in Russia, Shaw replied, unexpectedly using Stalinist phraseology, exactly in the leader's style: 'All the talk about forced labour is rubbish. There is no forced labour in Soviet Russia. Forced labour exists only in the countries of the West.... Soviet Russia is successfully carrying out the greatest experiment – I'm talking about collectivization.... There is no hunger in Soviet Russia,' Shaw emphasized (*Izvestia*, 1931, No. 211).

The camps were returned to their former state.

In August the OGPU authorities appointed L.I. Kogan as Chief of the White Sea–Baltic Canal Project, Ya. Rappoport as his deputy, M. Berman as head of the Main Board of Corrective Labour Camps (GULAG), S. Firin as head of the White Sea–Baltic Corrective Labour Camp and N. Frenkel as Kogan's assistant.[3]

Wielding full authority over hundreds of thousands of prisoners, they regarded them as a faceless 'work-force', supplied to them from the mass of criminals and 'wreckers' (Berman himself put this term into circulation). Later on Solzhenitsyn was to remark: 'And these were wreckers? But they are engineers of genius! From the twentieth century they were hurled back into the caves. And, look, they accomplished it!'

In 1923 Osip Mandelshtam, peering into the future, reminded us in the article 'Humanism and Modern Times' of the builders of ancient Egypt who 'treated masses of humanity as material that ought to suffice, that ought to be delivered in any quantity'. The poet was fearful lest a future social architecture 'crushed man, just like Assyria and Babylon'.[4] Ten years later the poet's apprehensions were realized as trainloads of 'manpower' were delivered for the building of a new Tower of Babylon, the canal, 'in any quantity'.

According to official figures in the book *The Stalin Canal* (1934), 100,000 people worked on the construction site; contemporary publicists mention 500,000, yet even this figure is hardly true.[5] When new prison transports arrived in the winter of 1932–33, efforts to file a card for every inmate did not always succeed. R. Suslik (Levko D. Rys), a former 'canal-armyman' (a term invented by Kogan), recalled his prison train from Melitopol in the hungry south: most of the passengers survived in the camp for no longer than 24 hours. The dreadfully emaciated people ate their fill of hot swill only to die of hunger colics. And since they were not yet all registered, and few knew one another, the corpses' faces had to be photographed in order to be identified.[6]

The huge prison transports of builders differed strikingly from the inmates of former years. They were mostly peaceful people who, prior to arrest, had minded their own business and refrained from conflict with the authorities. Many peasants, having left their families to die of hunger, could rely only on their physical stamina, for work on the canal exceeded all imaginable trials.

Another wave appeared – students, scientists and engineers, arrested for scholarly dissent, which was regarded as on a par with political crime.

The transports brought plenty of ordinary thieves and thugs, too, but they had no desire to work. Yet, because to write of them was permissible, the impression was produced that their hands had built the canal. From 1934 on Pogodin's play *Aristocrats* was staged all over the country. It showed how former gangsters were being 'reformed' on the canal into shock-workers, and admiring reviewers could find hardly any blemishes. Solzhenitsyn, on the strength of his own camp experience, subsequently noted that the thieves were 'far more intelligent than those depicted by Pogodin.... And if, when talking to a citizen-chief, or a newspaperman from Moscow, or at a silly meeting, they wipe tears from their eyes and put a tremor in their voice, this is just plain acting, calculated to gain some bonus or a reduction in sentence, yet all the while, in his heart of hearts, the rascal is jeering!'.[7] In the 1930s, though, a lively dialogue could cover up a lot....

In January 1933 boosted production was called for on the canal and played out as a military assault against nature: a headquarters was established and 250-strong assault teams were set up (including a women's blasting brigade). Brass bands boomed away, the musicians, the weather notwithstanding, moving on the run from one group of workers to another.

In spring a 'blitz' was proclaimed. The brigades worked on the canal route day and night, taking turns. People perished from exhaustion, illness and unbearable physical strain, so that the phantasmagoria of an improbable deadline, 1 May 1933, was reached after all.

Many were dazzled by the promise of preterm release, and hundreds of Solovkians volunteered. Varlam Shalamov noted later that in prison a strong soul grows stronger, but a camp with preterm release corrupts every kind of soul. This is certainly so; but how can the trust evoked by the OGPU's promises of preterm release and freedom be qualified as 'soul-corrupting'? Tens of thousands responded to the call of hope; many were cheated, although not at once, but later.

By 1 May Yagoda reported the project's completion. Artists, of whom the camp had many, painted more than 1,500 portraits of the best shock-workers. Stalin, Kirov and Voroshilov took a trip down the canal. The leader was not pleased: he found it narrow and shallow. Its purpose – the free passage of vessels, which was badly restricted by the severe climate (ice-bound for half the year) – was not attained. The supreme military task of moving submarines from the Baltic to the White Sea was possible only by stripping the vessels virtually of everything movable to reduce their weight.

Thus, the great project of the twentieth century dashed so many hopes and calculations, and proved a tragic end to thousands of unredeemable lives.

The leader was concerned with creating a favourable public opinion. In August 1933, at Stalin's personal command and at the expense of the OGPU, 120 cultural figures arrived on the canal. The guests were escorted by Firin. They were accommodated in four carriages, wined and dined, given chocolate and sausages – all free. Warm, fluffy sweaters were thoughtfully brought out of special storage lest the writers catch cold. There was the sound of merriment, laughter, epigrams galore....

A. Avdeyenko recalled the sight of the camp at Medvezhiegorsk:

> The barracks were carefully whitewashed. The paths were sprinkled with yellow and white sand, and to the right and left of them green grass alternated with flowers. Lawns and flowerbeds stretched all the way from one end of the camp to the other, for nearly a full kilometre. People sitting on brightly painted benches looked healthy and cheerful. Two-tier cots in the barracks had thick mattresses, sheets and blankets and pillows in clean pillow-cases. A table was covered with a clean oilcloth.[8]

It took the inmates a lot of effort to create this kind of eyewash. Did the writers understand where the truth about the canal lay? Judging by Vera Inber's notes, they would rather not have known. All of them? Not all. Boris Shklovsky brought back a feeling of horror: 'One day the door opened and Shklovsky came in. Without greetings, he sat down at the window and rapped out: I'm just back from the White Sea–Baltic canal. It's more horrible than in a war.'[9]

Publicly Shklovsky, just like many others, naturally reported feelings of rapturous delight. Why? Fear? Cynicism? Both, perhaps....

Romain Rolland, who visited the USSR in July 1935, made a curious entry in his Moscow diary. For years the writer had been confused by the contradictions of Soviet doubletalk and his own attitude to the new world. Rolland was a guest at Gorky's country house and was cosseted by NKVD big brass. He studied them. Yagoda was 'a mysterious individual – soft-mannered, soft-voiced, soft-glanced'. The Frenchman allowed himself to be deceived, looking into 'Yagoda's honest and diffident eyes'. Genrikh Yagoda and

Semion Firin ('he too, like Yagoda, is an idealist–dictator in the Jean-Jacques image') described in honeyed tones how they cared for the inmates' hygiene and suffered as a result of their own magnanimity toward the thankless....

Yagoda and Gorky decided to entertain Rolland with a concert prepared at the same corrective labour commune, Bolshevo, that Shaw had visited: 150 juveniles played balalaikas and guitars, sang in chorus the calumny aria from *The Barber of Seville* and brilliantly danced the 'Gopak'.

The writer was dismayed: 'In France this would seem an operetta.... The inmates, men and women, leap about and sing, to soften the Chief of Police, who shouts "Hurray!" (Respectable French bourgeois people would feel indignant over the enforced Punch and Judy show). But here the yardsticks are different....'[10]

For the OGPU–NKVD ideologists ('here') the yardsticks were, indeed, peculiar. They were convinced that, under coercion and fear, the individual could be programmed for any life. 'Reforming' was perceived as compulsory 'reforging', as the stamping out through hard labour of a uniform work-force and alert executives.

But other conceptions of man and of the purposes of art were also held – by the inmates, whom it was easier to eliminate than to 'reforge'. Many readily granted the probability of their physical end. A. Losev, an aesthete, who was given in 1931 at Svirstroy the safe position of a watchman, wrote to his wife:

> I know how they die here. So, when I croak from frost and cold on my watchman's post, under the fence of my firewood dumps, and cursing ruffians are forcibly dispatched to pick up my corpse and hurl it into the nearest pit, for no-one's going to volunteer to dig a normal grave in the frozen earth – it is then that the final end will come to my philosophical lamentations and aspirations.

However, on somewhat regaining his balance, Losev admitted that he felt 'a tremendous need to write *belles-lettres*, and that exceptionally, in the style of T.A. Hoffmann, Poe and Wells'.[11]

The urge for creative endeavour proved stronger than the fear of death. The attraction of the phantasmagorias of Hoffmann and Poe expressed the moral shock felt by a thinking individual in a world of mutilated forms, for it was impossible to adapt to a camp and canal in advance. Everything was so unpredictable.

Unexpected also were the forms of stagecraft current in the canal zone. The theatre at Medvezhiegorsk, which bore the resounding title of the Central Theatre of the White Sea–Baltic Canal (WSBC), was headed by two men, Uspensky and Rappoport, but largely depended on the tastes of the latter. The convicts recalled with horror *A Solovetsky Napoleon* by D.A. Uspensky, who had moved to the WSBC: a large, stout person with reddish curls and a tiny nose, remembered as 'a butcher, and a brute'.

The slow-moving, massive Ya. Rappoport appeared a different kind of personality. Before the revolution he had studied at Derpt (Tartu) University in Estonia. The Estonian *Vanemuine* Theatre was frequented with pleasure by the students, and Rappoport probably liked it, too. As a typical European urban theatre, it produced everything, from psychological drama to operetta and opera; it also presented concerts. The *Vanemuine* was a theatre for the entire town, for every taste. Repeated attempts to make it a drama theatre only were unsucessful, both under bourgeois government and in the Soviet years.

Perhaps the *Vanemuine* productions impressed themselves on Rappoport's mind as a kind of model? Whatever the case, he wished to have at his disposal a similar theatre, merry, pleasant – a court theatre.

And, just as in a real court theatre, members of the bosses' families – their daughters and wives – also played on its boards, for fun. Anna Louisa Strong, the British journalist, who in 1935 was perhaps the only foreigner admitted to Medvezhiegorsk (because of political sycophancy and ignorance of Russian), was delighted with everything she saw. A theatre in which free persons, and women at that, played alongside convicts was 'unique', she wrote, 'the only troupe in history'.[12]

The court theatre was a venue for the rest and recreation of the bosses and their families, the hired free builders and the guards, as well as the engineers and imprisoned scientists entrusted with the implementation of a unique twentieth-century project – the construction of a canal with wooden sluices and mechanization at the level of the wheelbarrow, the pick and the shovel. How could they switch over to the perception of art?!

All around were the rusty bogs of Karelia. Ill-appointed barracks and cold tents in which people perished. The darkness and frosts of long winter months. The hungry, grey world of convicts, filled with terror and hatred. Even members of the 'GULAG tribe' wished to forget all this, if only for a time, just as did the Chekists in their greatcoats and leather jackets.

It is hard to pinpoint the theatre's exact opening date, but in 1932 it was already functioning.

The small, newly-built, two-storey wooden playhouse, seating 330, was fine, with a good stage and orchestra pit, stalls and gallery, wings and dressing rooms, a decent foyer and even a sewerage system (something lacking in the bosses' homes). The auditorium's proportions reminded one of the cosy domestic theatres in the late eighteenth and early nineteenth century mansions of Russian aristocrats.

The main part of the Solovki troupe moved to Medvezhiegorsk, leaving at Kem a group of actors headed by Kalugin with the task of catering to the town and nearby camp sites (Vegeraksha, Babguba and others).

At Medvezhiegorsk a barracks was built not far from the theatre with rooms for five or six people and its own kitchen and dining room. For the actors there began a time of intoxication with a near-free existence: moving freely between the theatre and the barracks, wearing civilian clothes, in summer bathing in the lake. Those who were unable to appreciate these blessings were dispatched to the Solovki, or to camps along the banks of Vyg-Ozero Lake and the River Svir.

New actors were sought out from the WSBC files and at the major sorting station of Pindushi. For some a transfer to the theatre saved their lives.

Before his arrest assistant stage director Vladimir Tsekhansky had worked with a team of documentary film makers in Moscow, which had returned in 1932 from Tajikistan.

> Our cameraman had the ill luck to attend a reception at some embassy.... He was arrested, and from the addresses and telephone numbers in his notebook all the rest were swept in.... I got five years for 'failure to report'.... For half a year I never took off my boots.... In the spring we were ordered to clear a barracks stacked with frozen corpses.... To dig a grave was impossible.... The summons to the theatre saved me....[13]

The actor Ivan N. Rusinov reminisced:

> When a drama student, I lived in the Pavlovo suburb of Moscow. A fellow-student and I were preparing for our graduation examination a scene from Tolstoy's *Living Corpse* – the suicide of Fedia Protasov. I was walking to a rehearsal along Stoleshnikov Alley, carrying a small suitcase contain-

ing an undershirt, slippers and an old Browning pistol, bought from a neighbour. The delegates of the 14th Party Congress were emerging from the Bolshoi Theatre and coming out with them were Kalinin and Rykov. Interested, I joined the crowd of onlookers.

Then suddenly – 'Come along, will you...'. Well, they brought God's bondsman to a police station near the Bolshoi Theatre. 'What's in your little suitcase?' And there, under the undershirt was a Browning, and what's more – my father is a priest.... They slammed five years in the camps on me.... So, it turned out the theatre was to blame for it all.[14]

Raisa D. Zherebtsova (Evers), a student at Leningrad Conservatory and in camp assistant to the conductor and choir-master, had better luck: given a term of 3 years, she was appointed to the theatre at once. She turned up at the 'Medvezhka' in 1935 after risking 'earning a little more' as conductor of a church choir.

A large group of prominent musicians and artists (Moscow, Leningrad) were packed off to camp for homosexuality (a very cohesive stratum). At the time this sort of lapse earned one eight years. The ways to camp are truly inscrutable....

The work of the WSBC Central Theatre in 1932–33 was not advertised. Nor could we find any reviews. Inaccessible to prisoners, the theatre was, apparently, kept in the shadows. For a short time, another form of spectacle made an aggressive and vivid appearance in the work brigades – the propaganda theatre.

In the propaganda theatre, individuality is absolutely erased; it is replaced by a single political idea and by aggressive passion. Nature was enemy No. 1, to be conquered and subdued. 'Nature we'll train, freedom we'll gain', declaimed the propaganda brigade. The former 'Left' among the writers who took a ride along the canal welcomed this kind of theatre.

The canal's first genuine propaganda brigade emerged at Povenets. The most dramatically gifted, as it turned out, were the 'men of the 35th'. They possessed pathos, humour, sensibility and an ample assortment of smiles and intonations. They retained from their former life a knack for transfiguration, and here everything came in very handy.[15]

(*The Stalin Canal*)

A brigade of criminal offenders ('men of the 35th' according to the article of the code under which they were sentenced) appeared under I. Terentiev at the end of 1932 or early in 1933. Their number grew gradually from eighteen to fifty-seven performers. The orchestra comprised two guitars, two accordions and a mandolin. The texts of their limericks were provided by their stage director and by poets from among the convicts. This, of course, was not the 'first' camp brigade, for long before the appearance of the Povenets 'Comrade Firin Propaganda Brigade', the *Our Own* and 'Red Blouse' groups had appeared on the Solovki. Political scenes, couplets set to the tunes of popular hits and presentation were aimed at direct contact with the audience.

The Povenets brigade, neither the first, nor the last, proved interesting because it was led by a gifted director, active in 'Left' art in Russia – Igor Terentiev (1892–1937).

He was born in the quiet Ukrainian town of Pavlograd, his fault apparently to have been born into the wrong social milieu: his father was a colonel in the gendarmes, his mother hailed from a family of Prussian barons. Both in the Kharkov gymnasium and the law faculties of Kharkov and Moscow Universities, from which he graduated in 1915, the word 'gendarme' hardly evoked anything but annoyance. The youth early rejected his milieu and his family, striking root nowhere.

During the civil war Terentiev's parents emigrated; he never concealed the fact, perhaps thinking that he could thereby not be blamed for them. On the threshold of the revolution he was carried away by the crazy language of the Futurists and his own bold experimentation with words. In 1922 he emigrated, made appearances in a cabaret but the next year returned to Russia.

He was still in the grip of destructive ideas and emotions, starting with an anti-Easter propaganda piece *Snowmaiden*, after which he produced a stage version of John Reed's *Ten Days that Shook the World* at the Red Theatre (1924).

Terentiev proclaimed the principles of an avant-garde, extreme left-wing theatre: 'Sound-montage rather than music! Mounting rather than settings! Light-montage rather than painting! Literary montage rather than a play...'.[16]

In practice, of course, Terentiev was not so categoric. His work on John Reed won attention, yet his career as a stage director did not develop smoothly. He would delve into contemporary Leningrad's lower depths of thieves and prostitutes (*The Foxtrot* by

V. Andreyev), then switch to *A Little Knot*, a play of his own about embezzlers. In his stagecraft naivety went hand in hand with refinement, eccentricity and the farcical.

To counter the melancholic and tragic tone of Meyerhold's production of *The Inspector General*, in 1927 Terentiev staged Gogol's comedy as a farce about philistines.[17] The eccentricity of the costumes created by disciples of 'P. Filonov's school of analytical painting' is startling even today: there is something disturbingly contemporary in the clumsy clothes of the bureaucrats, reminiscent of the greenish-grey tunics of the Nazi army.

The play enjoyed a *succès de scandale*, but Terentiev's company, without premises and means, fell apart. An attempt to challenge Meyerhold's right to produce S. Tretiakov's *I Want a Child* (1928) were doomed in advance – the master still held full sway.

Early in 1929 Terentiev went to Kharkov, then the Ukrainian capital, either missing the point of the political changes taking place around him or dismissing them as unimportant: he was reckless enough to write about the 'social infantilism' of Leo Tolstoy!

He produced several plays for Ukrainian theatres, particularly with the Dniepropetrovsk troupe, which evoked varied reviews. In January 1931, when someone identified him as the son of a gendarme colonel, he was arrested and in September he received a five-year sentence. He must have arrived on the canal soon afterwards.

Quite a number of propaganda brigades made their appearance, then fell apart along the canal route and on nearby construction sites. For example *Ferroconcrete*, journal of the Svirstroy project, reported in its April 1932 issue on a young workers' theatre that presented a production written by a member of the company, A. Kudriavtsev. *At First Call*, about frontier guards in the Far East (settings by Khnok), was performed in the autumn in Svirstroy barracks Nos. 128 and 309. Presenting its art in barrack No. 106 was the "Derrick" propaganda brigade.

The writer Vera Inber described the appearance of two brigades before a meeting of timber-rafters at Nadvoitsy. Wooden platforms were thrown down on the ground and two men would stand on their edges to keep them from moving. That was the stage. A compère in a sailor's cap, with a scar across his face (a bandit with a record of five murders), announced in a screeching voice that they would hear a limerick.

Youthful female criminals with a record of many indictments sang with verve:

> Hey, shock-worker, come on!
> Hit the spade and press on,
> Hit the spade and press on,
> Raise your output higher on!

A band of two violin and three mandolin players (all thieves), shut their eyes and played really superbly. Then a second brigade swept onto the boards with a genuine gipsy dance. A young gipsy in a pink shirt and glove-leather boots nimbly hovered over the boards, followed by the gipsy girl Masha who, having stripped the previous dancer of his boots, gave a really 'classy' performance. In the past Masha had committed three murders, one of them at camp, where she killed a foreman for 'getting fresh'. She was now in charge of the cultural and educational sector.[18]

Brigades of this kind represented (ignoring the texts of the limericks) the lowest, yet eternal type of Punch and Judy show: some boards and an actor on them. As a means of influencing the masses, the Punch and Judy show fulfilled its role on the canal as well.

Terentiev's propaganda brigade at Povenets (a village on the Povenchanka river and the highest point on the canal) stood out for its leader's professionalism and drive. He managed to organize yesterday's thieves and prostitutes; moreover, once the stage director found his bearings and named his brigade after a high-ranking chief in the GULAG tribe, S.G. Firin, this secured it the boss's benevolence.

Most important, however, was that Terentiev, a professional with free command of a host of expressive means at his fingertips, moved from the avant-garde to the Punch and Judy type of show. He formed his group out of the dregs of society, in whom he had been interested even before imprisonment. By submitting them to his will, he accomplished the task of reforming man. In a word, at this new stage, he tried in a theatrical spectacle, just as had once been attempted in poetry, to combine the polish of refined culture with the crudity of Futurism and low farce. This amalgamation was brought about by the annihilation of the independent personality, completely subjugated to the State.

Aesthetically, this found expression in the creation of a political masque. Enthusiasm (sincere, or false?) in meeting the utilitarian tasks of the day apparently aroused the stage director's desire to dissolve art in the very life and work of the masses.

On the Solovki of the 1920s such efforts would have naturally provoked talk of venality and 'turncoats'. But the canal men lack that semblance of a public opinion found in a camp. They did not have the time to shape it. On the canal the only goal was to survive.

Performing in front of the canal men upon boulders or the boards which lined the bottom of a future sluice, the propaganda brigade members roused the exhausted men to another assault:

> Hey, lads, tell us
> Where, in which brigade
> They are lagging behind?
> We'll go and help them!
> Not merely by word,
> But by deed,
> Not only by bluster,
> But by bustle,
> Not only by song,
> But also with muscle,
> Not only by dance
> But in the sweat of our brow,
> Not only by art and culture,
> But also in bulk and volume.[19]

In fact, they took off their quilted jackets, set aside their guitars and seized shovels. And only when satisfied that work was well under way would they move on to the next group of canal men.

The Stalin Canal carries photographs of a superbly rendered playlet entitled *Treat Horses Kindly*. At the time a horse was valued much more highly on the canal than a human being, the death of the latter causing no ripple at all, while the fall of a horse would trigger a most stringent investigation, even including extreme measures.

The scene's pragmatism, however, is inflated by many literary and theatrical associations, above all by V. Mayakovsky's 1918 verse containing the poet's unexpectedly compassionate note: 'Kiddo, we're all in a little way horses, each one's a horse in his own special way'. One might also recall a play staged in 1922 under the same title in his Moscow workshop in N.M. Foregger, a lover of the Punch-and-Judy type of theatre.

Terentiev's limericks championed the 'horse' as an indispensable worker. The brigade's activities, judging by the scanty data at our disposal, led to the eulogizing of technology, construction and the canal to the detriment of life and personality. The limericks starkly oppose the old life to the joys of 'reforging' character.

The Joint, a full-length play on this topic was staged in 1933 and presented by Terentiev at a noisy rally of the canal's shock-workers at Dmitrov near Moscow, in a two-storey log clubhouse brought all the way from Medvezhiegorsk.

> And it was there that Liolia Furayeva, formerly a recidivist but now released preterm as the best shock-worker, sang a simple song, a song of hopelessness and despair, a song that brought a cold draught from the stage. The same Liolia Furayeva and her fellow actors performed a scene in the club with such verve and enthusiasm and merriment that the audience burst into applause.[20]

This last gathering of the canal builders was quite unexpectedly addressed by Chekmazov: 'Here I am, a former recidivist, who spent 15 years in prisons and the Solovki camp, today the director of the musical instruments factory at the Labour Commune No. 2'. The administration was quite ingenious in creating a myth of unity among all the project's participants. However, amid the trials they endured, there emerged a natural feeling of involvement in a cause in whose successful completion hardly anyone inwardly believed.

In June 1933 most of the shock-workers saw their terms cut. Some were set free and offered jobs on the Moskva–Volga Canal project. Terentiev and his brigade were among those who accepted. Various considerations decided the stage director's choice; not least, perhaps, the hope of receiving Firin's patronage and the promixity of Moscow.

Terentiev resumed contact touch with the film world, yet tried to keep under Firin's wing and worked as a free employee on the Moskva–Volga canal. But all his precautions were to no avail: on 28 May 1937 he was arrested, and on 17 June shot.

Let us pay homage to Terentiev's experience in the field of propaganda theatre, which, despite the brutality of the prevailing environment, was important in its own way. The meaning of this experience, despite its overall false moral charge, consisted in the endeavour to uphold man, forcing him to overcome his sluggishness and physical frailty. 'Hold out!' Terentiev appealed. And added: 'Only work brings salvation'. This was a slogan the convicts had learned long before.

11 Camp theatres and the Central Theatre of the White Sea–Baltic Canal

> *People grew dull, callous.... Showed no interest in
> things, even the theatre. Rehearsals passed in a
> slipshod way. It is amazing that plays were
> produced at all, and with invariable success, too.
> Only, perhaps, because there were truly talented
> people among the actors.*
>
> Vera Nikitina, *All that Happened*

In the autumn of 1933 the chief OGPU officers and many thousands
of convicts left Medvezhia Gora and the tenor of life in the camps
along the canal zone changed. The roads, the plants and factories,
the settlements around were awaiting their turn. From now on the
entire region was called the NKVD White Sea–Baltic Combine
(WSBC).

The camp owners were settling down for a long stay. A new
NKVD building was going up at Medvezhiegorsk. A huge two-
storey hotel with a high tower, the interior panelled with precious
woods, opened its doors in 1935. The former director of the Russian
Museum in Leningrad, Nikolai Sychev, now a prisoner, was on the
building site day and night, responsible for the hotel's interior decorations and furnishings.[1]

Grand plans were afoot to expand the GULAG country further by enlarging the camps and, particularly, the exiles' settlements.
Both the former and the latter were a nuisance: inmates tended to
escape. I. Chukhin cites figures from border guards' reports: 1,174
transgressors were detained on the Soviet–Finnish border in 1930,
2,488 in 1931 and 7,207 in 1932.[2] Escapees who put up resistance
were shot. Exiles sought to return home and a warning had to be
issued over the WSBC that 'henceforward exiles leaving without
permission shall be subject to criminal proceedings as for an escape
attempt'.

From the early 1930s hundreds of actors, artists and musicians were gathered in the canal zone. The more outstanding were
picked out for the Medvezhia Gora theatre; if they did not get there
at once, the convicts themselves protected them as best they could. A

legend has come down to us about the appearance on the canal of Mikhail Ksendzovsky, a well-known Leningrad operetta singer and a tenor of rare sparkle and mellowness.

> He had just arrived with a shipment of prisoners and as soon as he stepped down from the car was giving a concert when he was spotted by the camp chief Ivanchenko: 'Why is he here, why all the coddling? Off to the logging site!' Eventually, checking on the work-sites, he heard singing in the forest. Ksendsovsky was standing on a tree-stump, singing, and all around him convicts were chopping, sawing, working the logs. Ivanovsky was about to stop it, but the men begged him: 'Citizen chief, let him sing. It warms the heart. We'll do his quota for him.'[3]

The less lucky ones put together theatrical troupes that circulated from camp to camp, frequently changing their membership (an actor would be released, dispatched to a common work gang or another camp or die). These troupes were joined to escape the work gangs by people who had to be helped and adventurers of all kinds. Motley combinations took shape with a small core of professionals surrounded, at best, by not-too-young disciples.

An idea of the activities of the small theatres at Leiguba, Svirlag (Vazhino), Zaton and Lodeinoye Pole may be gleaned from the reminiscences of Vera Nikitina and Gabriel Ramensky. Nikitina, the first wife of the Moscow stage designer Leonid Nikitin, was arrested together with her husband and sent to the canal, where she worked in the theatre. Ramensky had studied in Leningrad at the Zubov Institute of the History of Art*.

The memoirs of Nikitina and Ramensky reflect the last years of the Solovetsky troupe, left to work at Kem. In 1931 the troupe, then led by Kalugin, was sent into the canal zone proper.[4] The company split into three small groups to cover the camp sites and adjacent settlements of the indigenous population. Each group had a leader appointed by the culture and education sector, but moved about without guards. The repertory of the group made up of Kalugin, Ramensky, Cheremisov, Zalesskaya and others included three plays: *Smoke (Mutiny)* by B. Lavrenev, *The Tempo* by N. Pogodin and *Grain* by V. Kirshon. They also gave concerts.

---

* The Institute was opened in 1912 by Count Zubov in his mansion at 5 St. Isaacs Square. The Count emigrated, and the institute, several times renamed and transformed, is still there.

They moved by foot or horsedrawn sled over the land of the former Olonets Governorship. Distances of 10–12 kilometres were easily covered in late summer, but even in early autumn were hardly passable. They had to play in all kinds of premises, often including unfinished clubhouses. Had they been built of stone we would now come upon striking fragments of a mad camp civilization!

The village of Vosnesenye, 35 km from the Svir on the southern shore of Lake Onega. Free territory. A log clubhouse is under construction: a reading room, gymnasium, quite a professional stage with an auditorium seating about 500. The village's population is no more than 300. The actors slept on the floor.

The village of Ostrechino. The clubhouse is unheated. When, in the course of a play, drinks were called for, the glasses contained ice instead of water. The actresses are miserable with cold.

Forest beyond Ostrechino. Concert for criminals (non-political offenders). No clubhouse. The night spent in the barracks.

Small village of Vorony. A camp-site deep in the forest, where there are unexpectedly many intellectuals. Performance in a clubhouse more like a cowshed.

On the right bank of the Svir, downstream from Ostrechino: a large camp, unfinished clubhouse. Auditorium seating 600, stage, cloakroom like that in a big town.[5]

What, then, was the goal of this arduous journey, a caricature of the perambulations of itinerant players in seventeenth-century Europe? It could not be simpler: hidden under the slogan of 'hitting the countryside' and the campaign to enlighten camp inmates was the camp administration's desire to make some money by the actors' efforts.

The actors were permitted to go for quit-rent, just as they had been in Russia during the demise of the serf theatre in the first half of the nineteenth century. Wealthy landlords, patrons of the arts, had once given their serf actors hand-outs of money: in 1832, for instance, Prince N.B. Yusupov's serf–musicians received 86 roubles per annum while the girls of the chorus were paid no salary, but, at full maintenance, were granted 5 roubles for tea and sugar.[6] Later, landlords on the way to ruin sent off their serf actors to make money (for quit-rent) or put them up for sale, the whole bunch or individually. By allowing the actors out into the free zone, the administration was making no mistake: the three plays presented at Voznesenye brought in around 2,500 roubles, promptly surrendered to the camp. The actors were attracted to such enterprise by the hope of eating a little better and earning something, however little, for those were hungry years.

The emotional semi-freedom the actors enjoyed during such trips could not but tell on what and how they performed. This ranged from inexcusable pot-boilers, which offended the more cultivated inmates, to unexpected interpretations of long familiar texts.

According to Ramensky, most success was enjoyed by Kirshon's *Grain*. The play presented a picture of State grain procurement and, given its falsity (difficulties were blamed on the kulaks and Party 'romanticists' who supported them), never left the convicts indifferent. Late at night in the Vorony forest camp a Professor Kirpichnikov shared his impressions with Ramensky: the actors' emotive force translated false words into a 'language of truth', the spectator understanding much more than the author wished to say. The anti-aestheticism of surrounding life and the pitiable props stripped the play of the allure of untruth. The truth – the forcible destruction of village life – was starkly revealed.

The money-making journeys ended in the elimination of the theatre, and after a spell in the common work gangs some of the actors were dispatched to the large camp at Lodeinoye Pole.

Since paid performances enticed the actors not only by illusory freedom, but also by the stupefaction of drunkenness, WSBC Deputy Chief Uspensky issued an order in the autumn of 1935 'prohibiting the propaganda brigades from giving paid performances to the local population'. Brigades found wanting were dissolved.

In 1934 the WSBC Central Theatre came out of the dark, making it possible for us to form some idea of it.

Those working in the theatre totalled between 100 and 110 persons; the ratio of convicts to free employees in 1934 was 88 to 31, in 1935, 81 to 23 and in 1937, 82 to 17.[7]

A combination of prisoners and free employees guaranteed a degree of stability in the theatre's repertory with the possibility of emergency substitutions in plays. The theatre even formed an extra company of some 50 persons for dispatch to Tuloma on the Kola peninsula, where a power plant was under construction. Several photographs have come down to us, giving some idea of the characteristics of the Tuloma troupe. In all probability, it had a strong musical element. One of the pictures shows a jazz-band of very young, frightened musicians. Another is of a scene between Pierrot and Columbine, closely resembling a similar one in Leoncavallo's *I Pagliacci*.

At the same time they staged quite realistic contemporary plays along the lines of Pogodin's *Aristocrats*, as well as vaudevilles and, apparently, Ostrovsky's comedies. The troupe was led by Igor S. Alander (1900–36?), who had been serving a 10-year term since 1931. At Tuloma it was hard just to survive. N. Krantsevich, a convict, wrote to his wife: 'The terrain here is very forbidding and morose: all around are rocks and mountains without forests, the skies are gloomy, and the sun seldom peeps out'. Is it any wonder that Alander was unable to withstand all the trials we know nothing about.... His registration card says 'Drowned himself'. No place, no date.

On the first night of the week the court theatre at Medvezhiegorsk staged a drama, on the second an opera and on the third an operetta. On the fourth night one could watch a ballet, on the fifth the stage was given over to the symphony orchestra and on the sixth to the theatre of miniatures and variety, while on the seventh a new film was shown.

The theatre's policy was determined by its leader, taking into account the tastes of the bosses, of course. Of the stage directors who came and went at 'Medvezhka', many are unknown to us. But chief stage director for the longest period, from 1933 to 1939, nearly as long as the theatre's life, was Alexei Alexeyev (Livshits) (1887–1985).

He had an eight-year term to serve under a non-political article. He lived outside the camp in a private apartment, and bore his misfortune with the help of cutting humour.

He was forgiven questionable witticisms, for the authorities trusted in his professionalism, and rightly so. They were dealing with a past master in a rare profession, that of compère, and an experienced stage director of minor forms and author of operetta librettos.

Alexeyev, the son of a well-to-do lawyer, started his career before the revolution in the theatre–cabarets of Odessa, Kiev and St. Petersburg, and when he received a lawyer's diploma in 1915 he promptly dismissed it from his mind. On the boards he quickly created his own persona: supple, but full of dignity, a polished gentleman in tails with a monocle in his right eye.[8] Witty, malicious, with refined manners – in a word, a society man, amusing his own kind.

In the early 1920s, when he gradually lost his audience and after someone in the audience shouted (without rancour) 'little Chamberlain' at him, he dropped the monocle, discarded the tailcoat and turned to operetta, doing so without claim to innovation or reference to special theories. The conventionality of operetta and its quiet, superficial psychology satisfied him as stage director. Having grown familiar with the half-masque on the stage, he came to feel comfortable with the half-truth and half-masque in life. He probably appeared at Medvezhiegorsk in 1933. Among dramatic directors who worked with Alexeyev were Sergey Taneyev (a relative of the well-known composer), Igor Alander, Alexei Larionov and other professionals.

The WSBC Central Theatre had resources and opportunities: at the time such words as 'none' and 'unavailable' were nonexistent where NKVD staff were concerned. That is why the glitter and richness of the costumes literally staggered the spectator. The properties department performed, indeed, excellently. The very talented chief stage designer Ivan I. Vovk, who got a 'tenner' in 1929, worked for several years at Medvezhiegorsk. In 1937, while in camp, he was indicted for group drunkenness, and was freed only in 1939. He returned, it seems, to the Ukraine where he died not long before the war. A gifted cartoonist, the Leningrad artist Mikhail M. Molodiashin, revealed a sharp, scathing brush and pen. His brother Leonid also worked at the theatre as ballet master. Another fine artist, Yuri V. Diachkov, also accused in the camp of drunkenness, adorned the foyer of the theatre with models (he was killed in action during the war). Also memorable was the work of the stage designer, a free employee, Natalia M. Nabokova. Undoubtedly, many others also contributed to the production of festive and beautiful spectacles.

The theatre's orchestra was maintained at a high level by Boleslav S. Pshibyshevsky (a relative of the Polish writer Stanislaw Przybyszewski), who before his arrest had worked in the arts sector of the People's Commissariat of Education in Moscow, and contributed to the newspaper *Soviet Art*, which depicted work in camp in such glowing colours.

For several years the core of the Central Theatre's company hardly changed, which helped produce a common style of performance, so important for a musical theatre. Numerous actors were on the rolls, but it can be said with confidence that most came from Moscow and Leningrad. Among the actors at Medvezhya Gora were the singer V.Ya. Armfeld (from the Leningrad operetta), the actor and declaimer G.V. Artobolevsky, the actress N.A. Bzozovskaya (Moscow), the actor I.P. Bomchinsky (from the Academic Drama Studio,

Leningrad), the actor N.P. Vronsky, the singer M.D. Ksendzovsky (Leningrad), the actor F.V. Krasnoshchekov, the actor A.L. Kremliov (from the Maly Theatre Studio), the actor V.I. Likhachev (from the former Nezlobin theatre, Moscow), the actor N.G. Lukianov (from the antireligious theatre, Moscow), the ballet dancer V.G. Morik, the bass A.P. Musatov, the actress E.F. Normai, the actor B.E. Panchulidze, the actress Z.I. Perevedentseva, the actor A.T. Podorozhny (from the 'Berezil' Theatre, Kharkov), the actor F.I. Poluyanov (from the 'Crooked Mirror', Leningrad), the singer S.F. Rakhmanov (from the Nemirovich–Danchenko Musical Theatre, Moscow), the actor I.A. Romanovich, the actor N.I. Rusinov (from the Yermolov Studio), the actor K.G. Svarozhich (from the Children's Theatre, Moscow), the actress N.A. Svetlova, the actor P.A. Strigushchenko, the actor and stage director S.A. Taneyev (Moscow), the actress M.A. Tolmacheva (from the Children's Theatre, Leningrad), the baritone L.F. Privalov, the singer S.M. Tukhner and many others. Working as free employees were the actresses V. Arskaya and N.N. Karpova, the wives of convict actors N. Lukianova and P.I. Vremenskaya, the stage designer N.M. Nabokova, the singer E.E. Rosenshtrauch and many more.

The theatre's aesthetic profile may be described only tentatively owing to the lack of reviews covering those years. The camp press of the early 1930s – the newspaper *Reforging*, the Svirstroy journal *Ferroconcrete* and others – did not cover cultural events. Attention was concentrated on emergency efforts and output and reports on the arrival of propaganda brigades are scanty.

Even the authors of *The Stalin Canal* avoided the risk of dwelling on the WSBC Central Theatre, for the obvious reason that the theatre was not intended for those slaving in the canal work gangs, although it had been promised at one time that a truckload of shock-workers would be brought to the theatre once a fortnight as a reward. However, without introducing the theatre, it was nevertheless condemned in passing for the type of concerts given.

> In the spring of 1932 a crash brigade of the Central Theatre was sent here from Medgora. They performed vocal and dance numbers, the overture from *Orfeo and Euridice*, an aria from *The Bird Dealer* and *Spanish Dances in a Tavern*.... It was a period when the Central Theatre did its best to emulate the Bolshoi and the Moscow Academic Art Theatre. They even staged the scene in the inn from *Boris Godunov, Krechinsky's Wedding* and the sketch *The Jilted One*.

Brigade members took their time in rehearsing, 'identifying with the character' and dreaming of marking the completion of the canal with a production of *Lakmé*.[9]

Of course, the sumptuously costumed *Spanish Dances in a Tavern* contrasted starkly with the bogs of the Karelian tundra and the convicts' damp boots. They were merely given a few morsels off the feasting Chekists' table.

Yet even fragments of classical art retained its essence. Its very source being highly moral, it invariably condemned falsehood and lies, the traditions of Russian realistic theatre ('identification with the character') proved sufficiently vital to preserve the characteristic features in excerpts from plays.

Igor Terentiev wrote in the article 'Actor on the Trail' (*Reforging*) that in the spring of 1933 the Central Theatre was eliminated, allegedly for failing to contribute to productivity, and its best performers merged with the Povenets brigade and sent out to the White Sea canal in two groups, referred to as the 'Propaganda Base of the White Sea–Baltic Camp'.[10]

In fact, the assault on the theatre was vigorous. In the same issue of *Reforging*, Terentiev's brigade was rebuked for a repertory that had nothing to say about struggle, breakthroughs or Soviet realities, serving up instead the ballet *The Little Hunchback Horse* and arias from operettas (*The Bird Dealer, Orfeo and Euridice*). Yet the reproach was couched in cautious terms for the Central Theatre was in the charge of Rappoport, not Firin.[11]

Having survived by 'reinforcing' the propaganda brigades, the theatre kept on with its work. In November 1934 it received a new stage director Lesia (Alexander) Kurbas (1889–1937), a Ukrainian with a five-year sentence in the camps for participating in a mythical underground nationalist organization. But Article 58 (54 under the Ukrainian Code) could shut the door to a decent professional life, and this became clear very soon.

Kurbas was an intellectual of the European type. Before 1917 a subject of Austria–Hungary, he had studied at Vienna and Lvov Universities, and acquired stage experience at the Ukrainian theatre *Russian Conversation*. In 1916 he moved to Kiev where he played romantic leads at the Sadovsky theatre. At Kiev, and then at Kharkov his stage-director's career developed swiftly: he revealed a gift for attracting talented people and channelling their efforts towards useful goals.

Kurbas' theatrical programmes at the Young Theatre (1917–19) and the *Berezil* Theatre (1922–33) changed drastically under the pressure of the times. However, their general evolution matched his inner development: having passed through the school of psychological theatre, the romanticist director rejected its lifelike forms, counterposing an art of conventional poetical forms, but free from the influence of Expressionism. In this way he found original interpretations of Taras Shevchenko's poem *The Haydamaks* and Shakespeare's tragedy *Macbeth* and produced a stage version of Upton Sinclair's novel *Jimmy Higgins*.

The greatest success and vexation of Kurbas the stage director was his meeting with the brilliant playwright Mikola Kulish (1892–1937). They created dismally prophetic pictures in *The People's Malakhy* and the drama *Maklena Grasa*. The appeal 'Put things aside and think of man...' went side by side in these plays with a depiction of the moral degradation of people of both socialist and capitalist persuasions and of historical time itself.

In the Ukraine, Kulish and Kurbas were hounded. In 1933, when Ukrainian towns and cities were combed for Galicians, Western Ukrainians and Poles, who were accused of being spies and wreckers, Kurbas was arrested, too. A year later Kulish was swept up in the 'Kirov stream' and served his tenner in solitary on the Solovki. All in all, seventeen actors and students of Kurbas fell into the clutches of the NKVD, most of them to perish.

At the Medvezhia Gora theatre the new stage director was given *Intervention*, a play by the Odessa playwright L. Slavin. Actors were drawn to the director, touched by his individual approach to each performer.

Vatslav Dworzhetsky, a Kiev student arrested in 1929 and the performer of the role of Marcel, had worked on the canal before getting to Medvezhia Gora; to the end of his life he spoke with feeling of Kurbas' remarkable professionalism.

In January the play was practically ready for the stage. There was even a draft poster: a zouave shielding with his body the red flag of revolution. However, Kurbas was not destined to bring the play to this audience (subsequently he produced *Intervention* on the Solovki). After 24 January 1935 his name disappeared from the list of actors at the theatre: he had 'departed'.

Assistant director V.I. Tsekhansky, the actor N.I. Rusinov and Person's wife M.M. Berger believe that Alexeyev was to blame for Kurbas' removal. Vexed by the fact that the newcomer somehow won the actors' affection too quickly and having promptly found common cause with Pshibyshevsky, Alexeyev sought the authorities, alleging that a convict under Article 58 could hardly be trusted to stage a play about the revolution. He also wrote a newspaper item describing Kurbas as a 'nationalist'.

The chief stage director's chagrin on sensing a strong rival is understandable. Kurbas disappeared.

The theatre continued to function, adapting to absolutely unpredictable circumstances. For the court theatre felt safe as long as Rappoport and Kogan, Firin and Berman, government decorations bestowed on them, flourished. In the wooden town of Medvezhiegorsk the actors walked along streets named after the Chekists, creators of the GULAG country. Still remembered were the years when convicts were issued camp money for settling accounts at the commissary signed by Bokii, Kogan, and Berman.

Suddenly, in the autumn of 1936, there was a rush to rename the streets! A wave of the Great Terror swept away the grouping that had held sway for nearly 20 years. The only survivor, who died peacefully in his own bed, was the artful Frenkel, now 'reforged' into an NKVD general.

The theatre at 'Medvezhka' opened its doors to another kind of spectator, playing four days a week for the town's citizens and three days for the convicts. Posters would announce: 'For camp inmates'.

The repertory for the 1935–36 season included the operas *Eugene Onegin* and *The Queen of Spades* by Chaikovsky, *Carmen* by Bizet, *The Tsar's Bride* by Rimsky-Korsakov and the ballet *The Red Poppy* by Glière. Many plays by Ostrovsky, *Woe from Wit* by Griboyedov, *Krechinsky's Wedding* by Sukhovo-Kobylin, *The Marriage of Figaro* by Beaumarchais, *The Six Loved Ones* by Arbuzov and Kirshon's *Wonderful Alloy* were also performed.

A poster for February 1936 marked 'For camp inmates' listed: *Platon Krechet* by Korneichuk, the Austrian film *Peter*, a concert, *Distant Point*, a play by A. Afinogenov, the film *Girlfriends*, Schiller's *Intrigue and Love*, the films *Aerograd* and *Arshaul* and the play *A Good Soul* by E. Karpov.

The same memorable year of 1936 saw important changes within the theatre: Person's term expired and Tsekhansky and other actors were released. Alexeyev remained the chief.

The theatre's planned repertory for 1938 included ten operas, among them *Tosca* by Puccini, *Tales of Hoffmann* by Offenbach,

Dubrovsky by E. Napravnik, Mascagni's *Cavalleria Rusticana* and Leoncavallo's *I Pagliacci*. It was also intended to produce fifteen plays, among them Shakespeare's *Twelfth Night*, Balzac's *Pamela Giraud*, Scribe's *A Glass of Water*, Gogol's *The Inspector General* and V. Shkvarkin's *A Plain Girl*. There were also plans for productions of two operettas: *A Lantern Wedding* by Offenbach and Lehar's *The Merry Widow*. And of course, all public holidays were marked by concerts.[12]

Not all these productions were realized, but their very number is testimony to a sturdy, well established theatre with a particularly strong musical department. The Medvezhiegorsk theatre had a clearly defined leaning towards opera and operetta. Excellent singers were available (Elly Rosenshtrauch, Sonia Tuchner, Leonid Privalov and others), while drama production was becoming an increasing source of problems.

At times Alexeyev was capable of miscalculation. An order of the day issued on 11 March 1938 by M. Timofeyev, chief of the WSB Combine, reprimanded prisoner Alexeyev for 'taking the liberty, as compère, of insinuating vulgar repartees, and behaving in an impermissible manner, arousing the indignation of the public,' at a Women's Day soirée. Alexeyev was warned that 'a repetition of such behaviour (would) entail more severe punitive measures'.[13] The chief of the WSBC also had problems: at the end of 1939 4,000 physically fit men were transferred and a further 16,000 sent to building site No. 105, turning the camps into 'invalid' colonies: who, then, was going to fulfill the plans? Timofeyev was upset.

Events developed in a way that made further punishment unnecessary, and the fate of the theatre took an unforeseeable twist. It could no longer exist as a theatre of the NKVD owing to an obvious shortage of both audiences and means.

The balance of convicts and free employees was also disturbed as those released, afraid of losing NKVD protection, remained in the theatres as free individuals who had to be paid (Privalov, Evers and others). Meanwhile, the new prison transports headed for other places.

The camps, extending ever further east and north, hidden in the logging grounds and mining shafts, were at first beyond the reach of civilization. Some gradually acquired a modest drama theatre, others only a propaganda or concert group.

But in the years of the Great Terror the bosses as well as the convicts lived under psychological strain. The example of theatrical

Medvezhiegorsk proved infectious. Iosif Girniak, an actor of the *Berezil* theatre in Kharkov, recalled finding himself in 1935 in the kingdom of Ya. Moroz: Chib'yu camp (today's Inta, the Republic of Komi).

> He conceived the idea of turning Chib'yu into the capital of the entire Ukht-Pechlag territory.... He began with the theatre, sending to it prisoner actors, musicians, artists and even writers from all departments.... Just as landlords used to boast about their serf actors, so the Bolshevist 'gentleman' Moroz ... had them play for him a diverse repertory of dramas, comedies, operas, operettas and vaudevilles and even present symphony and jazz concerts.
>
> The scope of construction at Chib'yu between 1935 and 1937 surprised even Moscow: a secondary school, a technical school for the children of free employees, a Young Pioneer Palace, a summer theatre seating a thousand spectators, in which not a single play was produced because of the short, cold summer, a huge stadium in Hellenic style, in which, at the time of my sojourn at Chib'yu only a few football competitions were held, many residential buildings for GULAG employees. A clubhouse named after Kosolapkin expanded into a professional theatre with a rotating stage, tall wings and all kinds of service annexes.[14]

The year 1938, when many NKVD officers were removed, allegedly for abuses of power, put an end to Moroz's antics. Yet the half-ruined wooden theatre may be presumed to have survived in a drawing by the camp artist B. Sveshnikov, who found himself in Ukht-Pechlag ten years later. *The Minuet* dimly depicts the open stage of a theatre surrounded by trees, and a lightly outlined dancing female figure. This, in all probability, is the chimerical theatre of Chib'yu.[15]

However, the time of phantasies on Hellenic and other themes was fast receding. And the theatre at Medvezhiegorsk remained a special, unique phenomenon in the camp life of the early 1930s.

Its fate was decided in 1940. In Moscow the camp authorities' theatrical whims had been watched with a good deal of annoyance. The drive for economy seemed a plausible pretext and an order was issued prohibiting the hiring of free employees for camp theatre work.

In an attempt to save the Medvezhiegorsk theatre, it was handed over to the Karelian–Finnish Republic as a theatre of musical comedy. The much diminished troupe was at Petrozavodsk when, in June 1941, war broke out. The actors formed a concert brigade and turned up on the Solovki. By then the prisoners had been removed to provide room for a naval cadet school and a naval base was being built.

The paths trodden by prisoners now served free actors. They were not to be sent to punishment cells or denied food and walks. They could no longer be exterminated, as their convicted brothers had been. But the very last page in the history of the Solovki camp will be told separately.

12 The theatre of the late Solovki

Oh, you, in whom free spirit is still burning,
Oh, you, who've not been deaf to human woe,
Sink down upon your honest, bended knees!
And, choking down emotion, harken
To the sad tale of vanished generations,
As told by every Solovetsky boulder....

G. Rusakov, 1926

The 1930s vigorously pushed the Solovki into the distant orbits of the Karelian and Murmansk corrective-labour camps. In the north the borders of this kingdom ran across the Kola peninsula and from Murmansk, through Monchegorsk, Apatities, Kandalaksha, Loukhi and Pangoma, to Kem. Then, embracing the vast expanses of the Leningrad Region and Karelia, they swept southward: through Belomorsk to Medvezhiegorsk, Kondopoga and Petrozavodsk, emerging at Svirstroy and Lodeinoye Pole. Not so far away was Leningrad, which had various ties with the camp zone.

In 1934 the Solovki were merely the 8th department of this empire, albeit in certain ways of special importance. Their population diminished with every passing year from a peak that was probably reached in 1930 (Nogtev's papers indicate 49,456 persons).

In June that year a very active OGPU commission (the Shanin Commission) sentenced some ten sadistic overseers to be shot. For a time this lifted the convicts' spirits and restrained the vengeful cruelties of the guards, putting an end to the times when defenceless prisoners had been beaten up with impunity.

The need to save the island from a new wave of typhoid solved once and for all the problem of bathing and laundry. A visit to the bath-house every ten days with a change of underclothes and the issue of camp uniform (dark-grey trousers, a quilted jacket and coarse boots, for some reason called 'Minsk–Moscow') became law. Inmates were also allowed to wear their own clothes.

Women prisoners, who particularly suffered from the filth, subsequently recalled the camp with gratitude! Aniza Potekhina, dragged on a prisoner transport from the Mongolian border through the transit prisons across the whole country, wrote of the Solovki in

1931 that the islands 'were an oasis on my road and, generally, for all prisoners, for here I could get a bath and wash my clothes, eat normally, even get some entertainment: go to the theatre, go skating, walk freely about the island without being hailed by the convoy'.[1]

Not all were so lucky. Having become cleaner and kinder to the prisoners, the camp retained its frightening unpredictability. Everything in it changed instantly, like the weather at sea.

Artistic activities had a special lure, although they were fraught with hidden hazards. However, the accumulation around the theatre of devastated people engendered banality and enhanced grovelling, even on the stage.

Solovetsky morals and customs, as portrayed in the novel *Solovki* by Anna Skripnikova, resembled only too well those of a royal court with its abject servility. This was doubtless demanded.

But to the end there also remained those who retained a sense of dignity and clarity of thought. Many were sustained at that time by links with their families, meetings with whom strengthened the spirit.

A meeting with relatives was permitted after a year (only in summer) and in the middle of one's term. Meetings were arranged at Kem and prisoners were transported there; sometimes they were arranged on the island itself.

Olga Sinakevich-Yafa was brought from Anzer to the Great Solovetsky Island for a meeting which took place at a tidy cottage surrounded by trees. A housemaid in a starched apron took orders for a dinner of several courses and served them. A veritable resort!

The family of historian Gavrila Gordon, sentenced for meeting a German journalist, were granted 'three days of general-type meeting' (his father was able to arrange for fourteen days). Mother and son lived in a single-storey wooden barracks comprising several small, tidy rooms (two trestle-beds and even a wash-stand with a zinc-plated sink). Meetings proper took place in a hall where, standing on either side of a partition and talking loudly, were about a score of people.

The guests were taken for meals to the freemen's 'club', a splendidly appointed dining hall with a Moscow cook, set up by Yegorov. Meanwhile the prisoners were kept on a near-starvation ration, for it was the third year of collectivization and the ruined countryside was facing famine.

After the valuable timber had been cut down between 1924 and 1929 the OGPU, unable to farm profitably on the rocks, found the Solovki's maintenance increasingly burdensome, while the White Sea–Baltic Canal needed experienced hands. So, in 1931, the island was unburdened: the old and infirm were sent into distant exile and woeful death, the able-bodied enticed to the canal by promises of reduced terms.

M. Rozanov recalled 1931 in the camp as a time of extraordinary 'liberalism'.[2] A curious confirmation of this was the creation in the kremlin at the end of 1930 or beginning of 1931 of a *Living Newspaper* group, headed by a member of the large Hessen family, which had contributed to Russia's cultural life at different levels. Daniil Yu. Hessen, sentenced to five years under Article 58 in April 1930, appeared on the Solovki at the height of the 'return to justice' period.

He took courage from the times and, together with Mussar (of whom we know nothing), put together the *Living Newspaper*. Targets for its criticism were the sellers of the camp's food store. Couplets by the newspapermen, who called the thieves and swindlers who robbed the inmates by their true names, aroused ire. The response was an illiterate and crazy denunciation, accusing Hessen and Mussar of all conceivable crimes:

> As responsible leaders of the *Living Newspaper* collective of the kremlin settlement, they reduced the latter to the utmost debauchery ... demanded the sales to them of foodstuffs out of turn and baited and persecuted the shopkeepers. Moreover, it has come to light that the said leaders indulged in debauchery from 10 o'clock in the morning to 10 o'clock at night, released their mistresses from hard productive labour, made use of counterfeit coupons and abetted stealing for their own benefit.[3]

The brazen denunciation ascribed to the newspapermen all the despicable characteristics of the camp's depraved Chekists and thieving dregs. The 'baited and persecuted' shopkeepers achieved their ends: Hessen was given an extra three years and the *Living Newspaper* vanished.

An amusing detail of Solovki theatrical life in the summer of 1931 is revealed in the reminiscences of Gordon's son, G. Gordon. The son brought with him the latest issue of the magazine *Krasnaya Nov*, which contained V. Katayev's play *A Million Anxieties*. Having glanced through it, his father promptly sent it over to the theatre. In only a fortnight the first night was announced, but neither Gordon's son nor wife were able to see it, having left a couple of days earlier.[4]

The following year the play was produced by the Theatre of Operetta in Moscow, and subsequently in Leningrad and other cities, as well as in 'left' theatres in France and Germany.

It goes without saying that Katayev's vaudeville is a striking example of a purely conformist potboiler. The life-loving author, just like his characters in those hungry years, wanted butter, sugar, sausage and good cigarettes. He hoped the theatres would help spectators swallow the coarsely delineated characters and ridiculous repartees.

But spectators on the Solovki where, unbeknown to the world at large, the vaudeville's opening night was held, were precisely the kind of Russian intellectuals (the children of lawyers) whom Katayev set out to mock. The play's main character, Anatoly Esperovich Ekipazhev, a loser at the race course, spits into a neighbour's soup, locks the toilet and issues the key only twice a day. He fears arrest, and is shaken upon learning that his son has joined the police and married a tram driver, while one of his daughters has married a worker with the indelicate name of Parasiuk. A Moscow bourgeois hailing from intellectual parents, he is made to look a moral freak. Coming to replace him are the true heroes – the workers.

How could this smelly concoction be presented on the Solovki? At any rate, the speed at which it was cooked shows full awareness of its potboiler status: the main thing was to serve it quickly and hot!

Apart from hackwork, the Kremlin theatre produced quite worthy plays. Likhachev maintains that 'the theatre staged excellent plays, with excellent actors, but getting to the theatre was more difficult than getting to the Bolshoy today'.[5]

As a railway repairman Igor I. Tukalevsky, a Ukrainian student who found himself on the Solovki in 1930, had no right or time to use the library and theatre. Yet several times, secretly, he was able to penetrate the auditorium and see the performances of a ballet dancer when she came for meetings with her husband. Those occasions remained for him 'the most radiant remembrance'.

At that time the theatre probably presented quite witty political propaganda items. The plays *A European Tavern* and *A Lyre for Hire* perhaps indicted the West's degradation and emigration; political reviews may have been combined with other material. So far as can be seen from a photograph, the set of *A Lyre for Hire* borrowed from Tairov's staging of M. Kulish's play *The Pathetic Sonata* (Chamber Theatre, Moscow, 1931). In Tairov's production the poet Ilko Yuga, sitting at a table, seems to listen intently to an argument by the two women characters – Marina, a teacher's daughter (A. Koonen) and Zinka, a prostitute (F. Ranevskaya). On the Solovki the scene was probably construed as a parody, and was stuffed with pertinent political content. Literary and musical parodies enlivened the performances. The winter of 1931–32 was marked, according to Likhachev, by a burgeoning of culture in the kremlin. After that came another outbreak of typhoid, accompanied by hunger.

Changes on the island since the summer of 1932 could be felt strongly. Foodstuffs stored up over the years and all the vegetables were taken away for the White Sea–Baltic Canal.

> The top bread ration of 1,300 grams was cut to 1,000. Young leaves of swede, turnips and stinging nettle went into the pot. Very soon seagulls began to disappear – the ruffians kept hunting them down in spite of an order of the day which threatened from 6 months in the punishment cell on Sekirnaya Hill to 3 years added term for each dead bird. Someone took the pet deer Misha into the woods and slaughtered him. That was the end of old, tame Misha, a fixture in the kremlin courtyard, everybody's favourite.[6]

The intensifying hunger manifested itself in much more dramatic ways. Yu. Chirkov recalled the intelligent, jolly, plump compère N. Andreyev who, in 1933 'was all but eaten up by thieves in the cellars of the Cathedral of the Transfiguration. They had already dragged him into the cellar, gagged him, and were discussing ways of killing and dressing him when they were attacked by a camp police squad. For this episode Andreyev made camp history not only as a compère, but as "cannibals' chow".'[7]

Another event that put an end to liberalism on the Solovki in 1932 was a fire that broke out at night in the Cathedral of the Transfiguration where, stored in the workshops under the cupola, were blankets. Inmates suggested that the blankets, on which loving couples used to settle down for comfort, had caught fire from a discarded cigarette.

The camp regimen was tightened up. The museum, lovingly assembled by inmates, was ruined and icons were destroyed. The guards' powers were restored, while the convicts lost whatever gains they had made over the years of confrontation with the administration. Nevertheless, some important 'Solovetski' traditions were retained – including the right to a theatre.

In a letter to his family in Taganrog in 1934, the convict Nikolai Krantsevich wrote: 'From time to time I enjoy theatre and cinema, which are well staged here'. In 1935 he wrote:

> On the eve of my day off I decided to divert myself from endless work and went to see *The Inspector General* at the theatre, but left in disappointment, perhaps because I had seen this comedy much better staged, several times, but more probably because the sets, music and movement remind me of better times, so that I feel some vague dissatisfaction. But generally, I'm sulking, and missing you all to distraction.[8]

The camp of those years could be rightly called 'silent'. Inmates were allowed to send only one letter a month and there was no news from relatives for months on end; the winter break in navigation (January to May) was a very painful experience. Everyone trembled for the fate of their families, who could be evicted from their homes, arrested and exiled. Even the theatre was unable to distract audiences from their troubled thoughts.

We know little of the Solovki theatre in those years, for those who could and ought to have left us their memoirs perished too early. The camp's intellectual élite was shot in 1937, while those lucky enough to live on until their release died soon afterwards, perished during the war or once again turned up in distant camps, from which they never returned.

We have a somewhat clearer picture of the fate of the director Lesia Kurbas, who disappeared from Medvezhia Gora in January 1935. V. Yereshchenko, a Kharkov student, met him at the Vian-guba camp on the banks of Lake Vyg, where the former 'was sweeping the sled road over the ice of the lake along which timber was hauled from the bank and loaded on barges'.[9]

Together with the Ukrainian playwright M. Irchan and a Czech called Urbanik, Kurbas had composed *A Dream at Vian-Guba* (a review? an operetta?) for the camp club. It was performed on Saturdays to packed houses.

Then a commission arrived. Apparently it was favourably impressed, for next morning its creators were transferred to the isolator and it was rumoured that the commission was taking them to the Solovki.

Meanwhile, 1935 saw a conspicuous change in the camp's inmates and the conditions of their existence. The numerous intellectuals, party functionaries, members of the Comintern and scholars worked conscientiously, but were confined within a circle of narrow themes and prospects. For the younger ones there was plenty of physically arduous labour.

Salvation for the soul through books somehow balanced a bare life full of anxieties. Professor M. Zerov translated Virgil's *Aeneid* into Ukrainian in the evenings. The theologian P. Florensky studied Racine's tragedies. At Kem he was robbed by convicts ('I was sitting under three axes, but, as you can see, escaped with my life, though I lost my belongings and money'). Now, holding a small volume of Racine in his hands, he was full of admiration for what he called the playwright's 'classlessness' and the daring contents of his dramas.

> It's amazing, that they let him stage such tragedies.... Above all, their structure is amazing; of course, this is not classical structure, but, in its own way, it is perfect. The entire tragedy is a monolith, without adhesions or fusions. The action moves swiftly ahead, unimpeded by archaeological detail, props or abstract thoughts, sentiments and words. Therefore there are no stops or useless narrative, everything is so purposefully streamlined. Here we have dynamism, pure and simple, stripped of the dead and immobile.[10]

The Solovetsky theatre could not stage Racine. But it, too, helped people to live. Aesthetically speaking, it in no way differed from other good theatres on the mainland. Perhaps the Solovki stage shed the starkness of the early 1930s as it addressed the classical and the psychological.

Between 1935 and 1937 the director was the well-known baritone Leonid Privalov. He sang in the few musical performances (including Anton Rubinstein's *The Demon*). Appearing opposite him was Erji Martnovna Normay, a Hungarian Communist, who revealed a pleasant soprano and a charming stage manner. In solo concerts Privalov was accompanied by Nikolai Vygodsky: high musical standards were maintained.

An elderly Georgian, Prince Andronnikov, supervised the group of dancers and helped Privalov in musicals. Nikolay Fershtudt (from Turkmenia, indicted in the canal-builders' case) organized a folk-instrument ensemble. The theatre's programmes (two have come down to us, for *The Aristocrats* by Pogodin and *The Devil's Disciple* by Shaw), suggest that the actors, both professionals and amateurs, were of many nationalities. There was, as usual, a shortage of actresses and males had to be dressed for the female parts (which delighted the homosexuals), so that any flash of feminine artifice aroused close interest.

Kurbas found it quite difficult to cast Susanna in *The Marriage of Figaro*. Irene P. Vasilieva, a pretty Moscow student sent to prison straight from her lecture hall because of her father who had been shot in the 'Kirov drive', was for a long time reluctant to venture onto the stage. Camp and theatre were incompatible notions to her.

Having given in to the persistent Kurbas, Vasilieva appeared twice in 1935, creating a vigorous and jolly Susanna seen in a sketch by the play's designer, P. Pakshin. The girl could not and would not, however, reconcile herself to entertaining the kind of spectator who sat in the front rows.

Kurbas produced various plays: as well as *The Marriage of Figaro* and *The Devil's Disciple*, they included *Intrigue and Love*, Slavin's *Intervention* and Gusev's *Glory*. The staging of Shaw's *The Devil's Disciple* (opening on 9 April 1936) seemed quite a risk for the producer, for the plot is based on an obvious error, which an English court of law will not recognize: Richard Dudgeon is sentenced to be hanged as the Presbyterian minister Anderson, yet the sentence remains in force after Dudgeon has been shown not to be Anderson.

The allusion here is clear. Sitting in the audience were absolutely innocent people, many of whom had not even been awarded a court hearing, but merely given a bit of paper to sign with their sentence. However hard they protested their innocence, they confronted a wall of cruel incomprehension. *The Devil's Disciple* begged to be placed in the repertory of every Soviet theatre! Kurbas's courage must not be forgotten.

Regrettably, no photographs from those years have come to light; we must refer to the evidence of eyewitnesses.

Mikola Zerov, a university professor and translator, wrote to his wife in Kiev: 'The theatre here put on *Krechinsky's Wedding* from the classical repertory and *Glory* by Gusev from the new one. Neither production was inferior to *Platon Krechet* at the Solovtsov Theatre, which you and I saw in March 1935, while *Glory* is incomparably better'.[11]

Professor Panteleimon Kazarinov of Irkutsk University, who worked as librarian in the kremlin, wrote to his family that Gusev's *Glory* was less popular than *A Distant Point* by Afinogenov.

After a production of *Intrigue and Love*, in which he played Ferdinand, the actor Valentin Tsishevsky of Moscow wrote to a friend at Chib'yu that, as a stage director, Kurbas 'outshone anything' he had ever seen before in the realm of stagecraft.

We do not know whether Kurbas was involved in preparations for the traditional gala New Year celebrations for 1937 or even whether he was in the kremlin at the time. Outwardly the camp betrayed no anxiety as it looked ahead to 1937. The appearance on the NKVD's political horizon of a new figure, People's Commissar Nikolai Yezhov, aroused both dismay and timid hope. The inmates of Solovki were quite sophisticated politically, yet the most discerning hoped that the guillotine of mad terror would be stilled after all.

The 1937 New Year gala concert was described by Yury Chirkov, who found himself in camp in 1935 as a 15-year-old school boy accused of intending to kill the Ukrainian Party Secretary S. Kosior and Stalin himself.

> We saw in the New Year of 1937 while still in the library, and on the eve a splendid New Year concert was held, the last in the history of the Solovetsky Theatre. All the performers had a premonition of this and played as if for the last time in their lives, giving the audience their all, their hearts and inspiration. How Privalov sang! How Vygodsky played Brahms and Rakhmaninov (Concerto No. 2)! Everybody was so moved and charmed. (By the way, Rakhmaninov, as a White émigré, is proscribed, so the concerto was annnounced as that of Chaikovsky.) What New Year miniature pieces were presented by comedians from variety and operetta! Andreyev, the compère, made the audience split their sides with laughter, including the camp bosses sitting pompously in the 'government' box. Andreyev's impromptu remarks were witty and daring. For instance, he impersonated two seagulls talking, one from the Solovki, arrived for wintering in southern Europe, the other from France. The Solovetsky gull lauded the Solovki so much that the French one wanted to fly there in spring. The Solovki gull was gripped with pity: 'Oh, God forbid! Mind, you're a foreigner, they'll surely frame you for S.S. (suspicion of spying)'. The bosses no longer laughed. Next day Andreyev was sent for three days to a punishment cell.[12]

Late in 1936 or early in 1937 something that involved Kurbas happened and he was dispatched to Anzer Island, considered a site for 'punishment assignments'. A Leningrad prison transport was unloaded on the island, many of the new arrivals having been implicated in the People's Commissariat for Land case and awarded long (10-year) sentences; nevertheless, Kurbas, with his selfless devotion to theatre, managed to find both actors and spectators there.

Igor Vekentiev, of Moscow, an engineer:

> I never worked on the canal; I got to the Solovki in January 1936 and was promptly dispatched to Anzer Island, which people try not to remember. We lived quietly on Anzer (some 300 persons), with the bosses far away, and when the straits froze over no news reached the convicts unless there was something urgent, when the telephone was used. Yet this was also a cause for anxiety, for our life depended entirely on what went on in the world at large.... On Golgotha Mount ... was a theatre built by convicts back in 1929 by partitioning the church. Quite decent premises, with good acoustics.... When Alexander Kurbas appeared on Anzer Island – I didn't know why he was removed from the kremlin – and started stage productions, I approached him. He already had an assistant, Dmitry Rovinsky. The two of them turned us into theatre people. In the spring of 1937, to mark a Pushkin jubilee, we staged *The Miserly Knight*. I played Franz.[13]

In all probability, the actors combined recital with the creation of character on the stage. How else could amateurs do Pushkin?

The Miserly Knight was perhaps the last work of Kurbas and his colleague, the Ukrainian stage director Rovinsky, as the quiet life on Anzer came to an end.

From the spring of 1937 terrifying omens of change in the status of the Solovki made themselves felt. Rumours spread of unceasing secret shootings. All meetings with relatives were cancelled for the year and correspondence was gradually stopped. In June, when the entire repressive machinery of the NKVD was overwhelmed with exertion, it received a powerful reinforcement: Stalin backed a Central Committee demand granting the NKVD extraordinary political powers.

That same June convicts were informed of an order of the day renaming the Solovetsky Special Purpose Camp a Special Purpose Prison, with the cellular confinement of prisoners. The convicts' life changed drastically. 'In a word, everything vanished (all and everything)', wrote Florensky in his last letter of 3–4 June to his family. All work without guards was cancelled. The library was in a shambles and the theatre ceased to exist.

In July 1937 the People's Commissar of Internal Affairs N. Yezhov signed an order 'On Operations Towards the Repression of Former Kulaks, Criminals and Other Anti-Soviet Elements'. The order contained a clause on the shooting of 10,000 NKVD camp inmates.[14]

The Solovki chief, Major Apeter of State Security, and his deputy, Captain Rayevsky, sent to Leningrad a list of more than 1,000 people for execution. It was alleged that, while in camp, they had engaged in counter-revolutionary activities and even manifested 'terrorist intentions'.

The inmates' files were prepared by the Third Division (camp security), which operated with the help of a wide network of stool-pigeons and secret agents. The latter would often submit their reports 'as requested', if only to demonstrate their vigilance.

The journalist Mikola Liubchenko remarked of the appointment of Yezhov to Yagoda's post: 'They put Yagoda in the People's Commissariat of Posts and Telegraphs because he is used to reading other people's letters'. The report of this was followed two days later, on 5 March 1937, by a new report: Liubchenko had visited another barracks and there had been talk about Odessa. 'Sentences were uttered in whispers, by allusion. Likvornik said the following: 'soon people will be eating each other alive'. I could not make out the meaning of it because Likvornik said some words that were not even in Russian (in which language I wouldn't know).'

There was also a report on the writer Vladimir Shtangey: 'On 11 March, sitting at his table in the laboratory, prisoner Shtangey sang: "Great and vast is my beloved homeland, Many are its rivers, lakes and camps. I don't know of any other country, Where so many suffer on the rack".'[15]

No doubt the stool-pigeons wasted heaps of paper on reports about the contacts of so conspicuous a personality as Kurbas. As a result Apeter signed the following reference:

> While in the Solovetsky camp in a position of leadership in the theatre, he persistently selected for the latter personnel drawn exclusively from among Ukrainian counter-revolutionary nationalists. Moves among Ukrainians – Irchan-Babiuk, A.G. Vladimirov, Gokkel, Genriks.... Shows interest

in political events. Believes the fate of the inmates depends on the international situation. Talking to convict Poturayev, referred to convicted Ukrainian nationalists known to him in the camp as 'being in high spirits'.... Intends to escape from camp.'[16]

All this was false, from the selection for the theatre of Ukrainians (the bills completely refute this) to the utterly fantastic intention 'to escape from camp'. It is doubtful that such a thought had ever occurred to Kurbas. Like many, he placed his hopes on Western intervention and a turn in international affairs.

The Leningrad NKVD meanwhile authorized the use of the death penalty in respect of the Solovetsky list. A three-man commission from the NKVD Board arrived on the island to see to the prescribed formalities as well as to extend the terms of other prisoners. The fates of thousands of inmates were decided.

As S. Podgainy and Yu. Chirkov have testified (there is still no official information), they made short shrift of the Solovkians. The first, not very large, transport was dispatched in July 1937 to the mainland, where new sentences were announced to the prisoners.

At the end of October all those in the kremlin's open cells were called out for a general roll call. A list several hundred names long was read out and all were told to be ready for departure in two hours in the same square. A terrible bustle started. People hurried off to collect their things and say goodbye to friends. Two hours later most of those leaving were standing there with their bundles.

More than a thousand convicts were moved from the Solovki on that dreary October evening. This was the second transport, called "a big one". A few days later a few hundred prisoners were driven in from Anzer and other camp sites about the Solovki. Early in November, with a section of the kremlin inmates, mostly Trotskyites, they were sent in the third transport to the mainland.

Following these three prison transports, the kremlin became quite deserted. Everyone was apprehensive: would there be a fourth transport? A terrible rumour spread, according to which the second transport had been sunk at sea. But, even without these transports, from early summer that year shootings by firing squad were going on in the evening all the time, and then at night as well.

According to certificates, Les Kurbas, Mikola Kulish, Miroslav Irchan, Dmitry Rovinsky, the youthful actor Eugene Perfilov and many, many others were shot on 3 November 1937.

The other actors, whose terms were to end shortly, were gradually evacuated to nearby camps in Karelia. Convicts with long terms still to serve were transferred north-east to Kotlas, Ukhta and further. Some of the inmates were transferred to the Vladimir and Orlovsk central prisons. The last prison ship left the Solovki in mid-November 1939.

Leonid F. Privalov, appreciated for his voice and talent, had moved to Medvezhia Gora; his 'fiver' was not due to end before 1940. He lived in a private apartment and was shaken by an unusual visit, of which he subsequently told I. Vekentiev. One evening a former Solovetsky secret-police officer called. In the camps such people are called 'god-fathers'. Having become fairly drunk, he lapsed into reminiscences of the Solovki's golden age. Shedding tears, he let slip that in the autumn of 1937 he had been involved in the executions and in one of the groups near Sekirnaya Mount had seen Kurbas.

The repulsive spectacle of a drunken executioner lamenting over his victim, is a fitting finale to the Solovetsky phantasmagorias and absurdities.

At the end of 1939, having destroyed all evidence of the camp years, the NKVD left the islands, which became a naval base and naval cadet school. War came and nobody gave a thought to the island's buildings, deteriorating under the impact of man's activities, time and the elements. It was only in the 1960s, when trips to the Solovki became possible, that a picture of desolation and ruin was revealed to the eyes of the first tourists. The monastery was given the status of a national historical and architectural monument and the few restoration experts conscientiously tackled their task. Yet, without assets of their own or sufficient authority, they could barely patch what was crumbling before their very eyes.

At last, in 1992, ownership of the estate reverted once again to the church. How will it cope with the huge buildings, the repair of which requires billions? Will it try to forget the heinous camp years? Is it capable of comprehensive consideration of the horrible experiences of those years?

Questions addressed to the future are only natural. For the Solovki fortress walls, raised 'not by human hands', are destined to stand to the very end of time.

Time has come full circle and summed up the results of the Solovetsky experiments. Much has already been said about the historical failure of Marxism and Bolshevism as atrocious utopias. Suffice it to repeat that no decree or order of the day can change human nature as if by the stroke of a magic wand, even though one can abuse man, scare, maim and physically annihilate him. 'Is it possible to reform human nature so that man regards himself as the world's sole law-giver?' Gorky asked. 'This question is answered definitely and positively by the Soviet experience of reforming "socially dangerous" people into "socially useful" ones through the system of work communes' (*Izvestia*, 14 July 1931).

In fact, history's answer is negative. It has refuted the absurd claims of Bolshevist ideologists to view man as the only 'law-giver' of the world, trampling upon the rulings of nature. The road from this idea leads to destruction, to a threat to mankind and nature itself.

Reforging through the camps has covered itself with ignominy for ever (which, of course, does not rule out the search for effective means of ennobling man). The Solovki clearly demonstrated the impossibility of obtaining a healthy work collective by destroying moral integrity. The truth that forced labour is unproductive was confirmed once again, although Trotsky relegated it to the category of 'liberalism's miserable and most vulgar prejudices'.

By turning the individual into 'man suffering' and deliberately annihilating the best, the thinking individuals in every nation, Soviet power has, however, achieved its purpose. It has altered the gene stock of the country's peoples, catastrophically diminishing the intellect and vital energy of society. The years of intimidation, terror and fear of retribution have inevitably taken a dreadful toll.

But the world of suffering and despair, the camp world, also elicited some of history's positive answers. Art, so easily suborned into becoming the handmaid of the administration, is nevertheless resistant to the corrosion of time and circumstances. The people working on the Solovetsky stage, subject, like all mortals, to shortcomings and physical ailments, did create an unprecedented world by the sum total of their selfish efforts. A world that lived according to its own special laws, which even the NKVD could not alter.

Man also learned that forms of art, once discovered, do not vanish, even if not recalled for centuries, but are retained, hidden, as it were, in memory. A political convulsion in society immediately revived organizational forms that were, perhaps, remembered by experts alone. At once the features and morals of the serf and court theatres became visible under the masques of the time.

The peculiarity of the theatres on the Solovki and the White Sea–Baltic Canal was that, in the fifteen years of their existence, nearly all the forms known to the Russian stage were represented. In the camps, history tried out all it knew, separately and in a daring blend. And pronounced the verdict that nothing worked because the creator of art – man – was debased too much to perpetuate on the stage that interplay and sparkle without which art has no life.

And so, whatever those gifted people did on the camp stage, they could not reveal anything new. At best, actors of every rank countered violence by their humaneness, their emotive power and the brilliance of their performances. Who at that time could do more?

The mysterious spark of creative endeavour, flaring up and vanishing, blazing up brightly again in one convict or another, exerted a pull that precluded any disappointment in art.

This was the encouraging result of that historical experiment.

References

Preface

1. B. Glubokovsky (1927) The Solovetsky Theatre. In: *Solovetsky Local History Society, Papers of the Criminological Section*, Issue XVII, Solovki, 106, 107 (in Russian).
2. Dmitry Likhachev (1991) *Book of Anxieties. Recollections, Articles, Conversations*, Moscow, 126 (in Russian).
3. MVD Archive of the Karelian Republic, Petrozavodsk. Case file of Georgy Mikhailovich Osorgin, No. 55/2128 (in Russian). Osorgin was sentenced by an OGPU collegium in 1925 to 10 years in camp for having in 1919 altered in an old document his date of birth from 1893 to 1883 and concealing his officer's rank, thereby evading call-up for compulsory service in the Red Army. Served sentence in Butyrskaya prison, Moscow; under a 1927 amnesty term reduced by one-third. At his own request dispatched to the Solovki, arriving there on 19 May 1928.
4. Bagne Rouge (1935) Souvenirs d'une prisonnière au pays du Soviets. *Istina (Truth)*, 50.
5. Dmitry Likhachev (1991) *Book of Anxieties*. Op. cit., 126.
6. D.S. Likhachev (1991) To the Editorial Board. In: *Sever (North)*, **4**, 99 (in Russian).
7. M.Z. Nikonov-Smorodin (1938) *Red Hard Labour (A Solovkian's Notebook)*, Sofia, 182–203 (in Russian).
8. Ivan Chukhin (1990) *Canal Armymen*, Petrozavodsk, 38 (in Russian).
9. See: I. Chukhin (1991) The Kremlin Conspiracy. Rehabilitation in Fates and Documents. In: *Sovetskaya Militsia (Soviet Militia)*, **9** (in Russian). According to Chukhin, the agents provocateurs Sergey Brylev and Ivan Shalayev drew trusting people into the conspiracy. The investigators' appetites were whetted: a picture was created of a tremendous conspiracy involving a 100-man Siberian group, a 40-man Ukrainian group and Caucasian, Kabardin and other groups. Then the scope was diminished, concentrating on former White Guard officers and intellectuals. N. Alexandrov, shot with the others, tried to explain to the investigator: 'I told the prisoners: Vanka is just raving mad and will have everyone put before a firing squad. Don't you believe him ... he is entangling all of us, dragging us down into an abyss'. V.K. Chekhovsky, dragged into the same abyss, exclaimed: 'What a pity I am innocent! (40).
10. See: Mikhail Rozanov (1979–87) *The Solovetsky Concentration Camp in a Monastery. 1922–1939. Facts – Conjectures – 'latrine buckets' (Rumours)*, Books 1–3, USA, FRG (in Russian).
11. Dmitry Likhachev (1991) *Book of Anxieties*. Op. cit., 130.

12. Case file of G.M. Osorgin. MVD Archive of the Karelian Republic. No. 55/2128 (in Russian).

1 From monastery to concentration camp

 1. N. Litvin (1926) The Ice of May. In: *The New Solovki*, **19**, **21** (in Russian).
 2. See: History of the First-Class Stauropegion Solovetsky Monastery (1899) St Petersburg (in Russian).
 3. D.S. Likhachev (1980) Solovki in the History of Russian Culture. In: *Architectural and Art Monuments of the Solovetsky Islands*, Moscow, 11 (in Russian).
 4. V.O. Kliuchevsky (1959) The Economic Activities of the Solovetsky Monastery in the White Sea Area. In: *Works in 8 Vols., Vol. 7*. 12 (in Russian).
 5. For the life of F. Kolychev and his relations with Tsar Ivan the Terrible, see the story *Palace and Monastery* by the nineteenth century writer A.K. Scheller (in Russian).
 6. S. Maximov (1981) *Selections*, Moscow, 210 (in Russian).
 7. See: Story of the Siege of the Solovetsky Monastery. In: *Literary Monuments of Ancient Russia. 17th c. Book 1*, Moscow, 1988 (in Russian).
 8. I. Ya. Syrtsov (1888) *Revolt of the Old-Believer Solovetsky Monks in the Seventeenth century*, Kostroma, 7 (in Russian).
 9. B. Veyev [Glubokovsky] (1926) Flowers from a Herbarium. In: *The New Solovki*, **33** (in Russian).
10. For the history of the Solovki prison up to 1903, see: M.A. Kolchin (1908) *Exiles and Prisoners Confined in the Jail of the Solovetsky Monastery in the 16th–19th Centuries. A historical essay;* G.G. Frumenkov (1965) *Prisoners of the Solovetsky Monastery. Political exile to the Solovetsky Monastery in the 18th–19th centuries*, Archangelsk, (Enlarged 4th edition, 1979) (in Russian).
11. G.G. Frumenkov. Op. cit., 83.
12. V.I. Nemirovich-Danchenko (1875) *The Solovki. Recollections and Stories*, St Petersburg, 356 (in Russian).
13. B. Detchuev (1990) The Last Year. In: *Sever*, Archangelsk, **9**, 125, 127 (in Russian).
14. Zorin (1926) The Solovetsky Fire of 1923. In: *The Solovetsky Islands*, **7**, 42 (in Russian).

2 The Solovetsky Special Purpose Camp – SLON

 1. M. Prishvin (1991) Diary, 1918. In: *Literaturnaya ucheba (Literary Study)*, Book 3, 118, 121 (in Russian).
 2. Zinaida Gippius (1991) Petersburg Diaries. In: *Daugava*, Riga, **3–4**, 182 (in Russian).
 3. V.G. Korolenko (1986) Unknown Letters. In: *Minuvsheye (Bygones)*, A Historical Yearbook, **1**, Paris, 300 (in Russian).

4. L. Trotsky (1920) *Terrorism and Communism*, Petrograd, 56 (in Russian).
5. See: Statements by political prisoners of Petrominsk and the Solovki, 1923–24. In: *Zvenia* (Historical Yearbook), Issue 1, Moscow, 1991, 245–8 (in Russian).
6. Major-General I.M. Zaitsev described this aspect of camp life in detail in the book *Solovki (Communist Penal Labour Camp, or a Place of Torture and Death)*, Shanghai, 1931. Julia Danzas commented on his recollections: 'Zaitsev's book is written very truthfully as regards the facts; it is regrettable that abundance of rhetoric diminishes the impression, yet I can bear witness to the full authenticity of the described facts.' (*Sever*, Archangelsk, 1990, **9**, 120) (in Russian).
7. F.M. Dostoyevsky (1972) *Letters from a Dead House. Complete Works*, Vol. 4, Leningrad, 155 (in Russian).
8. Yu. Bessonov (1928) *Twenty-Six Prisons and an Escape from the Solovki*, Paris, 159, 161. Bessonov escaped in 1926, in fact from Kem, from Popov-Ostrov, not the Solovki, and with four comrades reached Finland.
9. B. Shiriayev (1954) *The Inextinguishable Lantern*, N.Y., 31–2; facsimile publication Moscow, 1991 (in Russian).
10. Yekaterina Olitskaya (1971) *My Recollections*, Vol. 1., Frankfurt am Main, 265–6.
11. B. Sederholm (1934) *In a Robbers' Camp (Three Years in a Country of Concessions and the Cheka), 1923–26*, Riga, 284 (in Russian). Such an album was mentioned in *Recollections* by N.V. Surovtseva, but has not been found; in 1924 she lived in Vienna, expressed indignation over rumours about the ill-treatment of prisoners in Russia and was presented at the Soviet embassy with a 'large album of Solovki photos on excellent paper ... cosy cells, a well-appointed inn for visitors, and a lot more put me quite at ease... I left proudly carrying away the world's only camp photos' (Manuscripts Department, Central Science Library, Ukrainian Ac. of Sci., Kiev, f. 284, **83**, 15). A set of postcards with Solovki views was published in the camp in 1926 with drawings by Braz. In 1930 artists painted choice playing cards for Gleb Bokii and other big bosses in Moscow 'depicting the conditions and life in the camps' (*Zvenia* (Historical Yearbook) issue 1, Moscow, 1991, 338 [in Russian]).
12. B. Solonevich (1937) *Youth and the GPU*, Sofia, 312 (in Russian).
13. Natalia Iziumova (1986) STON (Solovetsky Special Purpose Prison). In: *Moskovskie Novosti*, 23 October (in Russian).
14. A. Solzhenitsyn (1989) *The Gulag Archipelago*, Vol. 2, 45 (in Russian).

3 The special purpose press: *The Solovetsky Islands* and *The New Solovki*

1. See: P.E. Shenberg. The Solovetsky Press. In: *The Solovetsky Local History Society*, Issue XVII, 1927; D. Driakhlitsyn. Periodicals of the Archipelago. In: *Sever*, Archangelsk, 1990, **9** (in Russian).
2. B. Shiriayev (1926) Pages and Years. In: *The New Solovki*, **19** (in Russian).

3. *The Solovetsky Islands*, 1926, **5**, 30–41. Boris Emelianov presented to readers the following picture of the general's well-being. The journalist visited Zaitsev at Isakovo and they went fishing at night. 'Suddenly I hear from behind a bush: "The Solovki? But it is paradise on earth, you'd never think it's a prison." I peeped over the alder thicket and there was the serious and intent general fixing a worm to a hook. Having fixed it, he spat in my direction: "Indeed, old chap. That's penal labour for you."' (*The New Solvki*, 1926, **25** [in Russian]).

4. Such formulations contained diverse, at times quite sincere, contents. The demoted Chekist, a Latvian, L.K. Ozolin wrote in 1934 in a statement to the Party Central Committee: 'To this day I cannot reconcile myself to the thought that in our Soviet reality one can, while absolutely innocent, spend seven years in a camp, with another three years to go.... I am so strongly sealed by blood with Soviet power that I cannot become a dissident.' (I Chukhin, *Canal Armymen*. Op. cit., 67, 69).

5. Tverie (1924) Mechanization of Language (Notes by a dilettante). In: *SLON*, **5**, 58, 59 (in Russian).

6. In B. Glubokovsky's book *49* (a non-political clause number under which criminal offenders were condemned) samples of literary efforts by convicts are collected.

7. N. Litvin (1925) Over the Solovetsky Islands. On Anzar. In: *The Solovetsky Islands*, **8**, 16 (in Russian).

8. Eugene Semionov (1924) On Labour–Education Activities. In: *SLON*, **5**, 39–40 (in Russian).

9. F. Eichmans (1925) On the Matter of Public Opinion in Camp. In: *The Solovetsky Islands*, **4–5**, 39 (in Russian).

10. V.I. Massalsky (1926) The Monastery – a Polar Industrialist. In: *The Solovetsky Islands*, **7**, 94 (in Russian).

11. A. Akarevich (1925) Professor Kal's Experiment. In: *The Solovetsky Islands*, **3**, 15 (in Russian).

4 Profiles and masques

1. N. Litvin (1924) In the Mikhailovsky Forests (a chapter from the story 'A General's Lapse'). In: *SLON*, **6**, Colonel Komov, *The Solovetsky Islands*, 1925, **8** (in Russian).

2. See: N. Kuziakina (1989) 'I Dreamed I Saw a Monastery...' About M. Bulgakov's *Flight*. In: *Literaturnaya Rossia*, **24** (in Russian).

3. N. Litvin (1925–26) At the Piers *and* About Monastery Legends. In: *The New Solovki*, **45** and **7** (in Russian).

4. Litvin's case file (No. 82/3404) is kept in the MVD archive, the Karelian Republic, Petrozavodsk.

5. B. Glubokovsky (1926) Journey from Moscow to Solovki. In: *The Solovetsky Islands*, **4**, 100 (in Russian).

6. B. Glubokovsky (1922) My Faith. In: *An Inn for Travellers in Beauty*, **1**, 12 (in Russian).

7. Shiriayev's story about the group of 'Russian Nazis' with whom Glubokovsky was arrested in 1925 requires careful checking. In connection with a similar story, G. Ramensky mentions the name of the stage designer Sasha Rodishchev, son of the stage director of the Trade Union Theatre in Moscow (?).

8. V. Komardenkov (1972) *Bygone Days*, 60 (in Russian).

9. Boris Glubokovsky (1926) *49. Materials and impressions*, USLON Press Bureau, 500 copies (in Russian).

10. See Chapter 11, The Performance in Dostoyevsky's *Letters from a Dead House.*

11. Dmitry Likhachev (1991) *Book of Anxieties.* Op. cit., 124.

12. An example. Shiriayev remembers the day of his arrival on the Solovki, 17 November 1923, when Nogtev killed on the piers, for the purposes of intimidation, the general staff officer Daller. According to Shiriayev, he was buried in an individual grave and on a wooden cross, burned out with a red-hot nail, were A. Blok's words: "I am not the first, and not the last one..." The historian A.G. Kavtoradze (*Military Experts in the Service of the Soviet Republic. 1917–1920*, Moscow, 1988) mentions on the officers' roll Colonel Vladimir Wilhelmovich Daller, in 1918 Chief of the Organization Board of the Supreme Military Council (chairman L. Trotsky). Meanwhile the officer who perished on the Solovki was Vasily Alexandrovich Daller, born 1875, date of death 2 February 1925. How we can unravel this contradiction is unclear.

13. B. Shiriayev (1954) *The Inextinguishable Lantern*, N.Y., 58 (in Russian).

14. Ibid., 80–1.

5 The Theatre of the 1st Department

1. B. Shiriayev. Ibid., 58.

2. Ya. G(inesi)n (1924) *The Abused One*, a play by P. Nevezhin. In: *SLON*, **5**, 34–6 (in Russian).

3. N. Litvin (1926) Icy Winter. In: *The Solovetsky Islands*, **2–3**, 26 (in Russian).

4. I. Armanov (1924) Basis of the SLON Theatre. In: *SLON*, **3**, 68 (in Russian).

5. An Old Theatre Goer, Resting at the Theatre. In: *SLON*, 1924, **6**, 57 (in Russian).

6. B. Shiriayev (1926) Idiots in the Twilight. V. Snail Horns. In: *The New Solovki*, **40** (in Russian).

7. March Repertory of SLON Educational Labour Department. In: *SLON*, 1924, **1**, 34 (in Russian).

8. M.Z. Nikonov-Smorodin (1938) *Red Hard Labour. A Solovkian's Notebook*, Sofia, 125 (in Russian).

9. Tiberius (1924) Unsavoury Habits of Our Cult. In: *SLON*, **7–8**, 60 (in Russian).

10. See: M. Prygunov, M.S. Borin (1924) *25 Years on the Stage,* Kazan (in Russian).
11. The 'Lyceum graduates' case occurred in Leningrad in the winter of 1924–5. No contemporary publications on it have come to hand. Klinger and Shiriayev differ. The case concerned a group of former high-ranking civil servants and members of the cultural élite, who had graduated before the revolution from the Tsarskoselsky Lyceum, an exclusive school which in its time gave Russia people of the highest cultural standing (A. Pushkin, I. Pushchin, A. Delvig and others).

    Delvig urged in 1817:

    > Keep up, my dear friends, keep up
    > Our friendship with the same good heart,
    > And our glorious aspirations,
    > The truth we love, the lie we chuck,
    > And in privations – noble patience,
    > And greetings to the stroke of luck.

    Lyceum graduates celebrated its anniversary every year and memoirists maintain that at their reunion in October 1924 former lyceum pupil Father Vladimir Lozino-Lozinsky conducted memorial services for the murdered Tsar Nicholas II. The GPU arrested, in addition to lyceum graduates, their friends and acquaintances; as a result, 54 people were shot to death, and about the same number found themselves on the Solovki (figures not verified), among them V. Lozino-Lozinsky, the Shilder brothers, Osten-Saken, Golitsyn and others.
12. B. Shiriayev (1954) *The Inextinguishable Lantern,* N.Y., 304–6. *Three Thieves,* a 4-act play by P.A. Arensky after a story by Notari, Moscow, 1924 (in Russian).
13. A. Klinger (1928) The Solovetsky Penal Labour Camp. Notes of an Escapee. In: *Archive of the Russian Revolution,* Book XIX, Berlin, 184–5 (in Russian).
14. Gennady Andreyev (S.A. Khomiakov) (1990) The Solovetsky Islands. In: *Sever,* Archangelsk, **9**, 20–1 (in Russian).

6 The smaller theatres – 'Trash' and the group of 'Our Own'

1. Tiberius (1925) About 'Trash'. In: *The New Solovki,* **10** (in Russian).
2. Rina Zelionaya (1990) Discordant Lines. In: Nikolai Erdman: *A Play, Interludes. Letters. Documents. Recollections by Contemporaries,* 313 (in Russian).
3. A Spectator (1925) 'Our Own'. In: *The New Solovki,* **22** (in Russian).
4. Tiberius (1925) March (A Short Feuilleton). In: *The New Solovki,* **1** (in Russian).
5. B. Glubokovsky (1927) The Solovetsky Theatre. In: *The Solovetsky Local History Society, Papers of the Criminological Section,* Issue XVII. The Solovki, 122 (in Russian).

6. M.N. Gernet (1925) *In Prison. Essays on Prison Psychology*, Moscow, 61 (in Russian).
7. Ibid., 62–3.
8. E. Mikhlin (1932) The Zerentui Prison Theatre. In: *Training and Cultural Work in Prison and Hard Labour Camps. Collected Articles and Recollections*, Moscow, 211, 214. *Apartment for Clandestine Meetings*, A 2-act comedy, 1906 (in Russian).
9. B. Glubokovsky (1926) *49. Materials and impressions*. The Solovki, 49 (in Russian).
10. Glubokovsky, op. cit., 124.
11. Glubokovsky, op. cit., 119.
12. B. Glubokovsky (1925) The Solovetsky Psisha. In: *The New Solovetsky Islands*, **9**, 9 (in Russian). The serf actress Psisha, the heroine of *Psisha*, a prerevolutionary play by Yu. Beliayev, destroyed in a confrontation with her master's despotism.

7 The end of the early Solovki

1. F.M. Dostoyevsky (1972) *Letters from a Dead House. Complete Works*, Vol. 4, Leningrad, 99 (in Russian).
2. MVD Archive of Karelian Republic, Petrozavodsk. Case under 1st Division's Register No. 72/3107; Central Archive, USLON, OGPU, No. 21956.
3. N. Litvin (1925) Over the Solovetsky Islands. On Anzer. In: *The Solovetsky Islands*, **8**, 21 (in Russian).
4. See: Malsagoff S.A. (1926) *An Island Hell. A Soviet Prison in the Far North*, Philpot; see also: Malsagov Sozerko (1990) *Islands of Hell. A Soviet Prison in the Far North*, Alma-Ata (in Russian).

8 At the crossroads

1. The late 1920s are reflected in the recollections of Julia Danzas, G. Andreyev (G.A. Khomiakov), Olga Sinakevich-Yafa, N.P. Antsiferov (*Thoughts About the Past*, Moscow, 1992), O. Volkov (*Age of Hopes and Downfalls*, Moscow, 1989) and D. Likhachev, among others.
2. F. Aliakhnovich (1991) In GPU Jails. In: *Polymia*, Minsk, **1**, 167 (in Russian).
3. See two documents of the A.M. Shanin Commission on the Solovki. Publication by I.I. Chukhin. In: *Zvenia* (Historical Yearbook), 1991, 357–88 (in Russian).
4. L. Ya. Reznikov (1967) *Gorky in the North*, Petrozavodsk, 5 (in Russian).
5. M. Gorky (1929) The Solovki. In: *Our Achievements*, **6**, 15 (in Russian).
6. The case file of Vadim Chekhovsky (age 27 years), shot on 29 October 1929, in the 'Kremlin Conspiracy' case preserved the text of his letter to Gorky: "Answer me, Alexey Maximovich. To you, an old man, whom I would like to respect, I dedicate this testimony. I have heard many things about you. To me you are a symbol of the GPU, the party and the

authorities – a symbol of a Sphinx. And it is this Sphinx that I am asking: Sphinx, who are you?.... The weak are broken and depersonalized by torture. If you need slaves in a system of state slavery, then fabricate them in concentration camps, but remember, the strong are not broken by torture, but tempered. So, who are you betting on, Alexey Maximovich? On the slave, scoundrel and coward, or on the knight?...” (I. Chukhin, *The Kremlin Conspiracy*. In: *Sovetskaya Militsia (Soviet Militia)*, 1991, **9**, 41 (in Russian).

7. For the treatment meted out to the 'Thompson Mission' see: I. Chukhin, *Canal Armymen*, Petrozavodsk, 1990, **3–4** (in Russian).

8. A daily paper *Trudovik (Labourer)* started to appear on the Solovki in November 1930 'not to be exported to the mainland'. O.V. Sinakevich-Yafa's archive preserved the first issue (National Library of Russia, f. 163, storage unit 303). A paper with the title *Solovetsky Listok (Solovetsky Leaflet)* was also promised, but no information on it is available.

9. The incident on the Chinese–Oriental railway (KVZhD), on which thousands of Russians were working, was resolved in 1935 in a typically Stalinist manner: the railway's Russian branch was ceded to China, and all the work-force, together with their families, were repressed on their return home.

10. See: A. Kenel (1929) Musical Accompaniment at the Solovetsky Theatre. In: *The Solovetsky Islands*, **3–4**, (in Russian).

11. O. Volkov (1989) *Age of Hope and Downfalls*, Moscow, 184 (in Russian).

12. F. Aliakhnovich (1991) In GPU Prisons. In: *Polymia*, Minsk, **1**, 186 (in Byelorussian).

13. Regulations on OGPU Corrective-Labour Camps. State Historical Archive of the Karelian Republic, f. 865, op. 32, d. 1/3 (in Russian).

14. Materials on the reorganization of SLON. State Historical Archive of the Karelian Republic, f. 865, op. 32, d. 1/1.

9 The theatre at Kem

1. I. Chukhin (1990) *Canal Armymen*, Petrozavodsk, 29 (in Russian).

2. A.K. Voronsky (1987) *Selected Prose*, Moscow, 481 (in Russian).

3. *Gudok (Hooter)*, Moscow, 1924, November 1 (in Russian).

4. *Archangelsk 1584–1984. On the Quatercentenary of the City. Fragments of History*, Archangelsk, 1984, 171 (in Russian).

5. USLON, Its History, Goals and Tasks. Report of USLON Chief Nogtev to a Workers' Meeting at Kem. In: *The Solovetsky Islands*, 1930, **2–3**, 60, 6 (in Russian).

6. See: Robert Conquest (1986) *The Harvest of Sorrow*, Oxford.

7. Recollections of O.V. Sinakevich (Yafa) *Augur Islands, 1928–1931*, are kept at the Russian National Library (Manuscripts Department, f. 163, No. 380). Excerpts published in *Our Heritage*, 1989, Book IV (in Russian).

8. Olga Viktorovna Sinakevich (Yafa) was sent to the Solovki in 1929, with the circle of A.A. Meyer (47 people). In camp, together with others (T.N. Gippius, V.F. Stein, K.A. Polovtseva), she cut puttees from potato sacks, while the former stage designer of the Mary Theatre, St Petersburg, the artist Pavel F. Smotritsky, worked as laboratory assistant and watchman at the farm; according to a character reference, 'a very decent, obedient and persevering worker'. His wife's appeal for preterm release of her husband, who was dying of anaemia and tuberculosis, was turned down. In 1934 Smotritsky died in the Sennukha infirmary (Kuzema station, Murmansk railway line). Certificate: 'On examination of the dead prisoner P.F. Smotritsky's mouth on 12 April, no gold crowns or teeth were found'. Document: '... the corpse is dressed in clean underwear, and lowered into a 1.5 m deep grave, head pointing west, in a dry place, chosen as cemetery outside the town boundary, to which effect the present document is done on this day, 21 April 1934'. (MVD Archive of the Karelian Republic, case file No. 228/9355).

9. See: Gabriel Ramensky (1954) The Theater in Soviet Concentration Camps. In: *Soviet Theaters. 1917–1941. A Collection of Articles*, N.Y., 203.

10. Gennady Russky (1991) The Solovki: Truth and Legend. In: Boris Shiriayev, *The Inextinguishable Lantern* (reprint, Moscow) 412 (in Russian).

10   The 'court' and 'vulgar' theatres of the White Sea–Baltic Canal

1. At the Commune established in the estate of the former chocolate manufacturer Croft the activities included amateur dramatics. See: E. Vatova. The Bolshevo Work Commune and its Organizer. In: *Yunost (Youth)*, 1966, 3.

2. Bernard Shaw (1969–70) *Autobiographical Selections from his Writings* (by Stanley Weintraub), N.Y., Vol. 2.

3. See: *The Stalin Canal*, Moscow, 1934 (amply illustrated).

4. O. Mandelshtam (1991) *Collected Works*, Vol. 2, Moscow, 352, 354.

5. B. Kostikov (1989) The Glitter and Poverty of the Nomenclature. In: *Ogoniok*, **1**, 14.

6. R. Suslik, Bloody Pages of Unwritten Chronicles. U.K., 254 (in Ukrainian). See also: *Famine. A People's Memorial Book*, Kiev, 1991; Procyk O., Heretz Z. *Famine in the Soviet Ukraine (1931–1933)*, USA, 1986. (in Ukr.).

7. A. Solzhenitsyn (1989) *The Gulag Archipelago*, Vol. 2, Part 3, Moscow, 408 (in Russian).

8. A. Avdeyenko (1989) The Excommunication. In: *Znamia (Banner)*, **3**, 15 (in Russian).

9. Emma Gernshtein (1989) New About Mandelshtam. In: *Our Heritage*, Book V, 112 (in Russian).

10. R. Rolland (1989) Moscow Diaries. In: *Voprosy literatury (Problems of Literature)*, **4**, 234, 238 (in Russian).

11. A. Losev and V. Loseva (1989) Overcoming Chaos. In: *Nashe Nasledie (Our Heritage)*, Book V, 83, 90 (in Russian).

12. Anna Louise Strong (1935) At Bear Mountain Lawbreakers Win Honour and Freedom. *Moscow Daily News*, 24 July. M. Geller justly called Strong 'a professional hack writer'. (*Utopia in Power*, London, 1986, 272).

13. V. Tsekhansky's recollections were recorded by the author.

14. I. Rusinov's recollections were recorded by the author.

15. *The Stalin Canal*, Moscow, 1934, 309 (in Russian).

16. Terentiev's Leftist excesses (he even eliminated the calling of play-wright) evoked an ironic snub from B. Lavrenev: 'Well, what can be done about such policeman philosophy? Here is a perfect repetition of the notorious reply of the Chief of the Gendarmes to a Third Department inquiry about the revolutionary movement; he wrote: "I have the honour to report that revolution in the Nth governorship is an anachronism"' (*Zhizn iskusstva*) (*Art Life*), Leningrad, 1926, **23**, 5 (in Russian). Could Lavrenev have known about Terentiev's father?

17. See: K. Rudnitsky (1987) Chasing Terentiev. In: *Teatr (Theatre)*, **5**, 58–79 (in Russian).

18. Vera Inber (1933) Programmes of the Nadvoitsky Camp. In: *Sovetskoye iskusstvo (Soviet Art)*, 26 August (in Russian).

19. Igor Terentiev (1988) *Collected Works*, Bologna, 332. Contains an article by M. Marzaduri: 'Igor Terentiev: Stage Director' (in Russian).

20. *The Stalin Canal*, Moscow, 1934, 391 (in Russian).

11 Camp theatres and the Central Theatre of the White Sea–Baltic Canal

1. N.P. Sychev was arrested and sent to the WSBC for resisting the sale of paintings from Leningrad museums to foreign countries. In Medvezhiegorsk he often came to the theatre and was on friendly terms with the actors.

2. I. Chukhin (1990) *Canal Armymen*, Petrozavodsk, 188–9.

3. Ibid., 177–8.

4. Vera Nikitina (1991) And All That Was. In: *Sever*, 7. At Svirlag this memoir-writer became acquainted with the Kem troupe headed by I. Kalugin, who 'was a truly cultured and intellectual person, but terribly tired, and because of that tiredness, he was absolutely unconcerned and indifferent to everything in the world'.

5. See: Gabriel Ramensky. Op. cit.

6. N.P. Kashin (1927) The theatre of N.B. Yusupov. In: *Transactions of the State Academy of Art Sciences*, Theatrical section, Issue 3, Moscow, 7 (in Russian).

7. State Historical Archives of the Karelian Republic, f. 865, op. 1, d. 1/6, d. 8/43. The lists of theatre employees are dated to 1935–38, but some had been working before or worked after those dates.

8. See: A.G. Alexeyev (1984) *The Serious and the Funny*, 3rd Ed., Moscow (in Russian).

9. *The Stalin Canal*, Moscow, 1934, 309 (in Russian).
10. I.G. Terentiev (1988) *Collected Works*, Bologna, 331.
11. The Art of Reforging and Reforging Through Art. In: *Sovetskoye iskusstvo (Soviet Art)*, 1933, 2 September (in Russian).
12. The Bolshoy Theatre in 1938. In: *Medvezhiegorsky Bolshevik*, 1 January 1938 (in Russian).
13. State Historical Archives of the Karelian Republic, f. 865, op. 1, d. 3/13.
14. I. Girniak (1982) *Recollections*, N.Y., 413 (in Ukrainian).
15. B. Sveshnikov's drawings were shown at the 'Camp Artists' Exhibition', Moscow, August 1990.

12 The theatre of the late Solovki

1. Letter from A.N. Potekhina of 14 August 1956 to O.V. Yafe. In: O. Sinakevich-Yafe, Augur Islands, Copybook 2. Russian National Library, Manuscripts Department, f. 163, No. 380.
2. M. Rozanov (1990) Solovetsky Trading Stations. In: *Sever*, Archangelsk, **9**, 88–9 (in Russian).
3. V.Yu. Gessen's personal archive.
4. I.G. Gordon's personal archive.
5. Dmitry Likhachev (1991) *Book of Anxieties. Recollections, Articles, Conversations*, Moscow, 97 (in Russian).
6. M. Rozanov. Op. cit., 89.
7. Yu.I. Chirkov (1991) *This Is How It Was*, Moscow, 100.
8. Letters from N.M. Krantsevich to his wife Z.M. Krantsevich (1933–35). Memorial Society archive. St. Petersburg.
9. M. Novikov (1989) Dream at Vian-Guba. In: *Sovetskaya kultura (Soviet Culture)*, 25 March (in Russian).
10. Pavel Florensky (1988) Letters from the Solovki. In: *Nashe Nasledie (Our Heritage)*, Book IV, 117 (in Russian).
11. Lettter of 11 January 1937 from M.K. Zerov to Sophia Loboda. Archive of the Ukrainian Museum of Literature and Art, Kiev, f. 28, op. 1, d. 142 (in Russian).
12. Yu. I. Chirkov. Op. cit., p. 133.
13. Conversation with I.A. Vikentiev. Recorded by I.A. Reznik. Memorial Society archive, St Petersburg.
14. A. Razumov (1992) August Nineteen Thirty-Seven: the Leningrad Variant. In: *Vecherny Peterburg (Evening Petersburg)*, **196** (in Russian).
15. Archive of the Ukrainian KGB. References and reports, collected in case file, 8 vols., common cipher 36546 F.P.
16. Archive of the Ukrainian KGB. Case file No. 3363. 'Gokkel' may be an error. There was an engineer I.M. Gakkel on the WSBC (1935).

Abbreviations

APG	Aesthetic Propaganda Group
CES	Culture and Education Section (a propaganda unit in a slave-labour camp)
Cheka	Extraordinary Commission for Suppressing Counter–Revolution, Speculation, and Malfeasance (Soviet secret police, November 1917–February 1922)
Chekist	Secret police agent; KGB officer
CR	Counter-Revolutionary
GPU	State Political Administration (secret police, 1922–27)
GULAG	Chief Administration of Corrective-Labour Camps
KGB	State Security Committee (secret police)
KVZhD	Chinese Oriental Railway
MGB	Ministry of State Security (secret police, 1946–53)
MVD	Ministry of Internal Affairs
NKVD	People's Commissariat of Internal Affairs (secret police, July 1934 to 1946)
OGPU	Unified State Political Administration (secret police, January 1927–July 1934)
RCP	Russian Communist Party
SLON	Solovetsky Special Purpose Camp
SSR	Special Solovetsky Regiment
USLON	Solovetsky Special Purpose Camp Administration
WSBC	White Sea–Baltic Canal
YCL	Young Communist League

ChK (Cheka); GPU; OGPU; NKVD; KGB: different names of the Soviet secret police throughout the history of the Soviet Union

Index

It has not been possible to ascertain initial or forename for every person mentioned in this book. Many entries therefore consist of a surname only.
References in italic indicate the illustration number, not the page number.

For Product Safety Concerns and Information please contact our EU
representative GPSR@taylorandfrancis.com
Taylor & Francis Verlag GmbH, Kaufingerstraße 24, 80331 München, Germany